One Child Too Many

Lesley Elliot

One Child Too Many

Copyright © 2020 Lesley Elliot

This is a work of fiction. Names, characters, businesses, places, events and incidents are either the product of the author's imagination or used in a fictitious manner. Any resemblance to actual persons, living or dead or actual events is purely coincidental.

For Carole - with love.

Table of Contents

Prologue

August 1978

I stirred on the chair in the public gallery as the woman was led into the dock and told to sit down. I nudged my husband, Peter. 'Look, there she is, oh my God, I can't bear it,' I whispered.

She was shaking as if she was ill. Her face looked ashen. Did we ruin her? Were we to blame? She'd always behaved as if she could have anything she desired, but perhaps we share her guilt? I knew that Peter would disagree. I thought that my nerves had been shattered when I'd had to give evidence, but it was nothing to how I felt now as I waited for the verdict.

It's strange how one person can tear a family apart. They were tangled snakes, but it was her venom that destroyed us – his wasn't that powerful.

1

December 1968

Even before my old, grey Morris Minor skidded awkwardly into the curve of the kerb, I could hear the music blasting from Lyn's room. I switched the engine off, grabbed my green, woollen gloves and wound a matching scarf around my neck. It was too bloody cold to be out, but yet again, I had no choice.

I half walked half slid along the icy tarmac path bordered on the left by a neat, yellow, privet hedge and on the right by a taller green one. Mom answered the door at the first knock. She must have been behind the net curtains keeping an eye out for me. She wore a blue, nylon overall over a shapeless, pink dress made from Crimplene – a cheap, synthetic material that I hated the feel of. Did we ever see her in anything else? My mind was roving as usual.

Mom was still an attractive woman, although she looked tired. The deeply etched lines around her blue eyes appeared swollen and red as though she'd been crying. I took my gloves off and held her cold hand in mine for a minute. It was so familiar. I ran my thumb over the calluses at the base of each of her fingers, a result of her favourite occupation, gardening, and then gave her a peck on her flushed cheek.

'Where is she?' I asked. Her record player was blasting out Barry Ryan singing "Eloise", insisting that the whole street should know where she was.

Mom nodded towards the stairs. 'Thank God you're here Sara, I can't get her to come out or turn the sound down. She's been playing it on repeat for almost two hours now. Be a love and see if you can make her see sense. She can't carry on like this – the neighbours – I'm surprised they haven't already complained. I don't know what's upset her.'

'I'll bloody well upset her if she doesn't pack it in,' I said.

I'd had my own home just a few streets away for the last four years, but coming to this house in Gorton on the outskirts of Birmingham and breathing in the faint aroma of spray polish mixed with fried onions always connected the dots – it smelt like home. It was a good place to live, just quiet enough to enjoy life, but not so quiet that it felt lifeless. Lyn was doing her best to liven it up lately, though. I didn't understand her; I'd always been an amenable teenager, and so had Janet and Michael.

I followed Mom along the short hallway with its cardinal red tiles. They no longer shone the way they did when I lived at home. I slung my coat and scarf haphazardly over the cream newel post and began to climb the red-carpeted stairs. Mom hurried into the sitting room and closed the door – she hated fuss of any kind.

The noise coming from upstairs was deafening. How anyone could be shut up in a small room for any length of time with that amount of decibels assaulting her ears I couldn't think. I took a deep breath; I didn't much relish the thought of having to deal with Lyn's shenanigans yet again. I loved her very much, but she could be a pain in the butt.

Three steps along the landing, where the oyster coloured Anaglypta was as familiar to me as my hand, past the bathroom and Mom and Dad's room, and then I thumped my fist on Lyn's

3

door. Lyn didn't respond. My brother, Michael, was out, or there would have been ructions. He'd recently started work as an apprentice turner in a local factory's machine shop and appreciated getting his head down for a couple of extra hours at the weekend.

I banged again and raised my voice above the noise. 'Come on, Sis, turn the bloody music down and open the door. What's the matter? Talk to me, love.' No response, then thank God the sound was muted. Minutes passed. I let my nails play a tattoo on off white paint and tried again – at least she was listening. 'What's up, Lyn? Open the door. I just want to help,' I said.

'Fuck off; I don't need your bloody help, just leave me alone.'

I could hear her sniffle. 'You know I can't just leave you; I need to make sure you're alright – Mom's worried to death.'

'Well, she needn't be, nothing's the matter – I don't know why she sent for you.'

I waited a few minutes for her to calm down. Nothing happened. My patience was wearing thin, but I tried not to let it show.

'I'm your sister and I love you. I haven't seen you for a fortnight – c'mon, open up so I can hug you. I'm going nowhere 'til you do,' I said.

I breathed a sigh of relief as I heard the bolt being drawn and the door cracked – I pushed it open and went in. Lyn sat as far away as possible in the corner of her bed. The intermittent light and shade from the window danced patterns across her dark brown, wavy hair. She had her knees drawn up to her chin – hands clasped – knuckles white. She was a mess; her hair that was usually her crowning glory cascaded to her waist in an unwashed tangle. It looked as though she hadn't brushed it in days. She kept her hazel eyes closed as I sat tentatively on a corner of the floral bedspread and surveyed the room with a critical eye. There was nothing to criticise because

4

it was tidy as usual. Her books and personal possessions arranged neatly in place along the two ample shelves that I had helped her put up a couple of years ago. The only things of note were about fifty soggy tissues strewn haphazardly over the faded lino that covered the floorboards. I glanced over my shoulder at the large, pine chest of drawers that had been mine to share when I was young. An almost empty bottle of Bacardi, and a half-full bottle of Coke with a glass tumbler balanced precariously over its lip, decorated its worn surface.

Anger at Mom's weakness flared and died. She must have given Lyn money to buy the alcohol even though she'd promised not to. Lyn always became maudlin when she drank, something she'd started to do about twelve months ago shortly before she was fifteen. At first, we'd not taken much notice, amused by her teenage need to experiment, but it wasn't too long before it became a problem.

'What's the matter, Lyn?' I asked. We sat in silence for what seemed like an age while I waited for her to speak. She burst into racking sobs.

I crawled across to where she was attempting to disappear into the wall at the head of the bed and pulled her awkwardly into my embrace. Eventually, she ceased to cry. I fished in my jeans' pocket, found a not too used tissue, and mopped her scarlet face. It subsequently joined the others on the floor. All the tension seemed to leave her slim body as she relaxed back against me.

'Can't you tell me?' I asked. She shook her head and began to sit up. 'Well, okay, I can't force you, but you can't carry on like this – is it Mom, has she upset you?'

Lyn still wouldn't look at me, but at last, she spoke. 'No, I'm sorry if I worried her. I just couldn't seem to stop acting up. Is she very mad at me?'

'Not really, just worried about you and the neighbours.'

'I know – I'm sorry.' She gave me her naughty girl smile and fluttered her long lashes. 'I won't turn the music up so high again.' As usual, she expected instant forgiveness.

'Well, if you do, I just might smash all your records,' I said. I wasn't sure it was a joke. I thought I just might resort to doing something like that. This time she looked directly at me with her eyebrows raised. I smiled at her. 'Are you coming downstairs now? You need to tell Mom you're sorry, I'm not doing it for you.'

She giggled as we shuffled our way off her bed. 'I'm going to the loo. You go down and tell Mom I'll be there in a minute.'

'Okay.'

She disappeared into the bathroom and I walked sedately down the stairs. I smiled as I remembered all the times that I used to sit on my bottom and bump down each step even when I was perfectly capable of walking properly. I had enjoyed it. I had to resist the temptation now.

I went into the living room where Mom was putting up the ironing board, a basket of laundry sat on the table. 'Is she coming down?' Mom asked.

'Yes, but why have you given her money to buy booze again? I thought we'd agreed you wouldn't. You know how it makes her behave.'

I made my way over to the table and picked up a shirt out of the basket, and sniffed deeply. Line dried, it smelled of fresh air. I sat on one of the sturdy, leather-covered dining chairs that had seen so many uses. I pictured our sister Janet and myself standing upright on the padded seat and holding on to the carved back while Dad cut our hair in straight lines. I was always scared that he would catch my earlobe in the scissors, but he never did.

On sunny days these chairs would find their way into the garden – no special outdoor ones for us. Sitting in a line, we would pretend that we were on a train and Michael was the engine driver. We often imagined that we went to the seaside, something we never actually did until I was much older. I gazed down the long garden to the railway embankment where we used to play in the tall grass. My mind swung to a memory of two of the chairs with their seats facing each other. They supported the carrycot that held our baby sister, Lyn.

Lyn had held us in her thrall until the last couple of years when she transformed from a sweet-tempered girl into an occasional monster. It seemed to me that the occasions were becoming more frequent with each passing month.

Mom bent down by my side and plugged the iron in, bringing me abruptly out of my reverie.

'I didn't give her money for that. She went shopping down the village, and I said she could buy herself something nice for going. I meant a bar of chocolate or some sweets. I never expected her to spend so much. She hid the bottle in her room.' Mom looked sheepish, and I didn't have the heart to carry on about it.

'Try not to let her have so much money, Mom. I don't know what's troubling her, but something is – her behaviour's worse than ever.'

Mom's eyes filled with tears as she nodded her acknowledgement.

'Don't worry. I'll talk to Janet when I phone her later, see if she can find out what's going on. Lyn might confide in her. She's at that funny age, isn't she?'

'Yes, she is and I'm just about fed up with it.' Mom said. She reached for her hankie again.

I edged my way to the door. 'Hey c'mon, stop now; Peter will wonder where I've got to. Ring me if there's any more trouble. I think she'll be alright now.' I paused at the door and stroked the silky Indian tapestry that had hung on the wall opposite the window since I could remember. 'Where's Dad this week? Have you heard from him?' I asked.

'He phoned last night, he's in Doncaster, sends his love and says he'll be home by the weekend. He needn't hurry,' she said. 'He hogs the telly.'

I glanced over at the screen to see the news that an eleven-year-old girl had been arrested and charged with the murder of two young boys. My stomach clenched. I couldn't understand how such a thing could happen. Dad could hog the telly if he wanted to because I didn't want to see the wicked things that they were reporting these days.

I kissed Mom and then shouted, 'Tarra' to Lyn, who had just flushed the toilet.

She sounded happy enough as she called, 'Tarra Sara, and thank you.'

I donned my warm clothing, hurried past the closed front room door, and pulled the house door shut. I walked gingerly on the frozen path as I returned to my car. I was anxious to see my husband and our daughter, Dawn, who was cute and entertaining at three years of age but definitely not being spoilt.

2

I watched the way Peter's tight, dimpled buttocks moved as he crossed our room on the way to the bathroom. He is beautiful, and, as usual, my stomach muscles clenched with desire even though we made love not much more than ten minutes ago. I love everything about his lean, long-legged form and his handsome face topped by a shock of blue-black floppy hair. Please don't get fat and bald, I thought with a grin. He turned and smiled at me as if he could hear my thoughts. Perhaps he can tell by my silly grin what's going through my mind.

It's Sunday morning and Dawn is very kindly still asleep in her room along the corridor – just a few steps from where I'm lazing in comfort. I've been expecting her to start calling us for the last half hour. Determined to take full advantage of her unusual sleepiness, I leaned across Peter's side of the bed and lunged for the packet of Bensons that he always had to hand. I scooched up the bed, leaned back against the padded headboard and, knowing he'll be back any second, light two cigarettes. I threw the gold packet and lighter onto my bedside table and watched as, predictably, the blue plastic lighter slid defiantly onto the carpet.

Peter sashayed across the room, giving me roguish looks that made me laugh, then he took his cigarette, and I snuggled onto his arm while we indulged in our guilty pleasure. I know it's bad for me, and I keep promising myself that I'll kick the habit; I'm sure that Peter would too if I managed it. Perhaps tomorrow, I think, with no real conviction.

Peter ran his fingers gently across my back. 'I love you, my darling,' he said.

I stubbed my cigarette out and listened for any indication that Dawn was awake. 'I love you too, but five more minutes, and we'll have to get up.'

'Okay, come here.' He drew me to him and began to kiss me. I returned his kiss and responded to his passion.

'Mommy come and fetch me,' Dawn shouted. She wasn't allowed to leave her room by herself yet. I was worried about the stairs, amongst other things.

'I'll go,' Peter said.

He grabbed his boxers from the bedside chair and fell back against the wardrobe in his haste to pull them on. I grinned. He left the room and returned with our daughter, who quickly jumped in between us and disappeared under the duvet where she did her imitation of a turtle.

'Okay, that's it; I'm out of here, time to get up my little turtle and have a bath.' I dragged her by her feet from under the covers. She wriggled so much that we both fell onto the floor in a giggling heap.

While we ate breakfast, I was miles away, planning the next day's shopping list, when Peter asked, 'What was yesterday's problem with Lyn all about?' I placed my second piece of toast that I'd slathered with honey carefully down on my plate – I sensed trouble.

I was surprised because he usually didn't want to know. He was fed up with the number of times my mother phoned and asked me to sort my sister out. It had caused us, on a few occasions, to have not a row exactly but strong words that had upset both of us. We rarely argue – both of us prefer to walk away from disagreements.

'Hard to say really,' I said. 'Lynn wouldn't tell me anything, but she did promise not to play her music so loud in future and apologised to Mom for taking no notice of her. She is becoming a nightmare, and she's still drinking.

'How can she afford the stuff?'

'She more or less stole the money from Mom this time to buy a bottle of Bacardi. Mind you, Mom's too soft with her. Sometimes I feel annoyed with both of them.'

Dawn had finished her cereal and pushed her bowl halfway across the table. 'Toast, please,' she said. Peter spread a piece of toast with honey, and, as he gave it to her, he planted a kiss on the end of her nose, making her chuckle.

He sat back in his chair and said, 'Well, you could always refuse to go when she rings – you aren't Lyn's keeper.' Peter sounded annoyed, and I could understand why. I had left him to mind Dawn yesterday and rushed off, even though I knew that he had a lot of papers to mark before school the next day. He taught Biology at the local Grammar School and was in line to become deputy headmaster when the current deputy moved to London in the spring of the following year.

'I'm sorry, love, I suppose I could, but you know I find it so difficult not to respond when Mom needs me. Lyn's such a handful at times. She needs a good slap, and sometimes I'm afraid that I'll lose my rag and give her one.' Peter grinned at the thought. 'I am sorry though that I left you to it. Did you manage to get the marking done?'

'It's okay. I can finish them later today. We're not going anywhere, are we?'

'No, but I didn't see Janet yesterday, so I'll take Dawn and drive over today if she's going to be in. That'll give you some peace.' I reached for his hand. 'I want to talk to her about Lyn and see if she can find out what's the matter with her. I'll give her a ring in a minute.' I stood up and kissed him on his cheek, which brought a smile to his face and a pat on my backside. I lifted Dawn from her high chair and noticed that she was almost too big for it now.

'Alright, love, give me a shout before you leave.' He dumped his plate into the sink and poured himself another cup of coffee before ascending the stairs to our third bedroom. It's small but big enough to make a decent size office, and Peter enjoys the time he spends there. Since he managed to squeeze in an armchair under the window, he refers to it as his den and occasionally escapes there to read one of the lurid murder novels he enjoys.

'Quick, come on in and shut the door – it's so bloody cold. I've got two jumpers on, and I'm still freezing.'

That's my sister, I thought with a smile. No, hello, nice to see you, just straight to the point. She was just like Auntie Freda, Mom's older sister. When Peter and I married, we had enough money saved to buy a house that was not too distant from Mom's, but Janet and Simon had had to rent a house from a private landlord on the outskirts of Birmingham. It wasn't ideal, but it was what they could afford. I enjoy driving, so I usually visited two or three times each week. It is probably too often for Simon, but not for Janet – I think she's often quite lonely as Simon goes out a lot. I wasn't too worried about what Simon thought. We got on alright, but he wasn't my favourite person – I thought he was arrogant and smarmy.

I followed Dawn, who skipped into the kitchen at the back of the house. It was cold despite the oil-fired central heating. I knew that Janet and Simon tried to be economical with it. Simon worked on the railways as a shunter, and the pay wasn't very good, so I said nothing. I was glad that both Dawn and I had sweatshirts on under our coats.

Janet made a pot of tea, then we sat at the kitchen table chatting about nothing important, just catching up, while her daughter, Michelle, who was almost eighteen months and

Dawn, who was a couple of years older, played together. They were drawing on a blackboard then cleaning their masterpieces off, sending clouds of white dust over the dog's basket and the surrounding floor.

'What happened then?' Janet asked. I'd already told her about Lyn's latest escapade when I'd spoken to her on the phone.

I pulled a wry face as I tried to order my thoughts. As usual, they side-tracked me into thinking about how much like me Janet looked. We could almost be mistaken for twins. We both had dark wavy hair cut in a neat bob, pale blue eyes, bow-shaped full lips, and high cheekbones. Her nose was less blobby than mine; I rather envied her well-ordered straight one with its very neat nostrils. We were both slim and able to eat more or less what we liked without piling on the pounds. "That's now my girl," Mom warned both of us at times, "you wait until you get older; it creeps on by magic." I always felt sorry for people with a weight problem, so I was determined that it wouldn't matter how old I became; I would keep my figure. What did I know?

I glanced at our girls, who fitted the same pattern. They were cute looking children, easy-going, and good at sharing. I pulled my thoughts back to Janet's question.

'Nothing more than I told you on the phone. I have no idea why Lyn was so upset; she just refused to say. I wondered if perhaps you could have a talk with her; she tends to be closer to you; well, we all do, don't we? You're the one we tell our troubles to.'

Janet smiled. 'Have you thought that she could just be telling the truth as she knows it – it could be teenage hormones. Perhaps nothing is the matter.'

I shook my head doubtfully. 'You might be right, but I am worried; I get the feeling that something is troubling her. She sobbed when I questioned her, so I'd feel much better if you had a word with her.'

'Okay, but I don't suppose she'll tell me any more than she told you. She's not good at confiding.' Still, she looked thoughtful, 'I'll make a point of seeing her tomorrow. I meant to go and see Mom anyway.'

'What's that clicking noise?' I cocked my head to one side; it sounded strange and quite loud.

'Oh that, I'm used to it. I barely notice it anymore. It's living on the corner; the wind sometimes howls out there like wolves on the prowl. The letterbox hardly ever stops clicking at times, so either the wind is whistling through it, or the postman stuffs things through it for a couple of hours at a time.' She pretended to glance up the hall. 'No, must be the wind.' She gestured with open hands. 'Hey ho, at least we have somewhere to live, and our landlady's okay.'

'Where's Simon at the club?' I asked to change the subject. I knew he went to Gorton Working Men's Club every Saturday and sometimes on Sunday too.

'Where he always is come hail, rain, or shine – at that bloody club. He asked me to go with him again, but I went last Sunday, and I don't want it to become a habit. It's not my idea of fun watching him playing dominoes or crib, and Michelle always gets dirty. The carpets are mingin', and I can't keep her off the floor.'

'I know the whole place needs refurbishing.' I pulled a face.

'I expect he'll be back at two o'clock for his dinner. Then he'll have a nap and go out again tonight, although I'm never sure where he goes. I've stopped asking – it only causes trouble. I love him, but I don't trust him to tell me the truth anyway, so it's better not to ask.' Janet shrugged her shoulders.

'Oh love ...' Janet didn't normally talk about Simon, who I had always suspected was a bit of a philanderer. I'd seen him flirting with a couple of women at the club on the odd occasion that Peter and I had gone there.

'It's alright. I knew what he was like when I married him, and I'm usually okay with it. I know he loves me and Michelle, and I have you and friends if I want company anytime,' Janet said.

'You do, and he always hands over enough money, doesn't he?' I asked.

Janet sighed, got up, and re-filled the kettle. 'He does, and we're okay. His main trouble is he's too good looking and sociable. Mind you, I wouldn't want him to be miserable. Oh, don't get me wrong, he's here every weeknight; I don't really have anything to moan about. You've caught me in a weak moment, so take no notice. I don't know how Mom has managed all these years with Dad on the road.' She smiled. 'I tell you what, let's have another cuppa and talk about something cheerful.'

I responded in a solemn voice. 'I'm thinking of putting our Christmas tree up next week. Dawn will be able to understand what's going on this year; I'm looking forward to seeing her face when she opens her presents. Mind you, so will Michelle, won't she? It's a lovely time when you're a kid, wouldn't mind being one again just for a little while, eh?'

Janet laughed. 'You're good at changing the subject, aren't you?'

3

I almost ran to answer the phone, which lived on an old wooden trolley just inside the front door. I'm not good with phones. The strident, demanding ring causes my pulse to hike up a few beats until I know who's calling. I think I always expect bad news, although I don't know why. I've never had awful news by telephone.

I breathed again when I heard Janet's mellow voice, 'Is that you, our Sara?'

'Hi, Jan, good to hear from you, I babble.' This amuses Janet, but I'm not sure why. Perhaps it's because I only visited with her yesterday.

'Listen, you daft bugger, I went to see Mom today and was going to have that chat with Lyn, but she wasn't there. Mom said she'd gone to school.'

'That'll be the first time in a month,' I said.

'Well, I thought that maybe Mom wasn't telling the truth; she looked shifty when I probed a bit. She said that she'd given Lyn money to buy her lunch from the chippy by the school, and when I asked her how much she'd given her, she didn't want to tell me. Anyway, I didn't pursue it. I'm not keen on causing her any more stress than Lyn gives her already. What do you think?' Janet asked.

'Hm, makes you wonder, doesn't it? I know one thing, if Mom is colluding with her, then there isn't a fat lot we can do, is there.'

Perhaps Peter is right, I thought. I should try to stop responding to Mom's pleas for help with Lyn. I didn't tell Janet that Peter was annoyed with my penchant for often flying to the rescue. I didn't want her to express any negative feelings about my husband. They got on well together, and I would hate to see anything alter that friendly bond.

'I suppose we could tell Dad when he's next home,' Janet said.

'Mom said he'll be back this weekend. I know he loves his job and is a good salesman judging by the commission that Mom says he earns, but he's no help to her, is he? Perhaps if he knew the way Lyn was behaving lately, he would come off the road for a while,' I said and sighed heavily.

Janet coughed. 'But she always seems to be "Miss Goody Two Shoes" when he's home. Mind you, it might encourage Michael to stay home a little more often if Dad was back. Mom said that he spends most nights at Derek's lately.'

'Yes, she told me,' I said.

'Do you think that he might be queer?' I could almost see the anxious frown on her face and could certainly hear the distaste in her voice. I didn't know that she was homophobic.

'Well, he might be – does it bother you?' I asked.

'Well, no, not really, but with Derek – yuk!'

We both couldn't stop laughing; Derek, with his acne, was not a picture of health and happiness. Not a partner we would have chosen for our young brother anyway.

I was the first to recover. 'I don't think that we should tell Dad yet. I'm not sure that Mom would be delighted to have him home every night. Let's just wait and see how things go, and if you do see her –well, you could have that chat, couldn't you?'

Janet sighed. 'Yes, I think you're right – okay, I've got to go and bath Michelle – speak tomorrow, eh? Love you.'

'Oh, hang on, I haven't told you what I've done – and I need sympathy.'

'What?'

'I've cut my hand.'

'What, how? Are you okay?'

'Well, when I was washing up after dinner, I cut my right thumb and little finger and across my palm, and it's killing me. It would have to be my right hand, eh?'

'Is this the start of a joke, you loony woman?'

'No, I was only washing a few things, but the coke glass broke as I delicately placed my hand inside to wash it.' Janet snorted. 'Okay, maybe not so delicately. Maybe it was more of a collision between the delicate glass and my fist.' I started to laugh. 'Anyway, it resulted in a lot of blood, and you know I'm not a lover of blood, especially my own, and I feel very proud of myself that I managed to stem the flow and apply the bandages all without passing out. Okay, the bandages were plasters, and as you know, it is so unlike me to embellish a story for the sake of sympathy.' I laughed again. 'So, on that note, as you aren't offering any, I'm going. Love you, speak tomorrow.' Giggling like a couple of school kids, we disconnected.

A couple of days later, I still hadn't decorated our tree. It remained living in the loft, where we had stored it, with never a thought, for the last twelve months. I had intended to spend the morning decorating it – one of my favourite pastimes – but Dawn developed a stomach bug and became very demanding, so much so that I couldn't leave her side. Although she was in pain, she asked for food and couldn't understand why I was depriving her. I hoped that only drinking water would see the problem off. Anyway, she did rapidly improve, and after a day and a half, she returned to her usual bubbly self. I felt dreadful that she couldn't understand what was happening or explain how she felt, and I wished that I had the bug instead. At least I could understand why I was hurting. I supposed all mothers, or at least most mothers, feel the same.

As a fortunate consequence of the delay, Peter and I decided that we would like to buy a real tree even if the needles made a mess as it dried out. So, the next weekend, wrapped up in our woollies and waterproofs, we drove to a farm by Cannock Chase and became ultra-fussy about the size and shape of our most important acquisition. Satisfied that we'd chosen the best pine tree available, we faced the problem of transporting it back home. The somewhat surly farmer had tied some of the branches together with twine, and Peter had then tied it onto our roof rack. This didn't seem to cause him much of a problem, as Peter was tall enough to reach without difficulty. Michelle and I were happy to watch him from inside the car out of the sharp wind that was whipping his face until it took on the same shade of red as Santa's coat.

All the way home, the wind velocity increased with gusts scraping, lifting and then smacking the tree back down onto the car roof. I was expecting any minute to hear it wrench free from its anchoring string and fly off the back of the car into some unfortunate vehicle that was behind us at the time. I kept telling Peter to slow down.

'I know how to tie knots, dear, so will you please give it a rest,' he said.

I shut up but swore that I would never do this again – the artificial one would do in the future. I changed my mind when we reached home without mishap, and the next day it was decorated with brightly coloured baubles and silver tinsel. It looked lovely with its even branches, and the sharp, sweet fragrance permeated the living room.

During the next couple of days, I would find Dawn sitting on the fireside mat, gazing with wide-eyed wonder at the twinkling lights that I purposely left on. I loved to watch the expressions on her face as she tried to comprehend when I told her that Father Christmas would be leaving gifts for each of us under its branches. I could scarcely wait for Christmas morning to arrive.

It did arrive and we opened our presents and helped our very excited child to open hers. Then we got ready and went round to Mom's. We were, as usual, all meeting up for a traditional turkey dinner. I looked around the room at my family – my Dad, with his thinning brown hair that was beginning to recede, sat by the fire smoking his briar and occasionally interjecting a good-natured remark. Mom, red in the face, was clad in a clean pinny that replaced her blue, nylon overall. She sipped a small glass of port and lemon while the dinner was cooking itself. Michael, for once, was not at Derek's house. He was playing with Dawn and Michelle, showing how strong his legs were as he stretched them out in front of him with both girls sitting astride while he lifted them in the air. He's filling out, I thought and becoming quite handsome. He was usually a quiet person and had always seemed to be a little uncomfortable within his family of girls, but he came out of his shell somewhat with the little ones who adored him.

Lyn sat on the settee by Simon and Janet, and for once, she too was quiet, no longer seeming to need to be the centre of attention. I wondered what she was thinking. She looked lovely dressed in new blue jeans and a Christmas jumper which had snowmen on the front, her present from Mom. She'd allowed her long hair to hang loose and added a touch of pink lipstick to her mouth. She's beginning to look very grown-up, I thought and remembered with a start that she was nearly sixteen – no longer our baby. Janet and Simon were the best-looking couple in the room. Despite being a Mom, Janet looked almost as young, if not younger than Lyn. I smiled to myself as I surveyed them all. We had always been a close family – problems – yes, we had them, but we were always there for each other. I felt such a rush of love for them all, and to hide my emotions – it was probably the port and lemon that Mom had insisted I had – went into the kitchen to check on the turkey that was roasting itself and the sprouts that had been cooking forever. Traditional, I thought with a smile as I removed the soggy mess from the heat.

Lyn remained quiet and sober all day, even refusing to have a small glass of wine with her dinner, but after Janet and Simon left with Michelle at about six o'clock, she became sour-faced and truculent. She went up to her room with a flea in her ear from Dad, who'd had enough of her moodiness. I could see that she was sneaking a half-full bottle of white wine off the sideboard to take up with her, but I ignored it. It couldn't make her mood much worse, I thought. I asked her quietly what was troubling her, and as she stood up, she shrugged. 'Weren't you happy with your presents, Lyn?' She shrugged again and bounced out of the room, slamming the door behind her.

'I'm off to Derek's; see you later.' Michael blew Mom a kiss and left the house by the back door.

Part of me wanted to go after Lyn, but I thought better of it and cuddled up to Dawn.

Mom said, 'Just ignore her. She'll get over whatever it is.' She poured us both a glass of Babycham and Peter and Dad a pint of Bass, and then we settled down to watch *Christmas Night with the Stars*. Dawn fell asleep on my lap, and after collecting all our paraphernalia together, we left for home at about eight o'clock to put her to bed.

There was no sound from Lyn as we called our goodbyes to her. 'Take no notice,' Peter said.

It had been a long, enjoyable day, and we were all tired, but I thought it was a pity that she had to try to spoil it at the end.

21

At least Dad was home for a few days, so I wasn't too worried that I would be getting a late phone call from Mom.

As we were drifting off to sleep, Peter said, 'She's getting worse, you know.'

'Mm, you've noticed.' I stroked his shoulder and drifted off, too content to be bothered.

4

As a treat for Lyn's birthday, Peter and I hired a self-catering cottage at the closed end of a valley near Dinas Mawddwy in Wales. Michael had agreed to come too, and so we braved the sleet, piled into our crammed car and headed for the hills. Well, mountains really, as we were staying very near to the Pass of The Cross, which is the highest single-track road in Wales, I believe. Peter and I had been there before on our memorable honeymoon in October of 1964. How young we both were, I was nineteen and Peter was only twenty-one, but we were very much in love – we still are.

We knew our way around that part of Wales but locating the cottage was difficult, to say the least. It turned out to be situated behind a five-bar gate and along a track through an overgrown field. We knocked on a nearby cottage door, and a helpful couple directed us to the old shepherd's cottage. Its three feet thick stone walls were whitewashed outside and in. They needed to be thick. Cold wasn't the word; it was freezing. There was only a wood stove in the sitting room that we had yet to light and a Calor gas heater in the kitchen. Other than the oven that we often lit and left the door open, the place was bitter. We all had to pluck up courage, throw a blanket around our shoulders and shiver our way to the bathroom and bedrooms.

Michael was the lucky one as he slept in the sitting room. It had its drawbacks, though. The beamed ceiling was so badly planked that there were inch gaps between the uneven boards. Every time anyone used the bathroom, the rest of us would press our fingers into our ears and sing or hum as loudly as we could. Michael told us that he had to do the same during the night whenever the sound of creaking boards woke him.

It was a memorable week; we went for long walks in the beautiful countryside, where we discovered shallow streams with sparkling waterfalls and strolled through delightful fairy glens. One day, we drove to Lake Vyrnwy across single track roads that were deserted by sane people at this time of the year. The views were magnificent, but the steep drops from the narrow tracks made me breathless with fear, and I could just imagine being stranded miles from help if we pushed our luck and made the return journey along those same tracks in the rapidly fading light, so even though we had enjoyed the experience I decided that we would drive back on the main roads

All in all, the week was a wonderful break, and Lyn showed no sign of being anything but happy and relaxed. I secretly thought that she was afraid of what Peter would do if she exhibited any usual sulky behaviours. He was family, but not the doting family that she was used to.

We'd been home for two weeks when Mom's next call for help came. 'Can you come, our Sara?'

'What's she done now?' I asked. I didn't want to interrupt my cosy evening snuggling up to Peter and watching a play on the television. 'Isn't Dad there?' But I already knew the answer.

'He's in London.' I could hear her beginning to cry quietly.

'Where's Michael?' I asked. Not that I thought he should become involved. He was inclined to be impatient with Lyn's erratic behaviour, and it sometimes made matters worse.

'At Derek's, please come, Sara.'

'Is she in her room again?'

'Yes, and she's saying she's going to kill herself. I'm scared that she means it. She's been drinking again.'

'Alright, I'll just tell Peter, and I'll be there soon. Try not to worry – she won't do anything – go and make a cup of tea.'

'Thanks. Love, I will.' The phone went down. I stood fuming for a few minutes, but I knew I'd have to go.

I went to give Peter the bad news. He shrugged and pursed his lips, but he didn't try to stop me. I tried to feel some empathy on the short drive, but I was pissed off with Lyn's constant attention-seeking. I had tried to be understanding so many times, but now I just felt angry with her. I knew that Mom would expect me to be gentle, but this time I couldn't. I was too annoyed, so I didn't bang on her door. I kicked it – hard.

'Let me in, or the next time I'm going to kick the hinges off,' I yelled.

'Fuck off and leave me alone.' Lyn yelled back.

'Okay, I'm going to count to three, then I'm coming in,' my voice lowered, 'one, two ...' I heard her jump off her bed and the bolt shot open. I stormed into the room and strode to where she sat; her face was a wet, blotchy mess. 'What the fuck do you think you're playing at? You've no intention of killing yourself, have you – you just want to upset Mom and the rest of us – don't you? Why? What has anyone in this family ever done to you, other than been kind and loved you – you spoilt sod you?'

Her crying became louder, and she flinched as I invaded her personal space until I could smell the alcohol sour on her breath. For the first time that I remember, I didn't feel any remorse for telling it straight; I was sick of it.

'Oh, shut up and get a grip.' I stalked to the chest of drawers and grabbed the nearly empty bottle of Bacardi that sat there.

'I'm going downstairs, and you'd better be down after me when you've washed your face – otherwise, I'm coming back up – and I don't know if I'll be able to keep my hands off you next time. Downstairs!' I left the room, slamming the door as I went.

Mom was waiting at the foot of the stairs; she'd heard every word. She gave me a reproachful look and went into the living room – I followed.

'You didn't have to be so harsh, our Sara. What if you've driven her to kill herself, eh?'

'Mom!' I banged my fist on the table. 'She is not going to do that; she enjoys the attention when she's been drinking – you know she does. Now, this has to stop, I don't care where she got the money from, but it has to stop. Do you understand me, Mom? I can't keep doing this.'

Mom's face crumpled as I put my head on one side and listened. I heard Lyn totter down the stairs and then pause for a few seconds outside the door before it was pushed open, and she came in. Her face was still blotchy and her eyes red-rimmed; she looked so miserable that I almost softened towards her until I remembered the look on Peter's face. This has to stop, I told myself.

'Sit down,' I said. She did – as far away from me as possible. 'And you keep out of it, Mom. I'm not doing this again.' She sank back into her chair, a look of resignation on her troubled face. I turned to Lyn, my fists as clenched as my stomach muscles. 'I don't know what caused this latest load of shit, and I don't want to know, seeing as how you refuse to say anything when I ask you. But I am telling you that this is enough, Lyn.'

Lyn went to get up and changed her mind. 'What's it got to do with you? You're alright sitting pretty with your smart husband and clever little daughter, I've got no one, and I'm bored,' Lyn said.

'For God sake, Lyn, you're sixteen – you don't want to go to school anymore – it's about time you stopped feeling sorry for yourself and started to pull your weight around here. You need a job. You've too much time to think about yourself.' I glanced at Mom, who was behaving like a noddy dog in the back of a car. Lyn stared straight ahead with her right hand holding her face as though she'd been physically punched. I was past caring how either of them felt, and I was determined that mine and Peter's lives would no longer be so disrupted by the two of them.

'I wouldn't know what to do,' Lyn said. But her voice was steady and less rebellious than I'd expected.

I tapped my fingers on the arm of the sofa. 'Well, there are lots of things you could do. You need to start by going to the labour exchange and applying for anything you fancy. You love kids, don't you, so what about a nursery assistant?'

'I'm not qualified for anything – do you think I could – I'd like to work with children,' Lyn said hopefully.

I could feel my anger dissipating like clouds forming different patterns as the wind shifts them across the sky. It was being replaced by the old, protective, loving feeling that had been the norm for as long as I could remember.

'I'll help you, I'm sure we can find something, but you have to stop drinking and being such a pain in the neck. I need you to promise me that you'll stop. I won't be running to your rescue next time Mom phones. Do you understand Lyn, I mean it?' I leaned back and waited.

I barely heard her as she said, 'I'm sorry, I know I'm a nuisance, and I can't explain why I'm like it, but I will stop drinking, I promise – I don't even like the taste.' She grimaced, and both Mom and I smiled. She was still the baby of the family.

'Do you want me to help you to find a job?' I asked. She smiled and nodded vigorously, making her hair swirl about her head. 'Okay, well, I'm thinking of returning to work myself so we can go job hunting on Monday. You need to let the school know that you aren't going back. It's your last chance with me, Lyn, so don't let me down.'

'I know, and I'm sorry,' she said again. She jumped to her feet and came to sit beside me on the sofa, where she proceeded to lean her head on my weary shoulder.

Mom hadn't uttered a word during my talk with Lyn, but I knew that she must be feeling relieved.

Do you want a cuppa love?' Mom got to her feet.

I needed one, and if I hadn't been driving, I would have asked for a tot in it.

I stayed a while longer, and we talked positively about jobs and family matters – Lyn didn't seem to be even slightly tiddly now. I wondered just how much she drank. Did she only pretend to be feeling the effects of imbibing alcohol to excuse her bad behaviour? She was devious, I knew that much, and she craved attention enough to make it a possibility. I thought no way to know, but if this doesn't work, maybe she just isn't wired up properly, and I would need to persuade Mom and Dad to seek medical help for her. I doubted Mom would, though. I kept these thoughts to myself; I didn't see any point in meeting trouble halfway.

It was eleven o'clock by the time I left, and I fully expected Peter to be feeling anxious and possibly more than a little annoyed. But I was hopeful that my intervention this time would bring about a change in all our lives. I know Mom is partly to blame, she's been the most indulgent of all of us, but I think she's reached the end of her patience too. I'd been thinking about returning to work now that Dawn was potty trained, and I thought she would benefit from spending some time with her peers. God knows the money that I could earn would be very welcome. I'd been a residential social worker before I married and would, hopefully, be able to return to a job that I enjoyed. I could envisage training to become a qualified social worker and liked the thought. I needed to talk to Peter about it, but not tonight. I'd see how the land lay after I'd had some sleep – I felt I'd earned it.

I needn't have worried about Peter; he was fast asleep and snoring gently when I arrived home. I stood looking down at him as I flung my matching navy-blue skirt and jumper onto the low nursing chair that I'd been so grateful for when Dawn needed to be fed every few hours in the night. Peter had already deposited his discarded clothing tidily on the chair's back. I wasn't so fussy, and mine stayed where they fell. I climbed into bed and tried not to let my cold feet touch his warm legs. Although I would have given a lot to warm them, I didn't want to wake him and perhaps start something that I might regret.

5

Peter wasn't up in time for me to discuss anything with him, and he didn't mention last night as he hurried off to school after giving myself and Dawn a peck on the cheek.

'See you tonight, love,' and he was gone.

I wasn't sorry; I was in no hurry to confront him with my intention to return to the world where they spoke nonsense in sentences rather than disjointed babble. Dawn was entertaining but hardly stimulating, and I was gradually becoming a couch potato and a *Play School* and *Jackanory* addict. Dawn would sometimes fall asleep during the stories, but I listened to them all. Although I found Bernard Cribbins's voice so soothing, I was surprised I didn't follow suit. I have to do something to retain my sanity, and I might as well be earning, I told myself several times during the day.

I cooked Peter's favourite cottage pie, and as soon as we'd eaten and I'd cleared up, I took Dawn up to his study. She settled on the rug with some toys, and I sat in his reading chair while he sorted papers from his briefcase into coloured folders.

'I need to talk to you, love.' I crossed my fingers out of sight.

'What about?' He eased himself into his adjustable office chair and swung round to face me. He looked mildly uneasy. Not surprising. It wasn't often that I was so formal when I had something to say. 'Don't tell me it's about Lyn again. I'm fed up with her tantrums.'

'No, well, not really, although she does come into it – I want to go back to work. I know we agreed that I shouldn't, but I'm becoming bored at home and I need adult company. Besides, the money would come in handy, wouldn't it?'

Peter frowned, beetling his brows together. 'And where does Lyn fit into this sudden urge to leave our child to the mercy of lord knows who?'

I tutted and then said sharply, 'Don't overplay it, Peter, it's not sudden; I've been thinking about it for some time.' I sucked in a breath. 'I've said I'll help Lyn to get a job too.'

He pursed his lips and slowly shook his head. 'Hrumph.' He sounded like one of Dawn's teddies – the one that growls when upended.

I tossed my hair back from my flushed face. 'Come on, Peter, how would you feel if you spent the majority of your days talking to a three-year-old. I love her to bits, but I need more, and she will enjoy going to nursery and mixing with other children.'

Peter looked thoughtful as he went off at a tangent. 'What time did you get home last night, and what was the matter with her this time?'

I felt relieved; at least he wasn't dismissing my plans out of hand. It would have caused trouble as I was determined that I should return to work. I smiled and went into detail about Lyn's behaviour. When I got to the part where I told her what a spoilt brat she was, a big grin appeared on his face.

'Well, you must have put the wind up her.' He began to laugh. 'I wish I'd been there to see my usually kind, placating wife turn into a shrew. I bet you scared the shite out of her.' He came and knelt before me and rested his head on my knees. 'It's up to you love, I don't want you to think that you need to go out to work, you do enough here, but if it's what you want,

I'm not going to object as long as you can find Dawn a suitable placement. Speaking of whom ...' He pointed to where our daughter had snuggled up to her teddy bear and gone to sleep. There were brown smears around her mouth, and her rosy cheeks still had remnants of her teatime meal.

I jumped up. 'Oh dear, am I a bad mother or what?'

'Or what,' his eyes twinkled, 'c'mon, let's get her to bed. Early night for us too?' He gave a rude leer.

The next couple of days passed too quickly for me to think any more about finding work. I did the usual household chores, shopped, and then took Dawn to change Peter's and my library books. She enjoyed being in our modern library with its tiny seats that fitted her backside but not mine. I had to sit on the floor while I read one of her favourite Winnie-the-Pooh books with her. I didn't mind, and I hoped that she'd develop a love of reading.

It was Friday before I phoned Janet to catch up. While I was dialling her number, I tried not to feel miffed that it was nearly always me that made the phone calls. Janet avoided making them unless she had to; Simon usually moaned about the phone bill. I thought that he moaned about anything that involved spending money unless it was on himself, but I'd never say anything to Janet; he was her choice after all.

As usual, she answered at the third ring. 'Hello.' Then her telephone number.

'Hi Jan, you okay you sound a bit chesty?' I could hear a slight wheeze as she spoke.

'I'm okay, just a bit of a cold, that's all. You?'

'We're all fine. Just been doing the usual, but I wanted to tell you about the latest episode with our dear sister.'

'You don't have to tell me. I had Mom on the phone for half an hour yesterday. She sounded quite chirpy, and so did Lyn when she spoke for a few minutes. She said that you're going to help her find a job – are you?'

'Mm yes, and not only that, I talked with Peter, and he's agreed that I can go back to work too.'

'Lucky you, I get so fed up being at home every day with Michelle, much as I love her, I could scream at times. We could do with the extra cash too, but Simon still thinks we're living in the dark ages, and I should stay at home.'

'Well, Peter didn't want me to go back either, but he's seen the sense of it, and when I can find someone suitable to mind Dawn, or a decent nursery that's not too expensive, I'm going to see if I can return to St. Phillips.' As I said it to Janet, it became real to me; I was going back to work. Carried away by my enthusiasm, I began encouraging Janet to rebel even though I knew that she didn't like the idea of facing up to Simon. 'Why don't you talk to Simon again if you're that peed off. I know you both want to buy a house and come back to live in Gorton. Michelle's almost two now, and that's old enough to be left.'

'Oh, I don't know, you know what a funny bugger he can be.' There was a short silence, then she said, 'Perhaps I will talk to him again about it. I'd certainly like to.'

To change the subject, I asked what she'd been up to since we last spoke, and our conversation turned to mundane matters. For the umpteenth time, I felt glad that I was married to Peter and not Simon. Janet had only been eighteen, and she was seven months pregnant when she and Simon married in December 1966. I think that she'd kept the fact that she was having a baby quiet as long as she could – worried about what Mom would say. Dad didn't come into the equation; he left all aspects of bringing us up to Mom. Janet needn't have worried; Mom was, as usual, kind and helpful. She just insisted that they marry before the baby was born. They had a quiet registry office wedding, and a few friends and family round to Mom's afterwards. I felt sorry for her, as I'd had a church wedding with all the usual trimmings, but she didn't seem to be sorry for herself. She loved Simon and was happy to be married; however, they'd achieved it. Finding somewhere to live had been difficult for them, but in the end, they'd rented a small terraced house. They seemed to be content enough until after Michelle was born, and then Janet had begun to feel the distance from her family to be a problem. She often talked about returning to Gorton.

Although I felt somewhat guilty for spurring Janet on to return to work, I dismissed the feeling. Why should women be expected to follow where their men led? There was no reason, these days, to stay at home and look after a houseful of children unless you wanted to. These sort of life-altering decisions should be made jointly. But when Janet made one of her rare phone calls to me the next day, informing me that Simon had gone ballistic when she told him her intention to return to secretarial work, I felt awful for precipitating a row between them. I gave myself a mental slap and reminded myself that it wasn't what I thought or wanted that mattered. I knew that I shouldn't have interfered in Janet's marriage, so I deliberately refrained from repeating my opinions and contented myself with making empty soothing noises while she was on the phone. I promised myself that I would keep my plans under wraps until she needed to know if there had been any progress.

The following Monday dawned wet and windy, and I was glad that Mom offered to mind Dawn while Lyn and I went to the local employment office, where we queued patiently. When our turn came, we registered and then spent a frustrating hour while a grey-suited lady, with a pencil, stuck amusingly through the knot at the back of her greying hair, trawled through boxes of buff-coloured cards in an attempt to find either, or both of us something suitable. Lyn's mood changed from hopeful and excited to disappointed and truculent as time wore on. There seemed to be nothing that we either fancied or were qualified to do. The lady turned away to search yet another drawer.

'C'mon, let's get out of this stupid place,' Lyn said. She didn't lower her voice, and I cringed.

'Shh, she'll hear you, and we'll be banned,' I whispered. I grabbed her by the arm and headed for the exit. 'Behave yourself; you don't expect to walk into something that you would like to do straight away – do you?'

Lyn frowned. 'Yes, I do; there were enough bloody cards in those stupid boxes and not one suitable thing. I don't think she wanted to find us jobs.' She snatched her arm from my grasp and began to stomp away from me.

The rain was lashing down as I pushed open the glass door and stepped outside. Oh, hell, I thought as I struggled to put up my umbrella; here we go.

I hurried after her. 'Look, you silly bugger, new jobs are being put onto those cards every day. We just have to keep going back and getting the woman behind the desk to look for us. It's no use you being a mardy arse – if you behave like this at work, you'll never hold down a job anyway – you'd get the sack. Come on, let's go and have some lunch, I'll buy you a burger and a shake, and we can make our plans. There are other ways to find work.'

Lyn stopped so abruptly that I bumped into her rain-sodden back, and we began to laugh together. Her mood had changed yet again.

'Okay, come on then.' She began to run towards the red and white Wimpey sign. I continued to walk behind her for a couple of yards and then broke into an unsteady run myself while the wind tried to tear my brolly from my hands. A pain in the bum she was, but she was also my little sister. She could make me laugh and jump through hoops at times, and this was one of those times.

6

Just after Mom's forty-ninth birthday in October, I decided I'd had enough of repeated unsuccessful visits to the unemployment office. Lyn was becoming increasingly despondent, so I put my sensible head on and phoned Mr Stanley, who was the head of care, at St. Phillip's Community Home with Education. I had worked there as a night officer and then as a residential social worker before I had Dawn. As I was waiting for him to come to the phone, I couldn't help but grin to myself as I pictured the first night I had been on duty. I was being taken around the establishment and shown the ropes by another night officer, a very tiny Irish woman. I followed her with interest as she chatted away, explaining everything she could think of. As we went through the main kitchen, she stopped to get her breath back and jumped up to perch on the edge of one of the enormous metal sinks, she had obviously done this before, but on this occasion, she misjudged her aim. I stood with my mouth agape as she disappeared into its depths with only her sandaled feet sticking out above the rim. I hastened to pull her out. She landed back on the floor with not a feather ruffled and continued to talk as though nothing untoward had happened. We became friends, but we never mentioned our introduction, although the picture of her sliding into that sink has remained and amused me on numerous occasions.

One Child Too Many

When he eventually arrived to take my call, Mr Stanley was, as usual, very kind and offered me a temporary post as a night officer again until a vacancy for an RSW should become available. I jumped at it. It would solve most of my babysitting problems too. When I explained that my sister, Lyn, had no experience but was looking for a job, he offered to let her start as a kitchen assistant or a cleaner in the hostel, which was on the main building's grounds. It was a big old house, modernised to accommodate social workers who didn't live in the city. There were three members of staff currently in residence. An on-duty sleeping-in person also had a room. It made it easy to contact them if there was a problem in the main building during the night.

Lyn's position would be a three-month probationary one, and I just hoped that she would be able to grow up and do a good job.

I hurried round to Mom's to tell her the news. 'Well, what do you think, eh?

Lyn wrinkled her nose. 'I'm not working in a hot, smelly kitchen at everyone's beck and call.'

'Okay, what about the cleaning job? I'm sure you'd like it. The hostel is a lovely place.'

'I don't know. Will I be able to travel by car with you?' Lyn asked.

'I'll be working different shifts, but you're quite capable of getting the bus; I'll show you where. You'll have to have an interview, so you need to ring Mr Stanley if you want the job.'

Lyn became very animated and asked numerous questions about St. Phillips and later arranged an interview. She got the job.

Peter's mother, Ivy, was happy to look after Dawn when necessary. She lived close by and loved her only granddaughter, who she'd minded overnight on the two occasions that Peter and I had been away from home.

It had been exciting and a real turning point for Lyn when she started her new life. After a few weeks, she seemed to be a changed person. Her moodiness had taken a back seat, and several of the staff mentioned to me what a delightful girl she was, always singing, very helpful, and also very good at her job.

I thanked my lucky stars that Mr Stanley had been prepared to give her a chance and to see Mom relax as she was able to spend her days looking after her precious plants, which made all my efforts worthwhile.

Mom's back garden was delightful, and we'd been glad of her obsessive hobby all the years that we were growing up. There was always somewhere beautiful to play, but we were in trouble if a ball went into any of the flower beds. They were an amazing array of perennials. Roses, lily of the valley, lupins, hostas and marigolds were her favourites, but she ensured that something was in bloom throughout the year. Although I valued our surroundings, mostly I appreciated that she didn't expect us to help in any way towards the result. I've never been one for digging in the dirt, metaphorical or otherwise. I hate intrigue and the feel of soil clogging beneath my long fingernails. Just seeing woodlice and orange wireworms and the results of exposed secrets have always made me feel like throwing up. I was sure when I was young that Mom loved her plants and Lyn more than me, Janet and Michael. Perhaps she did – she certainly gave them more attention.

That summer was well underway by the time I realised I had been living with an illusion. Lyn had seemed to be happy and content both at work and at home. She'd become friends with one of the social workers called Roy, who lived in the hostel and spent most of her off duty time in his company. He wasn't one of my favourite people; in fact, he was the type of man that I despised. He was nice looking and knew it, he was also arrogant and opinionated, but he was popular with the female staff – well, most of them anyway.

Roy was ten years older than Lyn, and I became quite concerned when she gained permission from Mr Stanley to live in the hostel during the week. Early morning transport to work had proved to be difficult. I wondered if she was having a relationship with Roy, but when I asked her about it, she denied they were anything but friends. I had to accept this as Roy merely laughed when I asked him if he was going out with Lyn.

'That's none of your business now, is it, big sister?' he said

Maybe he was right, she was sixteen after all, but I fretted until Peter said more or less the same thing, only in a nicer way. I tried to put it out of my mind as Lyn continued to look happy and chatted easily each time I saw her. Mom didn't have a lot to say about her youngest daughter's behaviour, either. She was enjoying the break from her problems and burying her head in the sand and her hands in the soil. I decided to bide my time and wait to see how things progressed. I didn't want to be –big sister – just sister would be enough.

Since Lyn and I had been working, I hadn't seen that much of Janet. Although we'd kept in touch by phone, our conversations had been somewhat haphazard, and I missed her. I knew that she missed my visits too, and so I arranged to take Dawn and stay overnight at her house on my next weekend off. We had often spent a weekend together before Janet had Michelle. Janet told me that Simon used to moan about it, but I didn't care too much as he never prevented her from coming to stay at my place, and he never mentioned it to me.

Janet was pleased to see us, but I thought that she looked less happy than usual. She did have her face paint on, but it certainly wasn't as carefully applied as she usually managed. I thought that she looked like a pale shadow, but I kept my thoughts to myself. I didn't want to upset her.

After we'd put the children to bed, and Simon had taken himself off to the club, we sat chatting for a while, then Janet said, 'I need to tell you something.' I raised my eyebrows; she looked so intense. 'I'm pregnant again. Simon doesn't want me to tell anyone yet, but I just can't keep it secret anymore.'

A long minute passed in silence, then I jumped up and went to sit beside her. She had started to cry. 'Hey, stop that, congratulations that's lovely news.' I hugged her then handed her a tissue as tears ran freely down her cheeks.

'Is it?' She mopped her eyes and sighed heavily.

'Yes, of course, it is, babies are never bad news; you'll love this one as much as you love Michelle, you silly bugger. What's the problem?' I didn't understand why she was so upset.

'It isn't a problem, really; I just feel trapped in a way. I wanted to go back to work, but Simon's made sure that I can't. It's not that I won't love this baby, but he knew that I didn't want to be a stay at home mom.' She shrugged her shoulders slowly. 'Oh, what's the use in crying about it? It's done, I'm pregnant, and that's that. I don't suppose we'll ever be able to move back to Gorton or buy a house now.' She shrugged again, dashed the tears from her eyes with the back of her hand and stood up. 'I'm going to make a cuppa; do you want one?'

I followed her to the kitchen and looked through the window into their tiny garden where the annual summer flowers had taken on a decidedly tired, straggly appearance. I've never been keen on this time of the year; it's like the way old age creeps up on a person, almost unnoticed, until infirmity and then death claims them. I shook my head to get rid of my morbid thoughts and turned instead to happy ones of the new niece or nephew that I would be able to love. I knew that Janet would love the baby too as soon as she became used to the idea. I watched her as she poured boiling water onto the tea bags.

'You know Jan – it's not the end of the world you'll still be able to return to work. Many mothers with quite young babies do these days. You just need to work on Simon and make him see how important it is to you. Have you told Mom and Dad yet – no, of course, you haven't – silly question,' I answered myself. 'You should; they'll be so excited to have another grandchild – when's it due?'

'The middle of March, about the sixteenth.' Her teeth clicked sharply against the side of her china mug.

I steered the conversation away from babies and brought her up to date about Lyn's latest escapade. But the subject quickly became about babies again, and as we talked, I could sense her slowly unwinding and seeing the future in a rosier light. Mainly hormones, I thought, but I could empathise with her wish to escape her humdrum life. I would have liked another child, but staying at home as a consequence didn't appeal. Peter and I had been trying to become parents again, but it just wasn't happening, and I was glad I had a job that I enjoyed. Plenty of time to let nature take its course.

The following Monday, I was called into Mr Stanley's office and told that a residential social worker's vacancy had become available. Although I enjoyed working nights, I preferred days. There was more interaction with the youngsters, and I had always gained satisfaction from helping them somehow rather than ensuring their overnight containment. I accepted with alacrity, but when I spoke to Ivy, she said she was sorry, but she couldn't be flexible enough to mind Dawn to accommodate my changing shift pattern. I didn't blame her. I knew that she led a busy social life playing golf, and she belonged to a sewing guild, as well as spending a day as a volunteer at a local hospice. I needed to find a solution quickly, so I did what I always do in an emergency, I asked my Mom if she could help, and she agreed temporarily. Problem solved, I looked forward to starting my new position, knowing that Mom and Dawn, who was now a four-year-old chatterbox, would be company for each other. Sure enough, after a couple of weeks, Dawn was becoming knowledgeable about plants and loved helping Mom in her garden.

After telling me that she was expecting, Janet had phoned Mom and told her the news. When I took Dawn for a visit a few days later, Mom said that Janet had sounded pleased to be having another baby.

'Another grandchild for you to love, exciting, isn't it?' I said.

'Well, it's better news than the last time anyway.'

I was taken aback to hear a definite spikiness in her voice. She wasn't over the circumstances of Janet's rushed marriage, but I wasn't really surprised as I was aware that she hadn't grown to like Simon any more than I had. I refrained from commenting. I knew that she would love her new grandchild as soon as it was born. I was more concerned that Janet should never find out how we felt about her husband.

'Have you told Lyn and Michael yet?' I asked.

Mom laughed. 'Well, I've told them, and you wouldn't believe how different their reactions were. Lyn was home for a change,' she sighed heavily. 'She's very excited and can't wait to be an aunt again. Michael shrugged his shoulders and said, "Oh right", and then wandered off down to the shed. He said he was going to mow the lawn before the rain set in. Dark clouds were coming over from by the railway bridge, and he thought we were in for a good old downpour. Did it pee down by you?'

'Yes, I think so.'

'All this rain,' Mom said. 'I reckon it's upset all our weather.'

'What has?'

'Men walking on the moon –what next?'

A big grin spread across my face. 'You are daft. It's nothing of the sort.'

It was only after Dawn and I were on our way home that I realised with a rush of guilt that I hadn't even asked how my Dad was or where he was. I did love him, but I wondered guiltily if he was becoming irrelevant to me. I made myself a promise that I would find out when he was next home and be sure to visit and have a chat with him.

7

To celebrate our birthdays in October, mine on the eighteenth and Janet's on the twenty-third, I booked an overnight stay at a small hotel on the banks of the River Severn at Ironbridge. We had always celebrated together. It had been a joke between us from as far back as I could remember. I don't know why, but Janet found the fact that I was two years and five days older than she was very amusing. She wrote the age gap on my birthday card every year. I often retaliated by commiserating with her because she looked older – sister's stuff, I suppose.

The hotel was very kitsch, and I found out that the owners were a couple of men. They were lovely and made us very welcome. It was a bit weird, though, to wake up in a room decorated entirely in black and chewing gum pink. Even the two small chandeliers had pink bulbs that cast a peculiar light around the room. Not unpleasant, but it made looking into the ornate mirrors a distorting experience. We'd found it a bit of fun, but I could imagine that it would annoy some people.

We spent the day visiting a couple of museums and walking along the tarmac path that followed the river's course. It was bitterly cold, and the wind constantly tried to push us into the water. I thought that it was a bit scary really, I'm not a strong swimmer. We were glad to return to the hotel, where we ate our freshly cooked meal and stuffed ourselves with indulgent puddings. I felt fit to burst and called a halt before I exploded.

One Child Too Many

Both Janet and I usually ate a reasonably healthy diet, but our birthday and Christmas were exceptions. We had a great time laughing and joking together as we always had, but by five o'clock, we were ready to go home, back to our little girls and, at least in my case, back to my kind and loving husband.

I dropped Janet home to her very sulky, disgruntled one. He resented not being able to go to his club, and his behaviour made me want to punch him. He barely said hello to me and didn't greet Janet at all except to say, "Michelle's in bed" before he donned his coat and left the house.

Janet's face was scarlet. 'Take no notice, if he had his way, I'd never leave the house without Michelle. He'll be sorry when he comes home after he's caught up with his mates and downed a few pints.'

'Fuck him!' I said. But I immediately regretted my outburst as I knew it would upset her. 'I'm sorry, Jan, but he annoys me at times; he can be such a selfish bugger.'

'I know you're right, but he's not always like that. I've told you before that he can be very kind. Are you stopping for a cuppa?'

'No, ta love, I'll be getting back; I want to see Peter, and I just might get to see Dawn before she goes to bed. You okay?'

'Yes, go on and get off home; we had a good time, didn't we?' she grinned. Her eyes sparkled at what was already a memory that we would both treasure. I nodded and hugged her as she said, 'Thanks for paying for me; I'll return the favour sometime – God knows when, though.'

'Don't be daft. I'm glad we could be together like that; it was worth every penny. I'm going home to redecorate our bedroom in pink and black. I wonder what Peter would say?'

We were still laughing as I got into my car, gave a quick wave, and headed home, where I knew my reception would be so different. And of course, it was – Peter was just getting Dawn ready for bed – they are so close these two-precious people. He was kneeling on the floor, trying to get Dawn to step into her pyjama trousers, and Dawn was deliberately missing her footing to make her Dad laugh. When I walked in, they both jumped up for a hug. I'd enjoyed my weekend with my sister, but I was so glad to be back in my comfortable, loving home.

'Have you had a good time?' Peter asked. I took over the task of getting our daughter ready for bed. She never played me up as much or laughed as often as she did with Peter, and while it meant that tasks were completed more quickly, there had been a few silly times when I'd felt quite jealous of their close bond.

'Yes, it was really good to spend some quality time with Jan – I miss our weekends together.'

I kissed Dawn goodnight, and then Peter chased her, screaming and giggling, up the stairs. I'd long since stopped trying to be a calming influence. Dawn usually settled down quickly, so I took no notice and went to make a cup of tea. When Peter returned five minutes later and sank into a chair pretending exhaustion, I went on to describe our hotel and how we'd spent our time. I left out Simon's behaviour. He was already Peter's least favourite person to spend time with, and I didn't want to make things worse between them – I knew he wouldn't think much of Simon's attitude.

Later, when we'd finished laughing over my threat to decorate our bedroom in pink, Peter said, 'I'm glad you enjoyed yourselves, but there have been a couple of phone calls from St. Phillips while you've been away. I asked if it was urgent, and they said no, so I decided not to tell them how to contact you and perhaps spoil your break.'

'I just hope it's nothing to do with Lyn. She's been a bit moody again lately, but I'll phone Mrs Darcy first thing and see why they want me. It must have been important – they don't usually phone us when we're off duty. I suppose I could ring Mom and ask if Lyn's okay, but I wouldn't want to worry her unnecessarily.'

I realised that I was nibbling at the cuticle on my thumb – something I always do when I'm worried. I guiltily pulled my hand away from my mouth. I've made my thumb very sore in the past.

'It's probably nothing at all. Try not to worry,' Peter said.

'I'm not worried, come on, let's get some sleep – or not.' I leered at him, making us both giggle like naughty youngsters as we kept shushing each other so as not to wake our daughter.

'Thank you for calling in Sara – how was your stay in Ironbridge?' Mrs Darcey, the school secretary, was a middle-aged woman with tightly permed, steel-grey hair. She had a steely manner too if she wasn't pleased with you, but she could also be very sweet, and I had always got on well with her. I gave her a very brief picture and then asked why they had tried to contact me.

'Well, it's really about your sister, Lyn; I wouldn't ask you; I know she isn't your responsibility, but Mr Stanley is worried about her, we all are.'

'Oh, dear, what's the matter?' I asked calmly. But I wanted to scream.

Mrs Darcey took a deep breath. 'She hasn't been to work for nearly a week or contacted us to explain why. I've tried repeatedly to phone her, but there's been no answer. We don't know if she's ill or if something else is wrong. Mr Stanley needs to know if she intends to return to work or whether she's resigned. Have you heard anything?'

I didn't know what to say; my initial reaction was annoyance – how could she let me down like this – but it quickly morphed into concern for her wellbeing. I would have to go around to Mom's and find out what was going on.

'I've not heard from either Lyn or my mother since last Monday, so it's been a week today. I'm worried now in case something is seriously wrong. I'll go to see them. I'll let you know what I find as soon as possible. I'm so sorry.' I wasn't quite sure why I was apologising, but I ended the call and tried to ring Mom.

There was no reply. I tried every few minutes while I got Dawn ready to go out, but there was still no response. I supposed that they could have gone out shopping or something, but why hadn't Mrs Darcey been able to contact them all week? It didn't make sense. I phoned and cancelled a lunch appointment with Mary, my friend of many years, pocketed the spare key that I kept at my house for emergencies, and then drove round to Mom's. By the time I got there, I'd convinced myself that something terrible had happened to them.

I turned my key in the lock and pushed the door open cautiously. All sorts of dreadful thoughts had been running through my head on the drive over: they could be lying there dead, what if someone had broken in and killed all three of them or all four if Dad was home? I slowed my breathing as I walked down the hall. I could hear the television was on quietly. I went into the living room, carefully keeping Dawn behind me, and there they were – very much alive. Mom in her chair by the fire, and Lyn sprawled across the red, chintzy sofa. They were watching an old wildlife programme.

I didn't know whether to be pleased to see them alive and well or angry that they were being so selfish.

'What do you call this?' I asked the foolish question quietly so as not to alarm Dawn, who had run to give them both a kiss and then settled herself on Lyn's lap.

I tried again. 'What is going on, Mom? I've been trying to phone you, but there's been no answer.' I threw my coat onto the back of the chair by the television and then sat down at the table. Mom looked sheepish and held up her hands, but Lyn shrugged her shoulders and continued to watch the telly. I could feel my anger growing, hot like a kettle coming to the boil. I got up and switched off the programme that they'd been watching.

'Hey, I was watching that,' Lyn said. Mom said nothing, just looked at her hands that were now twisting together in her lap.

'Mom, why haven't you been answering the phone?' I asked. I was well aware that my daughter was watching us with wide eyes. She knew something was amiss but couldn't fathom out why I had put the television off.

'I'm sorry, love, but Lyn didn't want me to in case it was St. Phillips for her. I'm sorry,' she repeated.

I looked at Lyn, who'd sat up and put Dawn onto the carpet where she sat with her thumb in her mouth, gazing from one to the other of us. 'I think you need to tell me what has happened at work, Lyn. You can't just hide here forever and let everyone, including you, down. And don't you dare say that it's none of my business.'

'Nothing much happened,' she shrugged, but her face reddened. 'I had a row with Roy, that's all and walked out.'

'What did you row about?' I asked. Lyn shrugged again and held her hands out, palms up as though she didn't know. 'Okay, don't tell me, but I need to know are you going back or are you resigning?' Lyn gave me a filthy look, got up and walked quickly to the hall door, but I moved faster and forestalled her exit. 'Oh no, Lyn, you're going nowhere until you tell me what your intentions are. I don't care what you rowed about, but I need an answer for Mr Stanley.'

She tried to push past me, but I pushed her against the wall and held her there – I'm much stronger than she is. 'Well, what am I going to tell them?'

'I'm not going back,' she said. Her face was full of fury as I released her, allowing her to escape to her room.

I went to Dawn and picked her up. I was sorry that she'd witnessed the scene, but at least I had the answer that I needed. I couldn't think straight. I supposed that I should be annoyed with my Mom too, but I knew how Lyn could make her behave, and I didn't have the heart to remonstrate with her. I fetched Dawn's coat from where it had fallen on the floor, and we left, after kissing my very subdued mother goodbye.

When I arrived home, I phoned Mrs Darcey, gave her the bones of what Lyn had said, and told her that I'd speak to her again when my shift started in the morning. I spent the rest of the day playing with Dawn, hoping that I could eradicate the nastiness from both our minds.

8

'I'm so sorry, Mr Stanley.' I apologised for my sister, who still hadn't had the decency to let him know that she no longer wanted to work at St. Phillips. I felt responsible as I'd asked him to give her the job, and I knew that he'd treated her kindly, even allowing her to have the use of one of the rooms without being charged. I couldn't explain her behaviour except to say that she could sometimes be difficult and repeat my apology.

'Well don't you worry, Sara, you were only doing the best for your sister, and you aren't responsible for her. I'm sorry we had to involve you, but we couldn't make contact with her, and I needed to know whether to advertise for someone to take her place. It's a shame because she was a good worker – I had no worries on that score.' He smiled, 'I would be happy to give her a good work reference in the future.'

I thanked him and started my shift on Shawberry, one of the units that were home to twelve youngsters, many of whom were there because they were out of parental control and placed themselves in danger. Although I loved my work, I was still smarting inside to think Lyn could be such an inconsiderate liability throughout that day. She didn't seem to care or have any understanding of how stupid I would feel. I felt even worse when two days later, as I was hurrying down the hostel drive to where I'd parked my car, I bumped into Roy.

'Hi there Roy.' I waved my hand politely as he passed and then continued along the drive. He came after me and grabbed the top of my arm in a vice-like grip that brought me to a standstill. 'Let go of me.' I said, louder than I had intended; I was so startled by his touch.

I was even more startled as he swung me round to face him.

'Tell that mad sister of yours that if I receive another letter like the one she sent last Friday, I'll take it to the head or maybe the police.' His warm spittle brushed my face. He let go of my arm and began to walk up the drive towards the large red-brick hostel. I ran after him and held onto his jacket.

'What's happened, Roy? What letter are you talking about? I thought you two were friends?'

His face twisted unpleasantly. 'I thought she was a sweet little thing and listened to her maundering on about the man that she loved and couldn't have. God, she nearly drove me barmy with it, but I felt sorry for her until she went too far.'

'What are you talking about? Who do you mean? I've no idea what you mean. I was worried that you might be having an affair with her – are you telling me that you weren't?'

I was totally confused, and my face must have shown it. His tone softened as he said, 'It's not me that you have to worry about – but I'll not betray her confidences, crazy as she is.'

'Well, tell me about the letter, why would she run off the way she has? There must have been a reason.' I let go of his arm and gazed into the handsome face that I so disliked – I needed to understand.

'Okay, I'll tell you what happened, but I still can't explain why she behaved like a madwoman. I don't know if you've heard that I'm going out with Barbara, one of the teachers from the school – we're engaged, but we keep it quiet – you know what Social Services are like they may not allow us both to work at the same establishment.' He looked expectantly at me, and I nodded my understanding, then he continued. 'Well, Lyn walked in on us at the beginning of last week and became upset for some reason. She threatened to tell Mr Stanley that we were sleeping together. I told her to get out and grow up and that I was sick of her childish fantasies. I was probably embarrassed more for Barbara than myself and became angrier than I should have, but the threatening letter she sent was way out of line. She sounds nutty. I hope it doesn't run in your family,' he sneered at me, 'anyway when you see her, tell her I said there hadn't better be any more letters and she'd better keep away from me in future.' His lips moved into a threatening half-smile as he finished speaking, but his eyes remained cold and insulting.

'Fuck off,' I whispered and turned to walk, with as much dignity as I possessed, toward my car. What had I walked into, and what on earth had she been doing? I liked being a part of St. Phillips very much, but at this moment, I couldn't wait to get away from the place; it felt hostile.

I waited until Peter and I had finished eating our pork chop and cauliflower dinner later that evening, then I told him what Roy had said and the way he'd behaved towards me. He listened with an occasional nod until I'd finished. Then he ran his hands through his thick, blond hair, something that I loved to do, studiously lined his knife and fork upon his plate, walked around the table, took me by the hand and led me to where Dawn was playing with her Lego in the sitting room. He sat in an armchair and pulled me onto his lap, all without saying a word. I was bemused.

'I want you to listen to me this time, Sara,' he said. I'd never heard him sound so serious. 'I think it's about time that you stopped being dragged into Lyn's problems. Ever since I've known you, you've run back and forth in response to her bloody awful behaviour. You've tried hard to help her and your Mom, but nothing you've ever done or said has made a lasting difference.'

'Oh but –'

'You need to call a halt. Let them get on with their lives, and we'll get on with ours. She's not going to change, you know; she's spoilt rotten and knows just how to yank you and your Mom's chain. You'll be looking after them for the rest of your life if you're not careful, and much as I love you, I'm not going to stand by and see that happen.' He pulled me gently towards him until my nose was breathing in his classroom smell and held me close. My heart was in my mouth. Would he leave me, I wondered, but I immediately knew I was being silly.

'What do you mean, are you thinking of leaving me if I don't stay away from them?' I couldn't resist asking.

After what seemed to be a long time, long enough to make me feel uncertain – like a Kelly doll that's been prodded until it wobbles – he leaned away from me until he could see my stricken face. 'Don't be silly,' he said. I exhaled heavily. I hadn't realised that I'd been holding my breath. He continued earnestly. 'I don't expect you never to see them, but I would move us far enough away from Gorton to make it too difficult for you to come to their rescue every time Lyn tried to make everyone pay for loving her and mollycoddling her too much.'

'Oh, but I –'

'No, don't say anything yet; I want you to think about what I've just said because I mean it even if it will cause us both to leave our jobs.' He moved to ease me from his lap, and I stood up. 'I'm going to put Dawn to bed now, and when I come down, we'll talk about it then, okay?' Peter said.

I nodded. I knew that he meant every word, and I didn't blame him; he'd put up with a lot from my family over the years. I walked into the dining room and cleared the dinner plates as he chatted to Dawn and helped her put her toys away.

One Child Too Many

I went about doing the chores automatically, my mind was in turmoil – first Roy's nastiness, and then this unexpected behaviour from my usually mild and accommodating husband had thrown me. They were my family, and all my life, I had pandered to them and been protective. How could I possibly stop now? I knew that I would have to find a way. Peter was my husband and my best friend, and as an only child from a stable and loving background, how could he understand the close family ties that existed – even in as dysfunctional a family as mine was.

My mind was still whirling when he came downstairs, and I went up to kiss Dawn goodnight. I knew that she'd heard what Peter had been saying, but I hoped she hadn't understood any of the implications. She was already very drowsy as I leaned down to kiss her, 'Night, night, my darling, sleep tight.' I turned her Winnie-the-Pooh bedside light off and began to close the door.

She gave an enormous yawn. 'Night, night Mommy, I love you.'

'I love you too, my baby; see you in the morning.' I shut the door quietly and went slowly downstairs to where Peter had poured us both a glass of white wine and was sitting reading in a pool of light cast by our old, wooden standard lamp with its floral shade. He put his book down and passed me my glass. I thanked him and then sat down opposite.

Anxious to get my perspective across, I said, 'I don't know what you expect me to do, love, they're my family, and I feel responsible. I know Mom's weak. She's always taken the least line of resistance, Lyn's a nightmare, and Dad's rarely home. Thank God for Janet and Michael, neither of whom is in a position to help. I don't see how I can suddenly change –what would you do if it was your sister?'

'She's not my sister. I don't have one and have never wanted one, so I don't know, but I do know that I've come to the end of the line with yours.' He sat back in his chair and looked at me with raised eyebrows and a downturned mouth.

I took a sip of wine and said hesitantly, 'I'll try Peter, I really will. I don't want us to move away, and you love your school. I can't say more than that – I will try.'

'Okay, that's all I need to hear; how about if we give it six months, and if there's been no change, I'll make sure we talk about moving again.' I had a lump in my throat and felt tears starting as I hoped that I only imagined a slightly threatening tone to his voice. I nodded my agreement, anything could happen in six months, and I felt determined to make some changes.

We were both feeling somewhat drained at this point, and after watching the news, we decided to have an early night and switched the telly off. I snuggled close to Peter, feeling scared by my brief thought that he might leave me. I felt certain that we loved each other too much for that to happen. I also felt certain a month later that that was the night when we conceived our second child.

9

When I got out of bed Christmas Eve morning, it hit me and my stomach started to cramp. I thought it was the start of my period, which was very late. I knew different when my lips began to tingle, and I began to retch. I didn't make it to the bathroom before I brought forth a stream of bile. I knew I must be pregnant. I had intense memories of vomiting yellow bile throughout the nine months with Dawn. I sat on the side of the bath and cried; the silent tears ran down my cheeks and into the corners of my mouth, I tasted salt, not unpleasant, but it was enough to stem the flow. I pulled some toilet tissue from the roll and mopped my face. I didn't know if I was pleased or sorry. We'd been trying to increase our family for a couple of years, but I'd only been back at work for a short time, and now I would have to leave again. I knew Peter would be delighted, and I didn't want him to see me crying when he came back upstairs with our early morning tea.

I quickly cleaned up the vomit and climbed back into bed without noticing that Dawn had snuggled down under the blankets, ready to surprise us. I let out a shriek of alarm as she tickled my toes, then climbed up my legs shouting, 'Surprise, Mommy.'

I decided to keep my news to myself for a while; I wasn't ready to hear other people's reaction until I'd worked out my own feelings. I thought that I should tell Peter, but I just didn't want to, even though I felt spiteful for not sharing with him.

Christmas Day was, as usual, spent at Mom and Dad's house with us all joining in and helping. Even Lyn pulled her weight. When she'd left St. Philips, Mom had told her that there was no need to find other work until she was ready, but off her own bat, at the beginning of December, she applied for a position that was advertised in the Evening Mail and was successful. The job was that of a live-in nanny. She'd be responsible for two boys whose parents were both Doctors and home every weekend, so the hours were only Monday to Friday. She also had several days off over the Christmas period. She spoke about it so enthusiastically that I couldn't help but be pleased for her.

One of her charges attended a private school near to where they lived in Edgbaston, and his parents dropped him there each morning, so Lyn's chores were not too onerous. She had to keep the boy's clothes clean and ironed, do a little light vacuuming and look after the three-year-old until she fetched the older boy from school. Then after giving them their tea, she was free for the evening. It paid well, and it seemed to be just what she needed. I had met the parents on a couple of occasions as Lyn had invited Dawn and me to have lunch with her so that Dawn could play with Henry while Charles was at school. Her employers told me when I visited her one evening that she was indispensable, and it was apparent that the boys loved her. She's growing up, at last, I'd thought with my fingers well and truly crossed.

Dad, Peter, and Simon had taken themselves off to the local pub for a few pints before dinner. They were all a little merry by the time they strolled back home just before lunch was ready to be served. Mom took one look at them as they shook the snow from their boots and hung their coats up in the hall.

'Men – trust you to stay out until everything's done.' She sounded annoyed, but she didn't expect men to help with household chores. 'Come on and get warm by the fire we're just about to dish up.'

My main present from Peter was a ruby and diamond eternity ring. I kept holding my hand under the Christmas tree lights to admire the sparkle of the gems. I loved it, and Peter kept smiling at me and nodding at my hand with a fatuous look on his face. I laughed each time and enjoyed the closeness that we shared. At times we didn't need words to get the message across.

The girls were excited by their new toys, especially the dolls and prams they had both received, and Michael seemed to be enjoying himself as much as they were. Dad sat in his chair by the fire and lit his pipe. He seemed content, but I thought that he didn't seem to fit in somehow – we were so used to him being away from home.

Peter and Simon stood with their hands held out towards the flames, and their bodies blocking the heat until Janet told them to move. They reluctantly went to sit on the sofa, and it wasn't long before Mom instructed everyone to find a seat at the table.

Even with the two leaves of the table pulled out, it was a squash for us all to sit down. Janet's bump seemed to get in the way of whatever she did, amusing everyone except for Michael, who averted his eyes. Mom had insisted that he stay home until after dinner. He wasn't happy, but I was glad he was there. He'd played with the girls most of the morning and kept them from under our feet. He'd refused to go with the other men to the pub. He'd told me once that he disliked the taste of beer and most other alcoholic beverages, so I surmised that he preferred not to go rather than run the risk of being teased if he didn't imbibe.

I glanced around the table at everyone as they filled their plates and pulled the cheap crackers that were a waste of money but so necessary, and inwardly smiled. I loved them all and knew how happy they would be to hear my news when I was ready to tell them. I wasn't ready yet, though – I had vomited a few times since that first day – but it was nothing like as bad as when I was carrying Dawn, so I wanted to wait until I was sure that I was pregnant before saying anything.

The cacophony of voices was deafening at times, but I wouldn't have missed the family Christmas for anything. Just the smell was enough. I hardly tasted what I was eating until I suddenly realised as I put a spoonful of Christmas pudding covered with a dollop of brandy sauce into my mouth that I was as stuffed as the turkey had been. Why do we do it, I thought, and dropped the spoon with a clatter into the half-empty dish? I rubbed my stomach and groaned, and everyone laughed.

Later, when everything was cleared away, we sang along with the carols playing on the radio. I studied the expression on each of their faces. I hadn't said a word to Lyn about Roy or work even though I wanted to ask her about the man that she was supposedly secretly in love with – and the letter. I knew that Peter appreciated my restraint. He'd drawn me aside after we'd all exchanged our gifts that morning and whispered in my ear. 'Well, it's working, isn't it? All's quiet on the Western Front.' He indicated Lyn's happy face.

'Yes, you were right, I took too much on myself; our lives have been a lot easier lately, thank goodness,' I whispered back.

Lyn still looked happy as she sang. She seemed to have a special glow on her pretty face, something I'd begun to notice since she'd started work again. I wondered if she'd met someone but quickly told myself to mind my own business. We'd know soon enough if she had.

10

Lyn's seventeenth birthday came and went, and to my amazement, she was still in a good place. She was content with the presents that she'd received and had shown no sign of shutting herself away or becoming intoxicated. I breathed a sigh of relief and began to think about the baby that was secretly growing inside me.

As the time plodded on towards the birth of Janet's baby with no more than filthy looks from Roy, which I ignored, I began to think that Lyn had probably been romancing about her feelings to get Roy's interest. It would explain why she'd been so angry about seeing him in bed with Barbara. She rarely went out at the weekends unless it was with her friend, Wendy, to the pictures or ten pin bowling, so I was sure that there wasn't a boyfriend on the scene. I soon stopped thinking about it, convinced that I was right.

By the end of the month, I knew for certain that I was having our second child and had come around to feeling happy about it. I waited until Peter and I were cuddled up in bed and asked, 'Do you want to know a secret?'

He pushed my hair aside and gently nibbled my ear. 'It depends, what sort of secret? Is it about your family?' He'd begun to sound wary.

I held my arms out wide. 'No, it's about our family.' He guessed what I meant straight away. He leaned up onto his elbow and rained kisses on me everywhere that he could reach.

'Oh, you're pleased then,' I said when I could breathe. I was glad that I'd waited to tell him until I had no reservations myself.

'When's it due? Have you seen a doctor yet?' He flopped down onto his pillow and pulled me back into his arms.

'No, I haven't, but I know it will be the beginning of August. I'd like another girl, but I bet you want it to be a boy, don't you?'

'I don't mind, my darling, as long as it's okay; another girl like our Dawn would be wonderful.'

I hugged my precious husband close and told him that I'd booked an appointment with our doctor for the following week. 'After it's been confirmed, we can tell the families, but I want to tell Janet now – tomorrow. She'll be so excited that we will both have babies so close in age; I know she will. If you don't mind, I will probably go over and tell her – I'll ring her first thing and see if she'll be in.'

She was in, and I made her put her feet up while I prepared lunch for us. While we were eating, with Janet balancing her plate on her very large bump, I grinned and said, 'I wish I had a portable table.'

'It's useful, but I'll be bloody glad when it's gone, I'm fed up of being a whale, and I can't wait to see if my bump is a son or another daughter,'

I laughed; I knew just what she meant. But I had loved seeing the ripples travel across my abdomen while I was carrying Dawn, and I was looking forward to being a Mom again, big belly and all. My only fear was that I would struggle to regain my figure after the baby was born.

I stopped thinking silly thoughts and said, 'Well, I've got some news for you.'

'C'mon spit it out, I thought you sounded, well, not exactly excited, but there was something different. What is it?'

'I'm having a baby in August, I can't wait, but I suppose I'll have to give up work again.'

Janet's plate slid to the floor and smashed into three pieces. 'Yeh, yeh, yeh.' She tried to do our excitement dance and struggled to get off the settee.

'Sit still,' I said, 'you'll cut your feet.' I went over, picked up the pieces of crockery, then sat beside her and gave her a hand to swing her legs to the floor. We did our excitement dance with our arms waving in the air while remaining seated. The noise brought the girls running.

'What's the matter, Mommy?' Dawn asked and ran over to us, followed closely by Michelle. Their eyes were wide and mouths open as they took in the scene of their mothers behaving like a couple of teenagers.

'It's okay, love. I've just told your Auntie a secret, and she was surprised,' I said.

'Can we know the secret, Mommy?' Dawn asked. She held on tightly to my hand.

'Not right now, but I will tell you soon, okay?' After being given kisses, the girls were satisfied and went back to the picnic they were having with their stuffed animals.

'You didn't say it was a secret, I nearly blabbed. Does Peter know?'

'Of course,' I assured her, 'but you're the second to know.' She hugged me as near as she could, and we continued to talk excitedly about babies for a while.

Janet suddenly became very animated. 'I've got an idea; how about if we both go over to tell Mom now? I know you should wait for confirmation, but I'd love to see her face when you tell her.'

It seemed like a good idea now that Janet knew, and I too wanted to see my mother's reaction to my news. 'Okay, come on, kiddiewinks,' I called, 'we're going to see Grandma; come and get your coats on.'

Mom was home on her own. She was overwhelmed to think that another grandchild was on the way and sniffled into her hankie until Janet and I laughed and told her not to be so daft. We didn't stay very long, as I wasn't keen on driving in the rush hour. We left Mom to break the news to the rest of the family. I was feeling a trifle tired of all the baby talk by the time I'd dropped Janet and Michelle home and could barely be bothered to tell Peter how my day had gone – much to his amusement.

'Well, now you've told your mom, I'd better ring mine and let her know – otherwise, she's going to feel left out,' Peter said. He looked like a proud teenager who has done something incredibly clever. I smiled at his retreating back and felt an intense rush of love for him. Ivy was, of course, overjoyed and sent me her love along with advice to take it easy and put my feet up.

Later that evening, Peter and I sat together and told Dawn that she was going to have a baby brother or sister. I wasn't sure if she would be pleased, but thankfully she was and shortly afterwards went scooting happily off to bed. As I climbed the stairs to tuck her in, I could hear her telling her favourite Pooh Bear all about the secret that was no longer a secret.

Janet had her second daughter on March fifth, two days before Michelle's birthday. They named her Karen Ann, and she was the image of Michelle when she'd been born. Both had a covering of wavy, jet black hair and startling blue eyes that remained the deep blue of bluebells.

Three weeks later, when Janet had just settled into the new baby routine and was beginning to get her strength back, she phoned me at work. I was panicking as I went to the phone in

Mrs Darcy's office, thoughts of doom clawing away at my mind; she'd never called me at work before.

'Hello love,' I said, 'what's up?' I held my breath.

'You'll never guess what's happened.' She sounded so excited that I breathed a sigh of relief; she was too hyper for it to be bad news.

'What, what's happened –tell me – I can't guess.' I could feel the excitement building up in me too.

'Simon's Aunt Beryl has died and left him some money.'
I knew who Beryl was because I'd met her at their wedding. She was quite an elderly, unmarried lady who spoke and behaved in a very gracious manner, but I wasn't aware that she had money.

'Oh dear, I'm sorry that she's died, but how much money has she left him?' I knew it had to be a substantial amount for Janet to ring me at work.

Janet's voice became a whisper. 'She died last month, but we've only just heard that she's left twenty-five thousand pounds between Simon and his brother, Paul.'

I gasped – so much money. 'Oh, my word, that's twelve and a half thousand pounds each, you lucky buggers. I've never seen so much money. What're you going to do with it?' A needle of jealousy pricked me, but it was quickly replaced by pleasure for my sister. 'You'll be able to buy a house in Gorton, won't you?'

'We haven't talked about it yet, but that's what I want to do,' Janet said.

'I'm excited for you, love, but I'd better go. Ring me tonight after you've talked to Simon.'

I went back to my charges hoping that there hadn't been any problems. There shouldn't have been; the youngsters were over in the school, hopefully behaving themselves. But my absence had left only one member of staff available.

I could hear the ruckus as I pushed open the door to the unit where I'd been on duty. I hurried into the kitchen, and my stomach turned into a jellyfish as I saw the knife in the tall, black girl's hand. She had pinned my colleague against one of the big metal sinks and was shouting. 'I'm not fucking going back there. I'll cut you if you try and mek me.' She was making ineffectual stabbing movements with the knife.

'Come on, Joy, don't be daft,' I said, 'put it down and come with me, let's have a cup of tea and talk about what's upsetting you – you don't want to hurt Judith, do you?'

Joy burst into sobs, her tears mixing with snot as they ran down her plump face. She flung the knife onto the draining board, where it slid and clattered into the sink. I took her hand and led her into the sitting room while Judith, who was visibly shaken, made some tea.

Joy was usually a reasonable girl, and we sat and talked for a while until she calmed down. It seemed that another girl had upset her in class, and she had run from the school back to the unit where she had expected to find me. She didn't know Judith very well and had become even more upset when I wasn't there. A little while later, I escorted her back to the classroom and had a word with her teacher, who I knew would decide on her punishment for leaving the school without permission. It wasn't unusual for this to happen, but it wasn't often that a knife was employed, and both Judith and I were somewhat shaken. We reported her behaviour to Mr Stanley, who said that he would speak to Joy after school. I was glad to end my shift and return home to some sanity. I couldn't wait to tell Peter what a bloody awful day I'd had and let him know Janet and Simon's good news. Any envy that I had briefly felt for their good fortune had utterly disappeared thank goodness.

11

Peter seemed to be distracted while eating our evening meal and remained po-faced later when Dawn put her head on my abdomen and talked to her baby. It was such a cute scene that I became concerned. It wasn't like Peter not to laugh with his daughter at bedtime.

I took Dawn up to bed a little earlier than usual and quickly skimmed through her current storybook. She protested, but I promised to read double the next night if she went straight off to sleep. As soon as she shut her eyes, I went down to join Peter. I was feeling intensely uneasy and wondered why he was in such a peculiar mood. It was so unlike him that I just had to fathom the cause.

No sooner had I walked into the sitting room than he said, 'I'm going up to do some marking.' He began to climb the stairs without cracking his face. I was certain that something wasn't right.

'What's bothering you; you're quiet, something wrong at work?' I called after him. I felt somewhat guilty as I'd spent ages telling him about the awful episode at work and Janet's good fortune but never asked him about his day.

As he came back into the sitting room, he frowned, drawing his heavy eyebrows together. He began to chew the inside of his cheek then walked over to gaze out of the bay window. He stood for a minute with his back towards me and then absolutely floored me when he said, 'I want you to pack in work. I don't mean when you go on maternity leave, I mean now, this week.' He turned to look at me, and I was bewildered; I could see that his eyes were wet with unshed tears. I couldn't understand why he was saying this; we'd discussed when I would start my leave.

'You mean it don't you? Why? What's brought this on?' I went to stand beside him and snuggled into his arms.

After a while, we sat down, and Peter said, 'I know it doesn't happen very often that the kids assault the staff at your place, but when you told me in such a matter of fact way what had happened with that girl …,' he took a breath. 'I was appalled to think about the danger you were putting, not just yourself, but our baby in.' He heaved a sigh and continued. 'Sara, I need you to stay home at least until the baby's born. Please, darling, we don't need the money, so there's no reason to work the extra few months, is there?'

He looked distraught, and I had a flashback to Joy, standing with the sun glinting off the blade of the carving knife as she threatened Judith. He was right. I was putting our baby at risk. I was so used to working with disturbed youngsters that I hadn't been thinking along those lines. Although I was four months pregnant, I hardly showed, so I was able to carry on much as I'd always done. There were often incidents at St. Phillips that ended with us restraining some of the more volatile youngsters, but I now realised that if I became involved in one of those incidents, my unborn child could be hurt. The thought made me feel queasy; no wonder Peter was upset and wanted me to give my job up.

It didn't take much thinking before I made a decision and said, 'Okay, love, I'll hand my notice in tomorrow and see how that will affect my entitlement. You're right. I just hadn't thought. I'm so sorry, Peter.'

'Thank God, I thought I'd have a fight on my hands because I know how much you love your job.' He beamed and gave me a resounding kiss on my forehead – all was right again with our world.

I talked with Mr Stanley the following day, and he was very understanding when I explained my fears. He advised me to see if my doctor could help with my need to give up work early.

Initially, I missed my job as I was very fond of some of the youngsters in care. But after a couple of weeks, I began to enjoy staying in bed late on the weekends and spending every night in my own bed instead of sleeping-in at work. Dawn was turning into a right funny little chatterbox, and she was good company. I knew that I'd miss her when she started school in September, so I spent every available minute with her.

Luckily it was a very good summer. The days were often sunny and warm, so we were able to get out and about and frequently went to places like Dudley Zoo, various parks and craft centres, or the seaside with Janet and the girls. Peter had taken up playing golf, but he often accompanied us. Simon hardly ever joined us as he had to work, but Lyn, who seemed to be as happy as ever, sometimes brought the boys to meet up with us. She couldn't seem to get enough of Janet's baby daughter, Karen, and tended to her every need whenever she could. I was surprised as she'd never taken an interest in either Dawn or Michelle when they were babies. She proved to be a good aunt now, though; she never seemed happier than when all the children surrounded her as she told a story or posed them for photographs. They all loved Lyn, and Janet and I loved our little sister too– her tantrums had faded like early morning mist fades when the sun shines.

The highlight for me that summer came on August the fifteenth when the midwife handed me our new-born son. We named him Paul Frederick after both mine and Peter's father. His father, Paul, had died of a cerebral haemorrhage when Peter was ten years old, and I knew that he'd never really come to terms with his loss – even though Ivy had married again. Peter told me that his step-father, Brian, was very kind and had treated him as if he were his son. He, too, passed away when Peter was fifteen. I hoped that calling our baby Paul might ease some of Peter's pain.

When we told my father, he was pleased that we'd included his name. Sometimes it doesn't take much to give someone a great deal of pleasure, and I was glad that we'd thought of it. He became the apple of his granddad's eye, and I felt sure that the babies were the reason why my Dad had begun to spend more time at home than he used to.

September was a month of highs and lows for me. Peter and I had watched the Olympics with excitement when Mary Peters won gold for us in the pentathlon and then two days later heard the news that eleven Israeli athletes had been taken hostage and then killed. I just didn't understand all the wickedness in the world, and I was thankful that my family were well and happy.

Janet and Simon moved into a big, old terraced house in Gorton. After installing a new kitchen and bathroom, it was an ideal home for them. It backed onto a park where Mom had taken us to row a small boat on the lake occasionally and feed the ducks when we were little. It was only a ten-minute walk from both Mom's and my house and quite close to Dawn's school, so our lives entered a new phase. Each day after our husbands had gone to work, either Janet would come to my house, or more frequently, if the weather was inclement, I'd walk to her house after I'd taken Dawn to school. Sometimes we'd stroll round to Mom's, but she was often busy in her garden, so we didn't always feel too welcome and didn't stay long.

Most weekends, Lyn could be found at Janet's playing the doting aunt. She rarely came to my house even though I always made her welcome, and at times I felt a bit left out. But I shrugged these feeling off as I preferred being with Peter whenever he was at home and wouldn't have wanted Lyn to spend as much time at our house as she did at Janet's. I think that Janet was grateful for the help, though, and Simon didn't mind; he wasn't one for looking after the children.

It was the second week in October when out of the blue, I received a phone call from Auntie Freda. 'Is that you our Sara? I want to come and visit tomorrow; I've got a present for baby Paul. I'll be wanting lunch; I'm not going to be eating in any of the places where they serve what they call food. I can't see how they prepare it, dirty buggers some of 'em.'

I smothered my need to laugh. 'What would you like for lunch, Auntie?'

'Anything will do as long as it's not fish. I can't abide the smelly stuff,' she sniffed loudly.

'Will shepherds' pie be okay?' I pinched my lips together to prevent a laugh.

'Yes, but I only want cauliflower and frozen peas with it, and apple pie and custard for pudding. I'll be there at one o'clock sharp – don't tell your mother I'm coming.'

She disconnected, leaving me with my mouth agape. I knew she was abrupt, but I felt as though I'd been hit with a table tennis bat. I couldn't think why she was coming to me instead of going to Mom's as she usually did, and why couldn't I tell her?

I lifted the receiver and dialled Janet's number. I knew she'd scream with laughter when I recounted Auntie Freda's behaviour. As her phone rang out with no answer, I hoped that Janet wasn't going to become even more direct like Auntie as she grew older.

The next day dawned wet and windy, and the sky was so overcast that I thought the rain was probably here for the day. I half expected Auntie Freda to call and cancel her visit, but she didn't, and promptly on the dot of one, she rang the bell.

I'd made sure the dinner was ready and had made a special trip to our local greengrocers to buy a cauliflower and cooking apples for the ordered pie. Every time I thought about her telephone call, I felt my lips twitch. She was certainly one on her own, our Auntie, but I knew that she was kind-hearted in her way, and I was looking forward to her visit.

As we sat at the table, Auntie said in a voice that brooked no argument. 'We'll eat first, and then I'll tell you why I'm here. She set to with alacrity and cleared her plate, then sat quietly until I'd put my last spoonful into my mouth. As soon as I finished, she jumped up and started to clear the table and then proceeded to run hot water into the sink, add washing up liquid and washed up. I joined her, feeling quite intimidated by this little woman who was about four foot ten and couldn't weigh more than six stone. She said very little while we carried out the chores, but as soon as we'd finished and sat in comfort in the living room, she thanked me for her dinner.

'I'm glad you enjoyed it.' I poured the tea that she had insisted on making and then handed her one of my good china cups.

'Thank you, Sara.' She settled back in the chair, making me smile as her feet, encased in fluffy, pink slippers that she'd brought with her, stuck straight out in front of her. 'Now I'm sure you are wondering why I'm here, aren't you?' She didn't wait for an answer. 'It's your mother's birthday next month – she'll be fifty – what are you going to do about it?'

My brain did a crazy jig as I'd given it no thought at all. 'I'm not sure. Janet and I have been so busy that we've not decided anything.' I could feel my face burning as though I'd been caught out in a misdemeanour of some sort. I suppose I had.

'Well, I thought as much, I know you've been busy having babies and such like so I've booked the function room at the Fox and arranged for catering, but I need to know how many to book for. I need to know by Friday, and you can book a DJ.' She watched my face as she finished speaking, and I just didn't know how to react. I knew that she was only being thoughtful, really, but it was Monday now, and I didn't think I could have a guest list ready by Friday, and I didn't know any DJ's. I said as much.

'Well, you'd better get your sisters to help you, hadn't you? It's all been left to the last minute, hasn't it, and I don't know about you, but I think becoming fifty deserves a party. I'm sure she'll be hoping one of you has arranged something for her.' Auntie Freda's feet jiggled up and down as she gave this onslaught.

Silence reigned while my brain continued to scuttle about like a panicked spider. 'How much will it cost, Auntie?' Not too much, I hoped. I waited and looked across to see her looking gleeful.

'You don't need to worry about that, I'm paying – it's my present to my only sister – but I expect you to decorate the hall, and you can pay for the DJ. Now can you get me a guest list by Friday? It's too late to invite our William – he'd never make it on time.' She frowned, making her sharp chin jut forward.

I knew I had no choice. Uncle William, Freda's twin brother, lived in Australia, and she was probably right. It was too short notice, but I decided to ring him and at least tell him about the party. I knew that Mom would love to see her brother.

'Yes, Auntie, I'll make sure I do. I'll get Janet and Lyn to help. Are we going to tell Mom, or is it to be a surprise? I'll have to get in touch with Dad and make sure he's at home that weekend.' As an afterthought, I said, 'Thank you, Auntie, I'm afraid we weren't being very good children. I'm sure we'd have done something, but we'd have left it too late for a party.'

She smiled, bringing her beaky nose down towards her chin, giving her a look of Mr Punch. 'That's okay. I'm happy to do it. I've got plenty of time on my hands and enough money, so don't you worry. Now I must go, I've things to do. You should think of a reason to get your mother there and make it a surprise – they're always nice.'

She was up out of her chair and had her coat on in no time. She gave me a swift kiss on my cheek and then was gone. She hurried along the street, her brown lace-ups splashing water as she trod through myriad puddles – her black umbrella held at an angle to ward off the wind. I knew that my Mom was younger than the twins by about two years, but Freda looked and behaved a lot older. Perhaps it's being a widow for many years and only having had one son, John, who she didn't see very often. John had married a girl from Lincoln and gone to live there. I knew that he'd asked Aunt Freda to move Lincoln, but she'd always refused to leave Gorton. Abrupt and straight to the point, she certainly was, but probably kinder than Mom, I suspected with affection as I watched her retreating figure hurrying to catch her bus.

12

The room looked lovely. It was decorated with brightly coloured balloons and streamers that Michael had risked his neck to put in place. I was glad that the radiators were on when we arrived – it was a freezing night.

When I had told Janet, Lyn and Michael about Auntie Freda's surprise for Mom, they were only too glad to rally round and help. We contacted as many of Mom and Dad's old friends and neighbours and family members that we knew and found that there were at least sixty to invite. Most of them accepted and managed to arrive before Janet and Simon came in with Mom and Dad. Janet had told Mom that they would meet Simon's mother, Helen, and then go to The Fox pub for a meal to celebrate Helen's birthday.

When she walked in and saw so many people gathered in one place, Mom's face was a picture of joy. She turned and kissed Dad on his lips, a real smacker. She must have thought that he'd arranged the party for her. I knew one of us would have to put her straight at some point. Not this one, though. I went to find Auntie Freda as soon as the initial noise had died down, wound my arms around her and gave her a bear hug.

'Thank you for being so very kind and thoughtful,' I spoke directly into her ear – the music was too loud to talk normally. At first, she was embarrassed but quickly regained her usual composure.

She placed her hands on either side of her mouth and used them as a megaphone. 'Well, she is my sister, and we were very close when we were young. It's a shame that life's little vagaries can push people apart, isn't it? Now go on with you, and I'm going to see if she appreciates your efforts. I certainly do – it looks lovely.' She gave me a gentle push on my arm and made her way through the knot of people who had congregated by the bar.

I went to sit at our table where Peter was doing his best to soothe Paul, who wanted feeding. Dawn was having a blast on the dance floor with Michelle, and Lyn was walking toward them, ready to join in. I took Paul into the ladies' toilet where the barman had let me have a chair so I could feed my now yelling baby. I enjoyed the sense of peace that breastfeeding usually gave me, but I was glad that the room was clean and didn't smell like the men's toilets invariably did. I've never worked out why the gents reeked so much whenever the door opened.

When I came out, I could see Mom talking animatedly with my Grandma Georgina. Granddad Bill was, as usual, propping up the bar. I waved to him and then went over and had a brief chat with Mom and Grandma. Dad and Auntie Freda, who'd been dancing and were red in the face, flopped down beside them.

I left them to it and went back to Janet and Peter and three of our friends. They were all singing "Roll out the Barrel" at the top of their voices, and I soon joined in enthusiastically, but I was glad when the DJ changed the music to Marmalade's "Ob-La-De Ob-La-Da", and the dance floor became full again. I looked around for Lyn and Michael but couldn't see either of them. I wanted to tell Michael that I was impressed with his choice of DJ who was interacting with the partygoers and playing such a wide variety of songs – I made a mental note to tell him later.

'Will you look after Dawn and Paul for a few minutes while Sara and I go out for a breath of fresh air – and I need a smoke?' Peter asked Janet, who was already entertaining both Dawn and Michelle by painting their eager mouths with her pink lipstick.

'Of course, but don't be too long though, I won't be able to move with the four of them to watch.' She indicated the two pushchairs with their sleeping occupants. I nodded, and Peter grabbed my hand and pulled me out onto the stairway and into the grounds, where he proceeded to light a cigarette. As we passed the dance floor, I noticed Mom and an attractive grey-haired man that I vaguely recognised were taking advantage of a slow number to dance together. Mom seemed to be enjoying herself, so I knew I had to hurry as Janet would be on her own. I felt a bit peeved with Simon and Lyn for disappearing just when we needed them. I didn't expect Michael to babysit as he'd brought Derek along, and I knew I couldn't have asked him and made him look wimpy in front of his mate. It was stupid because he often enjoyed helping with his nieces and nephew, but I didn't know Derek well enough to guess how he'd be.

After a few minutes, I'd had enough of the too-cold air, and I left Peter to finish his cigarette while I went back to the table. As I passed an open doorway that I knew led into the kitchens, I caught sight of Simon and Lyn, who seemed to be having quite a heated argument, but I wanted to get back to Janet, so I didn't stop. Not my business anyway, I thought as I remembered my promise to Peter not to become involved in Lyn's problems.

As the night wore on, I forgot about them and watched Mom as she waltzed around the room held firmly by the same grey-haired man that I'd seen her with earlier. He was a good dancer and hadn't lacked for partners, but I'd noticed that Mom and he danced together several times. I wondered mildly if she fancied him and wouldn't have blamed her if she did – he stood out from the crowd. Later, when I saw him at the bar talking to Dad, I felt curious and went over to them, thinking that he must be a relative; he looked so familiar.

Dad leaned forward and kissed me. 'You're a good girl for arranging all this.'

I shook my head. 'I've had something to do with the organising, but it was Auntie Freda's idea, and she's paid for it too. She's very kind.' I looked around. 'It's lovely to see so many of the family here, isn't it?'

The man that I was interested in said, 'Yes, it is. Do you remember me, Sara?' He smiled, showing even white teeth and raised his eyebrows.

I didn't and shook my head. 'Who are you? Where do you fit into this lovely family?'

He laughed and introduced himself as Tony Gardener. 'I belong to your Uncle William and Aunt Sarah – I'm their second son.'

I smiled and shook his hand. I knew that Uncle William was my Great Aunt Maud's son. 'They're over there,' he pointed into a far corner, 'I agreed to drive them here and stay sober; it's ages since they've seen you.' He took my hand. 'Come on over and say hello.'

As we pushed our way past the people edging the dance floor, I asked him if I'd seen him before.

'Yes, I visited a couple of times with Mom, and we stayed over, but it was some years ago now, and you were only young.'

I recognised Aunt Sarah, a small woman who reminded me of a mouse as she twitched her nose while she was speaking in a tiny, squeaky voice. She was delightful and told me that I was named after her – I inwardly wriggled as I hoped I wasn't too much like her. Her voice grated on me after we spent a little time chatting, and I was grateful when I was captured and dragged away by another distant relative. Her son, Tony, had wandered away after crossing the floor with me. I thought that he took after his father, who was still quite a handsome man.

The whole evening went by in a trice. There were so many familiar faces that I needed to speak to, but after a couple of hours, I found I was tired of smiling.

Around ten-thirty, when we'd all sung "Happy Birthday to You" as Mom blew her candles out then cut into her pink iced cake, I asked Peter if we should make our way home and get the children to bed. He was more than happy to go, so we hugged and kissed everyone goodbye, including people that we didn't know, and left them to it.

I was glad to be home even though we'd had a good time, and seeing Mom's face full of happiness as she greeted friends and family that she hadn't seen for ages was a picture that I'd hold onto for a long while to come. I was grateful that Auntie Freda had thrown the party as I knew that I'd been too preoccupied with my own life to even think of it. I resolved as I fell asleep to be more aware of people's needs, but by morning, I forgot the promise I'd made.

I rang Janet the next day after a late start; we'd all overslept, even the baby.

'Hi, hon, how you doing – what time did you get home?' I asked in response to my sister's weary greeting.

'Don't ask because I've no idea. By the time we'd put Mom, Dad, and a miserable Lyn – who were all squiffy – into a taxi and sent them home, it must have been gone midnight. Simon was a little drunk, and I wanted him to leave the car and take a taxi, but he insisted on driving, so I stupidly went with him – I was too tired to argue. I love him, but he can be such a bully at times. Anyway, I had my heart in my mouth all the way home, I know it's not far away, but it could have been miles and miles – I felt so scared. When we arrived here, he went straight up to bed while I just dumped the girls into their beds, still in their clothes, then fell in myself. I know I didn't drink very much, but I'm cream crackered this morning, and I've insisted that Simon take the girls for a walk in the park. I can't think straight. What about you?'

'Oh, I'm okay now, a bit tired still, but Dawn's been a star. She's fed Paul his breakfast, and he's napping while she's colouring in that new book that you gave her last night. Peter's still in bed, but I can hear him stirring, so I'd better go and make some coffee. What was the matter with Lyn?'

'Oh, I don't know, but she suddenly became snappy and seemed very down towards the end of the party. She'll get over it, whatever it was,' Janet said.

Did Mom say she'd enjoyed herself?' I asked as an afterthought.

'Oh, she did; she was so on a high when she left. I expect she'll tell you herself. I'll phone you tomorrow, or are you coming here when you've dropped Dawn to school?'

'Mm, I think so. Perhaps we can take a walk round to Mom's and let her tell us all about it if it's not raining.'

'Okay, see you then, love you, sis.'

13

We felt a bit like traitors as we'd always joined the rest of the family at Mom's for Christmas, but when Peter suggested, at short notice, that we do something different for this one, I jumped at it.

'Where would we go?' A big grin stretched my face. 'Do you mean abroad?'

'Well, no, it's a bit late to start making arrangements for that, but how would you like it if we went to stay at a hotel in Kent?'

I knew that he'd always wanted to see Canterbury Cathedral and visit Brighton, and I thought it would be fun to spend Christmas on our own – something that we'd not done before. We booked into a small hotel in Hyde, which had been recommended to us by Simon's brother. He'd stayed there in the summer and told Janet that it was ideal to use as a base to explore the surrounding coast and countryside.

On the nineteenth, I felt as though we were going on an adventure when we left home with everything but the furniture – we certainly hadn't realised how travelling with two youngsters for any length of time required so much gear. We also hadn't bargained for the weather, which turned our holiday into a real adventure. By the time we hit the A2, it had started to snow. It snowed and snowed until we thought it would never stop. It decorated all the trees and hedges in a sparkling white blanket – it was beautiful – but it made all our plans go flying out of the window. Fortunately, all the main roads had been gritted, and we reached the hotel without too much trouble, albeit slowly. Although I admit, I was a nervous wreck by the time we pulled up in their small car park. As if the driving wasn't bad enough, we found trundling the pushchair, carrying the children and getting our luggage inside – exhausting. I was beginning to regret not staying at home, but Peter was still as upbeat as ever.

For the whole of our two-week holiday, we never ventured more than a mile or two from the hotel, which, fortunately for us, was warm and comfortable – and the food was first class. Although we'd only booked for half board, as there were just our family and two other couples, who both had young children, the friendly owners agreed to supply us all with lunch and snacks when we needed them.

It worked out very well financially, and it was probably one of the best Christmases that we ever spent until the children were grown up. We made friends with the other guests and the proprietors and spent our days making snowballs and snow people and exploring where we could. The sea views were lovely, and I often stood to gaze at the ceaseless tides and enjoy the flocks of birds that I couldn't name.

In the evening's after the children were asleep, we played cards, read, watched television or just socialised. One of the couples, Gabriel and John, was from a place called Elliot in New England. They turned out to be a fun-loving family, and we remained friends with them for the remainder of our lives. Mary and Philip hailed from Nottingham. They, too, were lovely, good-natured people. I suppose I thought that we were all quite stoic, something I'd never thought of as a description of me before. I never heard any one of them complain anyway. It was so relaxing and peaceful, not at all like the usual hurly-burly of Christmas at home.

One Child Too Many

We rang home a few times to make sure everything was alright and see how their Christmas Day had gone, but otherwise, we felt isolated. It was as well that there were no emergencies at home because, to all intents and purposes, we were snowed in for almost a week. Peter said it was heaven, and we should do it every year, but I just laughed as I wasn't sure that I would always want to be away from my family at Christmas, and I didn't think that it snowed like that every year – even in Kent.

We returned home on New Year's Eve to find that Lyn had left her job and had been staying on her own in our house since Boxing Day after deciding that she didn't want to work for the Feltz family anymore. Mom was under the impression that she'd returned to live with her employers and had no idea where she was. She'd taken our emergency key out of Mom's purse and just let herself in.

Both Peter and I were furious. It wasn't so much the fact that she'd moved into our property without permission, but we didn't know how she could be so thoughtless as to simply leave that family in the lurch after they had treated her with every considcration.

We were both tired from the long journey, and our tempers were somewhat frayed. After putting the children to bed, Peter verbally laid into Lyn. She'd made coffee for us all and sat down.

Peter took a sip of coffee and set his mug down with a bang. The coffee slopped over, but he didn't seem to notice. He stared balefully at Lyn. 'Who on earth do you think you are, eh? What made you think that you had the right to walk into our home, switch the heating on and live here as though you owned the place?' He took a deep breath and pointed his finger at her. 'You are a spoilt, selfish little bastard. All your life, you've done just what you wished, never a genuine thought for how your behaviour affects other people. How could you just chuck that job in without any warning, those people relied on you, and I know that the children loved you. If you weren't Sara's sister, I'd throw you out right now. You're almost eighteen, and you should know how to behave!'

He subsided into his chair, and I ventured a look at Lyn. She was shaking from head to foot. Peter was justified in all he'd said, but I couldn't bear her to be so upset.

'Okay, I think enough has been said tonight.' I looked from Peter to Lyn. 'I agree with Peter, but it's nearly midnight. I think we can sort this out in the morning. Where have you been sleeping?'

'In D ...Dawn's room.' Lyn managed to say. Her face was as white as the snow that we'd just been enjoying.

'Come on,' I said. Lyn followed me into the hall, where I reached into the cupboard and fetched the blow-up mattress and spare blankets that we kept stored there. I placed the bedding on her outstretched arms. 'You'd better sleep in Dawn's room, but try not to wake her.' I didn't dare look into her face, I so wanted to hug her and make her feel better, but I turned and went back to Peter – leaving her standing there. I shut the door firmly behind me.

'What are we going to do with her, eh?' Peter asked. I was glad to hear he'd cooled down.

'I don't know, look, I can't think about it tonight, let's go to bed. We'll deal with it next year.' I managed a short laugh as our clock bonged midnight. 'Happy New Year, my love.' I went into his arms.

'Happy New Year to you too, my lovely wife; let's hope that nineteen seventy-one is our best year yet.'

'It'll have to be very good then; we've already had some good ones, haven't we?' Peter kissed me without passion, and then we wearily climbed the stairs while hoping that the children wouldn't wake too early.

One Child Too Many

The next morning, I was up at 5 a.m., woken by Paul, who was trying to wake the rest of the household by crying as if he was heartbroken. He wouldn't stop until I fetched him into our bed. The expression slippery slope came to my mind, but I ignored it, hoping that our snuggles would send both of us off to sleep again. It did, and I managed to snatch another couple of hours before his lively movements woke me up again. I took him into the shower with me, expecting any minute that Dawn would join us, but I was able to dress the pair of us before she arrived, rubbing the sleep from her droopy eyes. I lay Paul down on the bathroom floor and quickly helped Dawn to shower. It took longer than it used to as she wanted to shower and dress by herself and insisted on repeating most of my actions. I decided that I would allow her to do it while school was out, so it wouldn't matter how long she took. She was growing up so fast and becoming quite independent in lots of ways.

We were eating breakfast by the time Peter arrived. I finished my toast and left the children to Peter's care while I went up to see how Lyn was getting on. She was dressed, and her bedding neatly folded. She'd let the air out of the mattress, so I surmised that she didn't intend to ask us if she could stay. She was gazing out of the window with her elbows on the ledge, her hands supporting her face. As I went into the room, she turned and smiled weakly.

'I'm sorry, I'm such a bloody nuisance, and I'm no good to anyone, am I?' She looked a picture of misery.

My heart went out to her, and I couldn't help but put my arms around her. 'You're not a nuisance, but you do some things that make other people annoyed with you at times, Lyn.' I paused as she began to weep. 'I love you, my sister; you're still young, you'll learn.' I stroked her silky hair back from her face where her tears had stuck fine strands across her reddened cheeks.

She continued to cry as she said, 'I'm no bloody good, you don't know.'

'Now you're being silly and just feeling sorry for yourself. I know you've left the Feltz's, but I don't know why – do you want to tell me?' Lyn shook her head vehemently, and I didn't feel that I could be bothered to push her for an explanation. 'Did you give them any notice? Will they give you a reference?' Lyn shook her head again, so I continued patiently. 'They told me that you were good at your job, so you shouldn't have any trouble finding another one. I know Peter was angry last night, but he was tired, we both were, but what you did was wrong, and you know it. Anyway, it's over now, so come and have breakfast, then I'll take you round to Mom's, and you can explain – okay?'

'Can't I stay here; I could help with the children?' she said.

I gave an unladylike snort. 'Peter would never stand for it even if I would, so no, and you're going to have to live at home unless you've anywhere else to go. You're eighteen in three days, Lyn, and you need to sort yourself out and get on with your life – I'll help whenever I can – but there are some things that I can't help you with. Now come on, no more crying, come and have some breakfast.' I left the room, hoping that she would follow me downstairs. She did, albeit slowly.

As we entered the kitchen, Peter was just going up to his office and didn't say anything. He stayed up there until I called him to come and look after Dawn and Paul while I took Lyn home. He came down and stood on the bottom step looked sombrely at Lyn's belongings in the hall and then into her face as he said,' I'm sorry that I felt the need to say what I did last night, Lyn, but I'm not sorry that I told you how I felt. I want to forget how you've abused our trust, and I hope you'll be able to sort yourself out. Now I just want to forget it.' He turned away and went into the sitting room where Dawn was playing with Paul making him chuckle while she used a cushion to surprise him.

I helped Lyn take her stuff to the car, called out to Peter that I wouldn't be long, pulled the door shut, and headed for Mom's.

'Will you tell her what I've done Sara, I'm sure she'll listen to you if you tell her that I'm sorry,' Lyn asked.

'No way, you can tell her yourself. What are you worried about anyway? She always listens to you and lets you get away with murder? I'll be there, but you can make your excuses yourself.' Lyn didn't reply, and we made the rest of the journey in silence.

Mom greeted us cheerily. 'Oh, hello, you two, Happy New Year, do you want a cuppa?'

'Happy New Year, Mom,' I said and went to kiss her. Lyn followed suit, then sat down on the sofa, tucking her jean covered legs up under her. 'Come and sit down first Mom, Lyn has something that she wants to get off her chest.' Mom's face immediately became anxious, and her hands began to do their uneasy dance in her lap as soon as she sat.

'What's going on, Lyn?' she whispered.

I felt so sorry for her, and I knew that she must be heartily sick of Lyn, causing trouble somehow. I tried not to listen while Lyn began telling Mom what she'd done about her job and confessed to taking the key from her purse to move into our house.

When she'd finished, Mom shook her head, looked hard at Lyn and said, 'What now?'

Lyn shrugged her shoulders and smiled. 'I can stay at home, can't I, Mom?'

'Yes,' Mom said. Then she took a deep breath and spoke as sternly as I'd ever heard her speak to Lyn. 'But there's to be no more drinking, no more loud music and no more bloody sulking every time something doesn't suit you. You can have time to get another job, but when you do, I want you to start paying rent as Michael does. It's only fair. The others have always paid their way, so you should too. Shouldn't she, Sara?' Mom looked to me to back her up.

'Of course, we did, and you should.' I turned to Lyn, who looked shocked as though a beloved pet had turned on her, but she nodded her head in agreement.

She stood up. 'I'm going to take my things up to my room.'

We could hear her sob as she picked her belongings up from the hallway and carried them upstairs. I tried not to feel sorry for her, but I just couldn't help it. She used to be such a charmer, and I was sad for the way that she'd changed. I was certain that she couldn't help herself; she was spoilt and selfish, but we'd all had a part to play. I'm sure that she wasn't born like it, or maybe she was. I admitted to myself that I knew very little about nature versus nurture. The rest of us hadn't turned out like Lyn; could it be that we had loved and given in to her too much.

I went across and hugged Mom. She must have been thinking along the same lines as me as she said, 'Is it my fault, did I do something wrong? I'm sure I never treated her any differently to you or Janet or Michael.'

'We've all had a hand in spoiling her Mom, but hopefully, she'll learn that she can't always have her way. There's no point in apportioning blame, it's too late, and she is how she is. She'll grow up eventually and have her corners rounded, so try not to worry.' I finished on a positive note, and then after a little while and changing the subject to her grandchildren and my father, I left with Mom still sunk in gloom. I headed home feeling somewhat gloomy and inadequate myself.

14

Peter's jaw jutted. 'No, you go on your own, I haven't forgiven her yet, and I certainly don't want to go to your Mom's and celebrate her birthday.' I didn't try to change his mind.

'Okay, but I've bought her a cake and a present, and Mom's doing a special tea for her, so I've got to go. I'll take Dawn with me, but you know that Paul's been grizzly all day with his teeth, so I think he should stay here. Okay with you? We won't stay too long.'

'Yes, of course, poor little bugger, teeth can be a bloody nuisance. When can he have some more Calpol?' Peter asked. We both stood and surveyed our son's bright red cheeks, where he napped restlessly on the carpet with his favourite comfort blanket that I'd crocheted before he was born. I'd used white wool, but my washing skills aren't wonderful, and it was no longer white.

'Dawn, can you leave off colouring now, and we'll go to see Auntie Lyn for her birthday?' I spoke quietly – I didn't want Paul to wake just yet.

Dawn didn't want him disturbed either, as she came and whispered in my ear. 'Which shoes should I wear?' I smiled at her and fetched the blue ones that she was very fond of. I slung the strap of my tartan bag over my shoulder; we kissed Peter goodbye and then left him to cope when Paul woke up.

I was glad that we went to Mom's early because Janet, Simon and the girls were there. Janet had told me not to expect them as she thought Simon would go to the club and want his dinner when he returned home. She told me later that he was more than happy for them to come.

Mom and Lyn seemed to be okay with each other, and it turned into quite a party atmosphere. I gave Lyn the Clinique make up that she'd asked me for, and Janet had bought her a pretty silver bracelet. She'd had some money for clothes from Mom and Dad and even Michael, who rarely bothered with birthday presents, had offered to take her out for a meal and to the cinema to see any film that she fancied, so she was all sweetness and light.

How easily she bounces back, I thought. If a stranger walked in right now, they would think she never puts a foot wrong. I was glad to see her happy and enjoying her day, but there was a teeny, tiny bit of me that still wanted to shake her for her thoughtlessness and ongoing lack of contrition. She'd been a pain, but here we all were flocking round to ensure that she feels special on her birthday. It's no wonder she doesn't learn, I thought, but then pushed my negative feelings aside and joined in a silly game of wink murder that Lyn requested. We all still enjoyed being childlike sometimes.

After tea was over, we relaxed, too full for any more activities. We were chatting in a desultory way until Janet said, 'I've got some news.'

'You're not pregnant again, are you our Janet, Karen's only ten months you'll have your hands full.' Mom chuckled at her joke. Janet put her tongue out at her and carried on speaking.

'No, I'm not, thank you very much; my two girls are quite enough for me,' she grinned. 'Well, the thing is, Simon agrees that I should return to work if we can find someone reliable to mind Michelle and Karen; mind you, Michelle will be going to school in September so she won't take much minding, and

Karen's a good girl. Aren't you my darling little stinky bum?' She sniffed her daughter's nether regions, and everyone laughed and started to talk at once.

Again, I was surprised and couldn't wait to get her on her own and ask how she'd persuaded Simon to let her go. The last time we'd talked about it, he'd been dead set against her returning to work. Mom and Lyn went to make a cuppa for everyone, and I asked Janet if she intended to return to secretarial work.

'Mm, yes, but I've decided to train as a medical secretary. I fancy working for some consultant or other. I know someone who already works for a thoracic consultant at the General, and she says that the pay is much better than basic secretarial work.'

'Sounds like a plan. Is it expensive to train?' I asked.

'I'm not sure how much I'll have to pay, but it'll be worth it in the long run. I might as well earn as much as I can.'

Simon nodded in agreement. 'It has to pay well so we can employ a childminder and still have some left over. A silly idea if you ask me, I'd prefer her to stay at home,' he laughed, 'and be a domestic goddess, but it's what you want to do, isn't it, Jan?'

Janet nodded and got up to help Mom as she returned from the kitchen with mugs of tea on a large, floral painted tray that she'd had since the year dot. Lyn followed her in, and she was grinning from ear to ear.

'What's up with you? You look like a cat that's got a mouse to play with.' I smiled.

'Tell them, Mom – tell them what you've decided.' She looked about ten years old.

'If you are going back to work, Janet, then Lyn and I will mind the girls for you – if you'd like us to,' Mom said.

'You don't want to look after little ones again, do you, Mom, what about your gardening? You've just applied for an allotment, haven't you?' Janet said. She frowned while she tried to stop Michelle from wiping chocolate off her mouth onto the sleeve of her blouse.

Lyn took over. 'Well, I'd be doing most of the looking after, so Mom can still be as free as she wants to be. It'll give me a job, and I don't mind how much you pay me – I've only got to pay Mom some rent and have a small amount left for me – I shan't need a lot, and you know how much I love looking after Michelle and Karen. Oh, go on, Janet, please, I want to do this more than anything, and I won't let you down, I promise.' She held her hands out, palms up as she took a deep breath.

Janet thought for a minute then said, 'Oh I don't know, it'll mean you'd have to take Michelle to school and pick her up, you'd effectively be tied down from Monday to Friday, and what about if you suddenly change your mind as you did with the doctors? You still haven't told us why you left them. Why did you?' Her eyebrows almost met her hairline, and she stared intently at Lyn.

Lyn blushed then spoke hesitantly. 'I didn't get on with Dr Feltz after a few months. He was becoming too familiar and had started coming into my room without knocking. He caught me in my underclothes twice and pretended that it was an accident, but I knew that it wasn't.'

'What!' I exclaimed. 'Why didn't you tell us sooner I'd have gone to see him – did he touch you?'

'No,' Lyn said, 'but I know that it was leading up to that from the way that he looked at me – it gave me the creeps. I couldn't stand it anymore; that's why I never went back. I didn't tell you because I didn't think you'd believe me, and I didn't want to upset his wife – she doesn't deserve it – she was always nice to me.' Lyn's face was scarlet, and she gazed at her shoes while she spoke.

'Oh my God, how terrible, I'll be having words with him the bloody monster, and I thought he was so nice. I'm sorry we were awful to you about it, but we're not mind readers – you should have told us,' I said.

'You should have; we're your family, we'd have believed you,' Janet said.

'I did tell Mom but asked her not to say,' Lyn shook her head, 'I don't want you to say anything to him, Sara. It's in the past, and I just want to forget about it.' She turned to Janet. 'So, will you let us mind the girls when you get a job?'

Janet gave Simon an enquiring look; he nodded and said, 'Yes, why not. It's an ideal solution, and we know that they'll be loved and looked after.'

'Yes, they will, better than anyone else would; I'll treat them like my own.' As if on cue, Michelle came and snuggled into Lyn's lap as she continued by saying enthusiastically, 'Thank you all for my presents. I love them, but this is the best birthday present yet.'

I glanced across at Mom – her face was deadpan – I wasn't sure that it was what she wanted, but Lyn had always been able to get her to agree to anything. I mentally shrugged; it wasn't any of my business – I just hoped it would work out okay.

On the way home, I listened to Dawn as she recounted the good time she'd had with Michelle. She made me smile when she said, 'I love my cousin, you know, and I love Karen, but she's too little to play with properly.'

'I suppose she is, but she won't always be so little. She'll catch up with you just like Auntie Lyn is catching up with me and Auntie Janet – you'll see.'

'Well, I'm not sure I can wait that long so I think that Karen can play with Paul, and I'll stick with Michelle,' she said. I laughed. I found her profound way of speaking hilarious at times.

When I arrived home and told Peter what Lyn had accused Dr Feltz of doing, I thought that he'd regret being so harsh with her, but all he said was that she should have told us the truth.

It wasn't like him to be so uncaring, but I supposed that he'd had enough of her bad behaviour, and I left it at that. I certainly wasn't about to challenge him about anything. I was so relieved that he'd managed to get Paul off to sleep after giving him another dose of Calpol.

My hopes for a good night's sleep for both of us were shattered, however, and at two o'clock, I found myself pacing the floor with my hot, fretful son. Two hours later, I left a note for Peter, just in case he got up and wondered where we were, put Paul in his car seat, and then started the car. I hoped that I hadn't woken our neighbours up, but I was desperate. Driving anywhere with Paul usually sent him off, and this time was no exception; he fell asleep before I reached the bottom of our road. I headed back home, praying that he wouldn't wake up again as soon as I killed the engine. He didn't, and I was able to doze on the sofa for a couple of hours. When he woke again at seven still in his car seat – I hadn't dared to move him – it was like a magic wand had been waved and cast a spell; he seemed to be pain-free, and his cheeks had returned to their normal colour. He ate his breakfast and was his usual happy self. I couldn't believe our luck.

Although it was cold, wet, and windy, we needed to get out of the house, and so we went to visit the Botanical Gardens in Edgbaston. We'd been there several times before and loved the place. The weather was far too inclement to venture outside, but we ended up in the cafe where we ordered burgers and chips from the menu after wandering through the glasshouses. At nearly six years of age, Dawn was feeling very grown-up, as she was allowed to order her meal and sat drinking a cup of weak tea with her little finger crooked. We'd told her that's how posh people drank. We tried not to laugh at her, but she looked comical, and I could see smiles coming her way from a couple of other visitors. My eyes returned to Paul, who held a chip in his hands and enjoyed squeezing it through his fingers. I leaned forward to try and insert some food into his mouth – and saw him. My hand went to my mouth, and I could feel my pulse quicken.

'Look over there,' I said to Peter. He gazed around but shook his head. 'No, over there by the counter.' I pointed.

'Now don't you go saying anything to him,' he said firmly, as he spotted Dr Feltz, who had picked up a tray and was leaning down to speak to his two small sons.

I couldn't take my eyes off them as they collected their meal and sat at a table across the other side of the room. I wondered where his wife was – it was Sunday, so I didn't think she'd be working. I knew that Peter would be cross with me, but I had to go over and speak to him, although I'd no idea what I was going to say. I stood up.

'Where do you think you're going?' Peter said.

I ignored the warning in his voice and strode across to where the Feltz family sat. 'Hello, Dr Feltz,' I said as evenly as I could manage. I wanted to assault him, but I restrained myself, as I always do when these violent impulses sometimes raise their ugly head.

'Hello Sara, how are you, and how's Lyn?' He looked so friendly and innocent that I became puzzled.

'We are both well,' I said, 'could I have a private word with you over here.' I moved into a space a few tables away.

He told the boys to stay put and followed me – his eyebrows raised – as he said, 'What's this about Sara? I'm afraid we can't give Lyn her job back if that is what you want to ask me?'

'It's not,' I said, 'I want to know what happened to make her walk out?' I knew I sounded angry, but I couldn't stop myself – he was just a dirty bugger.

'Is that what she told you that she walked out on us? I'm afraid it wasn't like that at all. We had to dismiss Lyn because of her drinking.'

'What do you mean, drinking?'

I'm sorry that I have to tell you this because we liked Lyn very much, and the boys loved being with her, but we became concerned when she had such a bad hangover one Monday that my wife had to make other arrangements for the boys. I gazed open-mouthed at his face – was he telling the truth – but I knew immediately that he almost certainly was. I swallowed hard as he went on speaking, 'We accepted her story the first time when she told us that someone had spiked her drinks at a party she'd been to, and we simply told her that it mustn't happen again, and to be more careful. About a month later, on a Tuesday morning, in the run-up to Christmas, she never left her room until my wife went to call her, thinking that she'd overslept. She was incapable of standing upright. There was an empty Bacardi bottle on the floor by her bed, and the smell of vomit coming in from her bathroom was eye-watering. There was no excuse, and we had to dismiss her. I'm sorry.' He turned and checked on his sons, who were looking our way. 'I really must go back, Sara – I'm sorry, but if Lyn has a problem with alcohol, she needs some help.'

He started to walk towards his table, and I put my hand on his arm and said, 'I'm so sorry, thank you for telling me.' I walked back to Peter, who was mildly annoyed as I'd expected him to be.

Apologies were on the menu for me that day, and Peter accepted mine with a nod and asked, 'Well, what did you say to him?'

'Not a lot, really; I was all fired up to tell him some home truths, but thank God I didn't get started.' I pulled a face. 'I would have been in the wrong as she was lying.' I mouthed the last word so that Dawn wouldn't get it. 'I can't go on about it here, but I'll fill you in later, okay?' Peter nodded.

Dawn said, 'Can I go and say hello to Henry Mom?'

'I'm sorry, love, but not today; let's finish our meal, and there are lots more things to see, aren't there.' She looked disappointed, but it didn't last long as we soon left the restaurant and managed to get the birthday spirit back while we continued our visit.

When I told Peter that night what Dr Feltz had said, he was appalled that Lyn could have made up such an incriminating lie. 'It's a good job that you never got as far as repeating any of her allegations. Imagine the trouble that would have caused. No wonder she didn't want anyone to have a word with him – I suppose he could have sued.'

'She's a bloody nightmare,' I said vehemently, 'and I don't know what to do about it. Do you think I should tell Janet and Mom?' I took a sip of my wine and waited for Peter's advice – he usually knew what to do about most things.

15

Peter advised me to tell Janet and Simon what Dr Feltz had said, but I was still very torn. On the one hand, if I did tell them, it would be more difficult for Janet to make arrangements for the girls, and it would be devastating for Lyn, who was desperate to look after them. On the other hand, Janet had a right to know if Lyn was drinking and not caring for the children properly. I fretted over it for about a week, I didn't want to hurt either of my sisters, but I came to the conclusion that I should at least give Lyn a chance to tell me her side of the story, and then perhaps I could decide what to do for the best. I wasn't too worried as I knew that I could trust Mom to ensure that her grandchildren would be okay.

I didn't relish the thought of challenging Lyn's story about Dr Feltz, but I had no choice. I waited until the next sunny day when I was almost certain that Mom would be working in the garden or on her new allotment, and then I left the children with Peter once again and went to talk with Lyn.

I knew that she could lie when it suited her, but I hoped that I'd be able to tell if she was still drinking heavily and if it was unfair not to tell Janet what I knew.

I let myself in and called out, sounding more cheerful than I was feeling, 'Mom – Lyn, it's only me.' I walked through to where Lyn was hand washing some delicate lingerie. The kitchen smelled unusually fragrant. 'Hi you, what's that perfume?' I asked.

She brought her sudsy hands up and waved them at me as she said, 'It's Dreft, it does smell nice, and it's gentle. I think it's good for baby clothes, but I like it too,' she smiled, 'd'you want a cuppa, I'll make one in a minute, Mom's at the allotment – she's getting it ready to grow our vegetables.'

'You finish your washing, and I'll make it.' I leaned across her outstretched arms, filled the kettle, and then set it to boil on the gas stove. Lyn began rinsing her undies, and I said casually, 'I didn't come to see Mom anyway – I wanted to talk to you.'

'What have I done now? Hold on, and I'll just peg these out so they can drip outside.'

I wondered what she thought she'd done as I took the tea tray into the living room and watched her through the window as she snapped the last peg to hold a pair of stockings on the line. They began to move lazily in the gentle breeze making graceful ballet movements. She came into the room, still rubbing her hands dry on the kitchen towel. She sat down, and I handed her a cup of weak tea, thinking that I didn't know how she could drink such milky stuff. Mine had to be quite strong before I could enjoy it.

'Well, what do you want to talk about – knowing you it's bound to be something unpleasant? What am I supposed to have done?' She gripped the arms of the chair tightly. 'Has Janet sent you to tell me that I can't mind the girls?'

'No, but what I'm about to ask you could affect it. I need you to tell me the truth this time, Lyn, because a lot depends on it.'

Her expression became wary, her cheeks flushed. 'What the fuck are you on about – I always tell the truth.'

I took a mouthful of my tea, swallowed quickly and spoke in a matter of fact way. 'We both know that's not so; we all lie at times for various reasons – you're no different. I want you to tell me again why you left the doctors, and this time don't lie.' I watched as her face turned from pink to red, and she put her cup down sharply, making it jingle alarmingly.

'I don't know what you mean, I've told you –'

'Lyn, I met Dr Feltz by accident just over a week ago, and he told me that they had dismissed you and why.' I really couldn't bear to listen to her lies yet again. 'Tell me what happened.'

'You never told him what I'd said, did you?' she asked and licked her lips.

'No, of course, I didn't, but it was more by luck than judgement as he told me first what had happened. You are such an idiot, you slandered him with no good reason, and he could have sued, you know. Now no more messing, tell me what happened.'

I listened as she admitted what she'd done, but she made the boozing sound a lot less outrageous than it had been.

'Why, Lyn, why would you get so drunk? You liked your job didn't you?' I wanted to understand.

Lyn began to cry quietly. 'Yes, I loved it, and I miss the boys very much. I was feeling lonely, I suppose, I know I've only myself to blame, and I'm sorry I told such lies, but I couldn't bear for you all to know how stupid I'd been,' she brushed her tears away impatiently, 'I never dreamt that he might find out what I'd said. None of it was true. You won't tell Mom or Janet and Michael, will you?' she asked, her eyes wide. 'I haven't touched a drop of alcohol since then, and I don't want to either.'

'How will you cope, though, when you next feel lonely?' I asked. 'There are bound to be times when you feel like that again.'

She shook her head slowly. 'I've learned my lesson, Sara – it doesn't help – I've told you before that I don't like the taste.

I've felt lonely since, but I've found something to do or called one of my friends – I haven't drunk anything.'

She sounded sincere, and I believed her. I quickly decided that I wasn't going to tell Janet, but I would make sure that I kept a close eye on my youngest sister.

'Alright, I believe you, but you know if I told Janet the truth that she wouldn't trust you to mind Michelle and Karen, don't you?'

'Please don't tell her, I mean what I say, I won't make the same mistake again. I love those girls.'

'I know you do, but I'm going to be watching and listening out, Lyn, and if I so much as hear that you've been drunk while minding them, I will tell Janet everything. As far as I'm concerned, this is your last chance to show that you can be trusted. I'm sticking my neck out for you, don't let me or yourself down.'

She nodded thoughtfully and then said, 'Thanks, Sara, I'm sorry I lied, but I think that you can understand why I did, can't you?'

I nodded, I could understand, but she was so glib I wondered what other lies she'd tell if it was expedient. She came and kissed my cheek, full of remorse and then said casually as she walked over to her record player, 'I bought a new record it's called "My Sweet Lord", have you heard it? Shall I put it on?'

I marvelled once again at her ability to bounce back as soon as she thought she was out of trouble. Perhaps Peter was right when he said that I'd end up feeling responsible for her for the rest of my life. I'd certainly stuck my neck out this time as I'd have to keep an eye on her for the foreseeable future. I didn't feel very clever as I berated myself for getting involved yet again. I listened to her new record and then made an excuse and left before Mom arrived home.

When I told Peter that I'd decided to keep mum about the reasons that Lyn had lost her job, he reacted, as I thought he would, by saying that he'd better begin to look for somewhere to move us to, but I knew by the twinkle in his eye that he had no intention of doing so yet.

'You know, my love, I haven't forgotten my promise not to keep responding to problems with Lyn. I'm not going to be checking up on her every five minutes, believe me.' I chuckled, and put down the never-ending washing that I was folding and went into his arms. 'And we're staying right here.' I hoped I would be able to keep my word.

July was a month of warm sunny spells and celebrations. First Dad's – then Dawn's sixth followed on the twentieth – by Michael reaching his twenty-first birthday. We celebrated the first two with small family parties, but we thought that Michael's warranted a real knees-up at the Fox, although it took us a while to persuade him that it was necessary. He enjoyed being the centre of attention, though, and Lyn managed to allow him to have centre stage for once.

Towards the end of the evening, Janet told us that she'd landed a job in our local hospital's respiratory department. More congratulations followed, and as I glanced across at Simon, even he looked pleased. I just bet you are happy, I thought scornfully – he would know that she'd be earning more money than he did – more for him to spend at the club. I told myself to stop being so vile. Janet called Lyn over to our table from where she'd been entertaining the girls.

Lyn plonked herself down on a spare seat next to Simon with Karen on her lap and said, 'What, what have I done now?' She grinned at Janet, who asked her if she wanted to carry on minding the girls. Lyn looked apprehensive. 'Of course, I do; I've been minding them alright while you've been studying, haven't I. I love them; you know I do.' Karen put her head down onto Lyn's chest and touched her cheek. 'It's alright, my baby, I'm not upset,' Lyn said and lifted her into her arms to cuddle her.

I looked into Lyn's soft eyes as she gazed adoringly at Karen, and it triggered a memory of when she'd been born. I could picture us being taken by our father into the front room where Mom was sitting up in bed, drinking a cup of tea. I'd climbed carefully onto the bed and kissed her, wondering why she was in the front room and not in her bedroom. She'd drawn our attention to a straw crib that was nestled in the alcove by the side of the fire, and Dad told us to come and look. We stood and gazed in awe at our new little sister. Her hands were like pink shells that an Auntie had brought back for us from a holiday in Weymouth. They were tiny and delicate, looking as they lay alongside her face. I leaned in, kissed her gently on her soft cheek, and smelled a wonderful mixture of warm milk and Johnson's baby powder. I thought that she was beautiful, the most beautiful thing I'd ever seen. Then she opened her eyes and seemed, for just a second, to focus on my face. I was hooked. A tiny bubble formed and burst from between her pink lips – she closed her eyes again. I felt such an overwhelming sense of pride and possessiveness. She was my sister, and she had chosen to love me. Somehow that feeling of being special had never disappeared; eroded undoubtedly, but never wholly ceased. I still thought that she was beautiful, just not quite so beautiful on the inside. I shook my head and returned to the present to hear Simon trying to reassure Lyn of their intentions.

'What Janet is trying to tell you, you daft bat, is that she's starting work Monday week, and we want you to mind the girls for the foreseeable future.' Simon raised his eyebrows and put his arm around Lyn's shoulders as he looked to Janet for confirmation.

'Yes, you are a daft bat, you've been looking after them beautifully, but now I'll be able to pay you a proper wage instead of some pocket money. I've got a job at the hospital.'

Lyn shrugged away from Simon's arm and stood up. 'Well, congratulations, that's good news. I'm going back to the girls now.' She walked away with Karen bouncing on her hip.

I don't know how we all expected her to behave at the news, but Janet turned her hands' palms up and shrugged. We all laughed and carried on discussing very little as the DJ had started to play "Da Ya Think I'm Sexy". I didn't want to discuss anything; my head was whirling unpleasantly. I had intercepted a look that passed between Simon and Lyn as she walked towards us, and it brought to mind the night of Mom's party when I'd seen them having a blazing row. At the time, I'd dismissed it – I was in a hurry and thought no more about them – now I felt a sharp stab of fear. Surely they weren't carrying on with each other. I took a sip of my white wine and decided that I'd imagined the look – I just didn't want to go there. I turned to Janet and asked her to tell me exactly what she'd be doing at the hospital.

As the evening wore on with no signs that I could see that Simon or Lyn were interested in each other, I gradually convinced myself that my imagination had been working overtime. I wonder with hindsight if I'd deliberately looked the other way so as not to precipitate trouble. Could I have prevented future events had I acted on my thoughts? I'll never know.

Janet started work on the second of August after dropping the girls off at Mom's. She phoned me the same evening to say how strange it felt, but how pleased she'd been to spend her day with other adults.

'You know it made me so excited to see Michelle and Karen when I picked them up from Mom's. Lyn suggested that it might be a good idea to let them sleep there Monday to Friday so I could have more time weekday mornings, but I couldn't do that,' she was silent for a couple of seconds then continued in a rush, 'although it would make sense wouldn't it?'

'You'd miss them, and I'm sure they'd miss you too. Hmm,' I mentally shrugged and went on, 'I suppose a couple of nights might not hurt, but what do you think Simon would have to say about it?'

'Oh, I don't know – I haven't thought it through –but I might ask him what he thinks. It would be nice sometimes not to get them ready every morning, but I don't know if I could do it; I'd feel guilty. It's bad enough that I'm leaving them each day. It's a good job that it's with Mom and Lyn; otherwise, I don't think I could do it. Anyway, it's too soon to think about it. I'll see how things work out. Are you okay?'

I answered briefly in the affirmative and then said, 'I'll phone you later on; bye, for now, hun.' I could hear Peter calling to me from the sitting room. My thoughts were jumbled as I went to see what he wanted. I understood that Janet was tasting freedom for the first time in four years, but I hoped that she'd take her time before making such a big decision. I knew that I'd have to see my two every night.

When I told Peter what she'd suggested, he pulled a wry face and said, 'I don't expect Simon would agree to that anyway.'

'No, maybe not. What did you call me for anyway?'

He beamed as he lifted Paul to look at me. 'Our clever son just said Dada. Say it for Mommy Paul, Dada, Dada.' Paul gave a big yawn making me double up.

'He finds you boring. Come on; son, let's see if you can say, Momma.' I took him and sat on the floor while Peter and I had a contest to see who could get him to speak. Neither of us won, but we enjoyed trying until Dawn lost her patience.

'Please will you two stop – I'm trying to think.' She chuckled and then said, 'Paul say, Dawn. Come on, say,

Dawn.' She knew that it would provoke her dad into action, and he was hot on her heels as she fled from the room. I didn't go to see, but the shrieks of laughter coming from the kitchen were infectious, and I found myself laughing too – business as usual, I thought.

16

By November, I was initially dismayed to find that I was, yet again, pregnant. Paul was only a year old, and I was just getting over that first baby year when everything revolved around ensuring that the little one's needs are planned for and met. Thank goodness it didn't take long before I accepted my fate and began to look forward to another jump onto the merry-go-round. I thought that the timing couldn't have been better as Peter still loved teaching, and the pay was good enough so that I didn't need to go out to work – we were happy.

My happiness stemmed from a feeling of deep contentment. The whole family, well, those that I care about anyway, seemed to be settled. They were getting on with their lives without any need for my intervention. Mom and Dad still spent long periods apart, which, to us, children was the accepted norm. Janet was enjoying her work, and Simon had advised her to leave the girls at Mom's Monday to Friday, so that was the arrangement they came to. She often popped in to see them on her way home from work, sometimes staying until they were asleep, but she seemed content not to take them home until the weekend. Lyn was in her element and treated the girls as though they were her children, especially Karen.

After a couple of months, when Michelle told Janet that she called Lyn, 'Momma Lyn,' there were some very strong words forthcoming until it changed back to Auntie Lyn. Since going out to work, Janet had seemed to be able to assert herself more, and she wasn't going to allow Lyn to undermine her place in her children's world.

Michael had used some of his savings and his birthday money to buy a cheap, second hand Cortina, and he still spent the majority of his time, when not at work, with Derek, his friend, since school days. He hadn't said so, but we were now convinced that he was different. We saw no reason to bring the subject up with him as he seemed perfectly at ease with his sexuality.

I sometimes envied the boys happy go lucky ways and admired how they'd use their free time to take off to whichever seaside resort or Welsh mountain range that took their fancy. I'd never felt entirely in charge of my life and didn't see myself as a decisive person. There had always seemed to be someone else whose feelings I had to consider before I could decide what I wanted. I was glad to see that Michael had that free spirit no matter what problems he might have to face because of his fairly obvious sexual orientation.

As the month wore on, I found that I had lots of time on my hands despite two young children. Peter agreed that we should invite the whole family to our house for Christmas, and everyone accepted. Mom jumped at the chance to have a change that meant she didn't have to cook. It was hard work, but I enjoyed the day until my bubble was burst again by an incident that I witnessed between Lyn and Simon.

Tea had been cleared away, and Janet and Simon were getting ready to leave when Lyn asked if they would leave Karen to go home with her. Janet refused, and Lyn burst into tears. 'Oh, but I'll miss her,' she wailed, causing eyebrows to rise.

'She'll be back with you in a couple of days, and we need her too, you know.' Janet laughed and pulled an exasperated face at her sister. Lyn's crying dissolved into sniffles as Janet left the room and headed for the bathroom. I chose to ignore them, took a couple of cups hanging about into the kitchen, swilled them and left them to drain. When I returned, I was just in time to see Simon run his fingers gently across Lyn's damp cheek and say something that I didn't catch. I sensed that it was intimate as the look in her eyes spoke volumes. She appeared to have been kissed.

I went back into the kitchen, sad and confused. This time I knew that I had imagined nothing. I was going to have to do something, but I couldn't think what. Whatever I did, someone that I loved was going to get hurt. I wondered how far things had gone between the pair of them, was it possible that they were having an affair. I wouldn't put it past him, but surely Lyn wouldn't be so wicked as to carry on with Janet's husband. I thought that she might well be flattered that he should pay her some attention, he was, after all, very good looking, and she was highly impressionable. What if he'd been using her as a plaything since she was very young? It would explain the moodiness she'd exhibited since her early teens and the drinking too. At first, my mind ran on and on, rejecting the notions that entered my head and then finding affirmation for my crazy suspicions. By the time our last visitor had left, I was feeling sick and edgy with apprehension. I wanted to tell Peter how I was feeling, but I couldn't – my thoughts just felt too horrible to be put into words.

I had a nightcap of whisky, thinking that it might help me to sleep, but it didn't, and I tossed and turned all night; for once pleased when Paul woke for his milk at six-thirty. We were going to Peter's mother's house that day and then planned to spend Monday, the Boxing Day bank holiday, at home. So, I knew that there was nothing I could do other than try to put my mind at rest until I could get to see Simon. I had worked out that it would be best to tackle him rather than face yet another battle with Lyn, who would probably lie anyway and rightly or wrongly resent me for interfering. Simon's reaction wouldn't bother me as I liked him less and less every time we came into contact. But I knew that I needed to face up to the inevitable unpleasantness. If my suspicions were correct, I had to protect Janet and her children, and if unfounded, I needed to stop him from tormenting Lyn. I wondered how much, if anything, Mom might know, but I couldn't bring myself to ask her. If she was aware of anything and hadn't tried to stop Lyn from hurting Janet, I would be so angry with her that I would not be supportive. I needed to be sure before I said anything.

We spent Sunday at Ivy's, and it was really like a more relaxed version of the previous day, except I found that my traitorous mind insisted on raking my suspicions over and over. I was worried and frustrated, and I wanted to storm over to Janet's and confront Simon. I wasn't a stirrer, and the thought of all the upset that would follow should I behave so impulsively prevented me from following my inclination. A picture of my grandfather with his thin, white hair whispering across his nodding head, telling me always to keep a wise counsel, came into my mind. I didn't understand at the time, but I did now, and I hoped that I was doing just that. Our family had always been close-knit, and I couldn't bear the thought that anyone could drive a wedge between us. I decided that I would confront Simon when he was at the club.

I managed to contain myself the following week until Saturday when I phoned Janet, and during our conversation, ascertained that Simon was at the club. Peter said that he would mind the children while I had some downtime and visited my friend Sylvia, who lived not too far away by Olton station. I rang her and asked if she would mind if Peter rang her to tell him that I'd just left. She agreed but asked what I was up to.

'Not messing about, are you, Sara?' She laughed, and I managed a chuckle too.

She knew me better than that, and I easily fobbed her off with a story about needing to shop on my own. I then headed to the club. I walked into the somewhat noisy, stale smelling place with its host of small wooden tables that housed couples and families enjoying their leisure time together. I immediately spotted Simon propping up the bar talking and gesturing to a red-haired young man. He looked as though he was explaining how to do something. I thought that I'd seen the man before, but I wasn't sure and dismissed him from my mind as I walked across to them. My brother-in-law's eyebrows almost touched his hairline as soon as he caught sight of me, but he quickly regained his usual composure and said, 'Hi Sara, what brings you here?' He looked over my shoulder. 'Where's Peter – you here on your own?'

'Yes, I came to talk to you,' I said it casually, but to my eye, he immediately flushed and began to look guilty.

'Can I get you a drink?' he asked. 'Come on and sit down.' He excused himself from his companion and, placing a hand under my elbow, led me to a table at the end of the bar.

'Do you want a drink? What'll it be?'

'No thanks, nothing for me.' I sat down. Simon placed his beer on the table and then perched on the stool opposite.

'Okay, what can I do you for?' He asked in his usual jaunty manner – but I could sense that he felt as uneasy as I was. I could feel my heartbeat power up a notch, and I'm sure that I felt the baby quicken in my womb. My face burned as I stopped being a wimp and looked him in the eye.

'What is going on between you and Lyn?' I asked.

'Eh? I don't know what you're talking about,' he said. His already pink neck turned a darker shade, and I watched as it spread into his cheeks.

'I think you do, Simon; I've witnessed some intimacy between you both on a few occasions.' He opened his mouth to speak, but I forestalled him. 'Don't bother to deny it, or I'll go straight to Janet and tell her what I think.'

My hands trembled in my lap. I tried to steady them and reached for my red leather gloves from where they lay on my matching handbag.

Simon picked up his glass and took a long pull, downing about a quarter of his pint. He pursed his lips, and his eyes were cold as he looked at me with deliberation. 'I don't know what you think you've seen, Sara, but it can't be much because there isn't much to see. Lyn's had a schoolgirl crush on me ever since I've known her and made that obvious to me, but I've never responded to her in anything other than a kind way. She's a very mixed up kid. So,' he leaned forward and stuck out his chin in an aggressive manner, 'so if you want to go and try to cause trouble for me and my wife, then you'd better do it – she's the one that will get hurt. She knows how Lyn feels, but she won't appreciate anyone else seeing, believe me.' He opened his eyes wide and held out his long slim hands palm up. 'There is nothing to tell. I've made my position clear to Lyn, and at times I think I've done a pretty good job of helping her grow up and settle down. So, do your worst Big Sista, but you'll be doing no one a favour.'

He said the words Big Sista with such sarcasm that I felt small – very small. I stood up, gathered my things and said, 'Okay, I believe you, but if I ever find out that you're lying, I will make you very sorry.'

'You could try, but you'd be the loser, Big Sista.' He stood and walked away, leaving me by the table, feeling very foolish. I should have realised that it would be Lyn's attention-seeking behaviour that I was witnessing. Simon wouldn't risk his marriage by having an affair with his sister-in-law, who could be somewhat flaky at times. I felt sure that he had a few other women that he could see if he wished. I left the club feeling glad that I hadn't confided my thoughts to anyone else and relieved that now I wouldn't have to. I needed to try and mind my own business.

17

My heart went out to Lyn. I could imagine how it would feel to have a crush on a man and not have it returned, especially a man she couldn't avoid. No wonder she'd had such a difficult time throughout her teenage years. It explained an awful lot of the depressive behaviour, the drinking, and the inability to confide in either Janet or myself. Again, I wondered if Mom knew – perhaps that was one reason she was so indulgent towards her youngest child. I decided that I wasn't going to waste any more of my precious time dwelling on the matter. It wasn't any of my business unless my family were going to be badly hurt, and it seemed to me that no one was. Janet knew about Lyn's crush, but she hadn't bothered or wanted to tell me about it, and I suppose I was a trifle miffed about them keeping me in the dark. I resolved as the week wore on, and the New Year began to concentrate on my own rapidly growing family. It was one I'd made before and never been able to keep, but this time I was determined.

An unexpected break from the family assisted my resolve. Peter had booked us into the hotel in Kent where we'd stayed the previous year. It fitted in nicely with the half-term holiday, and he explained it by saying it was his late birthday present to himself. I didn't mind what the reasons were; we'd had such a good time when we were snowed in that I couldn't wait to pack up the car and go. No snow this year, and we managed to spend a lot of time exploring the surrounding countryside. I fell in love with the whole of Kent, well, the parts that we saw anyway. My favourite was a place called Faversham. Such a step back in time and hardly touristy at all, the cobbled streets on the walk down to the creek were something that I wanted to experience every day. I was hooked, and Peter agreed that we should move there at some point in our lives. I said that we should move before our children became enmeshed in their lives in the Midlands and didn't want to move, and he agreed.

Term time beckoned, and we had to return to reality, but for as much as I'd decided not to be concerned about my family, I found my stomach knotting up as we neared home.

As soon as we were settled, I phoned Mom. Keeping my tone light, I said, 'Hi Mom, how are things?'

'Is that you our Sara,' she said, 'Oh, I'm glad you're home. It's been hell here,' I could hear a sniffle, 'Lyn's gone.'

I took a deep breath. 'What do you mean Lyn's gone, gone where?'

'She's living at Janet's.' My heart jolted.

'What?' I couldn't believe that I'd heard correctly.

'She's gone to stay at Janet's. She said she couldn't stay here with Michael anymore.' I could hear Mom beginning to cry quietly.

'Put the phone down, Mom; I'll be there in a few minutes. Make yourself some tea.'

'Okay, love, see you in a minute.' We disconnected, and I went to tell Peter the news.

'Bloody hell, I think she waits until we go away and then decides to make everyone's life miserable. Well, I suppose you'd better go and find out what's happened. I know you won't settle until you do. Don't be too long, though.' He took me in his arms and kissed me passionately. I prolonged the kiss. We'd been so close while we were away, and I knew just

115

how he felt. We wanted to live in our little bubble, not have others sticking pins into it.

'I'll be as quick as I can.' I patted his bum and gave a cheeky grin as Dawn came into the room.

'Hey, rude,' she said, 'can I come to Grandma's with you?'

'Not this time, but I'll take you soon. Look after your Dad and Paul for me, will you?' She rolled her eyes and went back to whatever television programme that she'd been watching.

When I arrived at Mom's, I could see by her red-rimmed eyes that she'd been crying for a while and gave her a long hug before asking what had happened.

Words tumbled from her mouth as the tears began to flow again. I couldn't understand what she was saying, but it had something to do with Michael.

'Mom,' I said firmly, 'stop crying and tell me properly.'

She mopped her eyes and gave me a look, but the crying ceased. 'Well, Michael came home the other night and found that Lyn had put some of the children's toys into the wardrobe in his bedroom. He took them out and flung them into her room. As soon as Lyn saw what he'd done, she started screaming and shouting that he was a selfish bugger who didn't need his room because he always stayed with Derek. Michael retaliated by telling Lyn that she was the selfish one and had no right to go into his room when he wasn't there. Next thing I know, there's a lot of scuffling happening on the landing, and I hear Lyn call Michael a fucking queer. Then everything went quiet for a minute, and I started to climb the stairs only to hear Lyn say that Derek had been trying to get off with her, so he was bi or something. That's when Michael walloped her across her face. She staggered against the wall and then slid down until she was sitting on the floor.'

Mom took a deep breath, and the ready tears spurted out again.

'Stop crying,' I said automatically, 'what happened then?'

'Everything, Michael started to say he was sorry, but Lyn jumped up and grabbed his jacket and began to hit him around his head with her fist. Michael managed to shove her off, went into his room and banged the door shut. I told Lyn to go into her room. All the fight seemed to go out of her, and for once, she obeyed without another word. I was so shaken that I went and lay down on my bed. Next thing I know, I can hear Lyn on the phone asking Janet if she can go and stay there and mind the girls as she can't spend another night in this house with Michael.' Mom dropped her face in her hands and began to rock gently in her chair.

'She said yes, didn't she – when did this happen?'

'On Friday, Simon came and helped Lyn to move her stuff into their spare room. I haven't seen or heard from her since, although Janet has rung and said its okay. She seems to think that it's only a temporary thing until they make it up. They usually get on so well together – it was such a little thing to set them off. I've never heard Lyn say such awful things – it felt as though she deliberately wanted to hurt him. I don't know what I've done to deserve her; she can be such a bugger at times much as I love her. Do you think that you could have a word with them, Sara? I don't know what to do. I didn't want her to leave home,' Mom said.

'What's Michael said about it?' I asked.

'He just said that she deserved it and she could stay away for all he cared. I told him off for hitting her, but she was pretty horrible to him, so ...' Mom shrugged.

I had a dreadful sinking feeling in my stomach as I said, 'You know Mom, I'm sorry this has happened, but I'm not going to get involved. It's up to Janet and Lyn what they do.' Her hands moved to cup her tearful face, but I was determined not to intervene. 'Do you need me for anything else because I promised Peter that I wouldn't be too long – we've hardly had time to unpack, and it's school tomorrow?'

Mom shook her head. 'Did you have a good time, love?'

'Mm, yes we did; I'll probably pop in tomorrow after I've taken Dawn to school; we can talk then – I'd better go.' I kissed her cheek and resisted looking back at the door. I didn't want to see if she had started to cry again. I wondered if I was becoming hard-faced as I got older, but I thought I was probably just becoming more sensible.

That summer was fairly uneventful; we did the usual picnics and seaside visits and made a big fuss on Dawn's seventh birthday in July. Dad had managed to get some time off, so we celebrated both their birthdays together with a family tea at our house. Michael opted not to attend, so there was no friction between Lyn and him. I was proud of myself as each time I had gone to visit Janet and Lyn had been there, I'd resisted the temptation to ask questions regarding their arrangements. They seemed to be getting on very well, and I most certainly didn't wish to rock the boat, so I never mentioned what I knew or didn't know. I realised it meant that I was slipping away from the closeness that I'd enjoyed with both my sisters in different ways, but my energies were directed well and truly at my own family.

Dawn was still a quick-witted delightful girl, and Paul was at the hysterically naughty stage that I remembered her going through. I couldn't wait for our third baby to put in an appearance. It was due around Paul's second birthday, but you can imagine how embarrassed I was when my waters broke early on the third of August whilst I was in an aisle at our local Woolworth store. The staff were very helpful and reassuring. They ensured that I was comfortable and brought a chair for me to sit on while quickly cleaning up my mess.

Our new daughter waited until the ambulance came and whisked both myself and Paul off to the hospital. Peter subsequently collected him and deposited him with his mother before returning for the birth. I was back home by the next day, as this time, it had been a very short labour, and I felt so well. We called her Jennifer Sara; she was beautiful and looked remarkably like Dawn when she'd been born.

Despite the tension between Michael and Lyn, when Autumn arrived and Lyn still hadn't returned home to live, we all ceased to be concerned. Janet enjoyed her work too much to do anything more than appreciate the freedom that she'd gained. Lyn took excellent care of Michelle and Karen and never seemed to want time for herself. I still had my doubts about the wisdom of allowing her to be with Simon daily, but it wasn't my problem. I enjoyed my life and didn't want to face something that I couldn't do anything about.

The weather that had us wrapping up in our winter clothing was probably the only thing we had to moan about until Dad had a TIA. After the initial assessment, he was transferred by ambulance from Halifax, where he'd been working, to our nearest hospital. I didn't know what a TIA was but soon found out that it was medical terminology for a mini-stroke. We were all horrified. He'd only been a small part of our lives, but he was always there in the background. He was fifty-five years of age, and I don't think he'd had a day's illness in his life. He was only in the hospital for a week as there didn't appear to be any lasting consequences. When it happened, he'd lost power down the left side of his body and was unable to move his arm, but he recovered rapidly and was allowed home. The cardiologist recommended a change in his diet, prescribed blood pressure medication and signed him off work until his GP would pass him as fit.

Altogether, it was a very testing time for Mom and Dad – I had memories of them being demonstrative from when I was young – but it was many years since I'd seen evidence that they loved each other. The only time had been a kiss when

Mom mistakenly thought that he'd planned her birthday party. Now they were thrust together, and I think that Mom resented his constant presence. She wasn't used to having to consider her husband before she did what she wanted to do. Although there weren't many things that she needed to do in the garden or on her allotment at this time of the year, she fretted when she felt restricted by him. Dad had been warned that he shouldn't drive for a while and was sensible enough to heed the warning, but he became increasingly restless to get back on the road. I spent as much of my time as I could just being about and having a chat with him. I got to know much that I hadn't known about this enigma that I called Dad. For the first time that I could ever remember, he talked about the injury he received during the war while fighting in France. He'd had several operations to remove shrapnel from his abdomen and right leg, and that was the end of his war. He told me that his leg had permanent damage and scarring, and I wondered with some guilt how I'd never noticed that he was in pain on occasions – but I never had.

While I was there, Janet popped in a couple of times, but Lyn never came. Mom said that she hadn't been home since her row with Michael, but she seemed to be okay with that. When she still hadn't been to see Dad after three weeks of him being at home, I told him that I would go and see if I could persuade her to visit perhaps when Michael wasn't at home. His reply, which came out of the blue, was probably the biggest shock I'd had so far in my life.

He shrugged his shoulders and said calmly, 'Don't trouble yourself, Sara, I'm not bothered about seeing her. She's not one of mine anyway.'

I peered closely at him to see if he could have had another TIA, I could hear his words, but I couldn't interpret what he meant. Surely, he didn't know what he was saying, I thought.

I laughed. 'Well, whose is she then?' I challenged him with no thought that he meant what he'd said.

'Perhaps you'd better ask your Mom. I've already said too much. I thought perhaps she might have told you by now what with all the trouble that Lyn has caused.' He sat back in his chair by the fire, and I studied him for a couple of minutes before asking him again in all seriousness this time.

'What do you mean Dad, you can't say what you have and then expect me to leave it there. If she's not yours, then who does she belong to – is she adopted?'

'I'm saying no more. You'll have to ask your mom.' He seemed to shrink into himself, and he looked drained as he shut his eyes.

I leaned forward and kissed his cheek. It didn't feel right to carry on pushing him. 'Okay, Dad, why don't you try and have a nap. I will ask Mom when I see her, don't you worry about it.'

18

Peter walked into the kitchen, flung his car keys onto the breakfast bar, ran his hands through his hair, and collapsed onto a bar stool. 'That wanker!' he said and gestured towards the front door.

I didn't need to ask who he referred to as he'd just returned from driving Simon up to Halifax. 'Bad journey, my love?' I said.

'You'd better believe it. I think that another hour in his company listening to him boasting about himself, and the fact that he has two women to wait on him, would have resulted in me dumping him out at the side of the road. He thinks he's God's gift. Got any coffee on the go, love?'

I hurried to boil the kettle and make him a fresh cup of instant and then kissed him tenderly with an apology in my look. It was my fault that he'd had to put up with Simon because I'd asked them to go; I couldn't think of any other way to get Dad's car back for him.

Dawn and Paul were spending the afternoon at their Grandma Ivy's as she'd offered to give me a break. I'd just put Jenny down for her afternoon nap, so we took our coffee into the sitting room where I snuggled up to Peter as though he'd been gone for days. I wanted to share some of the things that were troubling me.

'I want to talk to you about something; I'm afraid it's about Lyn though,' I said.

Peter sighed. 'Go on, then what's she done this time?'

'Well, she hasn't done anything.' I repeated what Dad had told me.

'Are you sure he wasn't rambling, love?'

'I don't think so, but I haven't plucked up the courage to ask Mom about it in case I stir something up that's better forgotten about. What do you think I should do?'

'Well, do you think you can put it out of your mind unless you do ask her? I doubt you can – it'll eat away at you, won't it?'

I nodded. 'Hmm, it probably will – it's hardly the sort of thing I can forget.'

'Well, get it over with and ask her; that's what I'd do anyway.'

'Okay, I think you're right. I'll talk to her in the week. I know I'll be glad when Christmas is over this year, I don't feel like celebrating with Lyn and Michael still not speaking and Dad and Mom being antagonistic towards each other. Thank God he's been given the all-clear to return to work in the New Year.' I said and snuggled even closer now I'd finished my coffee. There's nothing that I can't face with Peter to support me, I thought.

Later that week, I began to make plans for the Christmas Day meal. There would only be Michael and Derek and Mom and Dad this year. Janet and Lyn were staying at home, but Janet said she'd be round on Boxing Day with the girls. Although I thought that Peter was right and I needed to ask Mom about Lyn's birth, I'd decided to leave talking to her about what Dad had said until after Christmas – perhaps when Dad had returned to work.

Despite my misgivings, I thoroughly enjoyed Christmas Day and Boxing Day. It was delightful to see Dawn and Paul's happiness as they opened their presents from Santa. When Michelle and Karen arrived, they brought some of their new toys with them, and I was pleased that all four of them were good at sharing. It made for a very pleasant time so that Janet and I could relax, leaving Peter, who had volunteered to clean up in the kitchen, on his own. I again resisted asking about Lyn and Simon, but Janet told me anyway. Simon had agreed to spend Boxing Day and overnight with his brother, Paul's family, in Nottingham. Lyn had said that she just couldn't be bothered, arsed was the word Janet said that she'd used to join in all the shallowness of another day like the one before and was going to stay in bed and read and eat chocolate. It made me smile as I remembered that she was still only nineteen years of age, and to her, it was probably the best thing that she could do.

'I'm surprised that she didn't want to stay with Michelle and Karen,' I said, just for something to say.

'Well, I must admit I was surprised too; she barely lets me do anything for them anymore. I often have to insist – she treats Karen as though she is her child – oh, she loves Michelle too, but it's Karen that she dotes on. I'm not always sure that it's healthy for her. She doesn't seem to have any interest in going out with her friends or finding a boyfriend. Mind you; I don't know what I'd do without her – she makes life very easy for me. Do you know she does most of the housework and often cooks meals for us all? Sometimes I feel very guilty; I mean, I pay her a pittance, it's all we can afford, but she'd be much better off working for a family like the Feltz family. They paid her well.'

I could feel my anxiety hike up a level; I wished that I'd said nothing at all as I just didn't know how to reply. My brain scurried around like a meerkat after food while I searched for safe words that were non-committal. I wondered whether to tell her about the information that Dad had given me but decided that I'd rather talk to Mom before sharing just in case he'd been rambling. I didn't think so; he'd seemed to be thinking clearly enough when he was with us the day before.

I settled for, 'I'm sure that Mom misses her living at home too.'

'Well, it doesn't look as though she has any intention of returning; we don't charge her rent either, so I suppose that she is marginally better off. I'm not sure that when I agreed to her coming to stay that I thought it would be long term, and I admit that there are times when I would like her to go back home, especially when Simon and I need some privacy.' She shrugged. 'Shall I refill your glass? I could do with another drink.'

I thought I detected a note of despondency in her voice, and as she walked towards the kitchen, her shoulders seemed to be tense, not at all like her usual relaxed walk. I felt sure that my imagination was working overtime as when she returned with our replenished glasses of wine, she seemed to be in her usual good spirits. I wondered if I was looking for trouble where there wasn't any.

We went to sit with the girls, and I was able to stay on safe ground for the remainder of the visit. Later, when Peter joined us with Jenny, who needed feeding, the conversation became light-hearted, and we all had a good time as we'd always done when we were together. I missed Janet, but I recognised the inevitability of change.

Peter and I were beginning to establish a tradition of bringing in the New Year without the company of extended family. So, as midnight struck, we were happy to kiss each other and give our friends Bob and Sally, who were also teachers at the Grammar school, a peck on the cheek. We'd spent a pleasant evening in each other's company and went to bed feeling hopeful that this would be an even better year than the last one.

The following week I walked Dawn to school, even though she protested that at seven, she was old enough to go on her own. Then I took the two little ones to give Lyn a new wristwatch as it was her twentieth birthday. She seemed pleased to see us but didn't offer to make us a drink, and I got the distinct impression that she wasn't keen on us staying. She'd not long returned from taking Michelle to school and said she was planning to visit a friend with Karen. I thought that she looked pale and tired, but for the first time, I couldn't bring myself to comfort her in any way. I just didn't feel that we were very close anymore. It saddened me, and I very soon made an excuse and returned home. I had an awful sinking feeling when I pictured her face later that day. I wondered what was up with her. I didn't think that it could be anything I'd done; I barely saw her these days. I wasn't sure that I wanted to know, but I was about to find out.

'Whatever's the matter?' I spoke through the door with some acerbity as I unlocked it. I'd been reluctant to answer the insistent ringing of the doorbell at seven-thirty in the morning, clad in crumpled, none too clean pyjamas, and with a crying baby in my arms. Janet stood on the step; her tall frame hunched over, giving her lofty appearance an air of vulnerability – quite unlike herself. A bulging blue suitcase leaned against her booted feet.

She looked dreadful; her hair was stringy and looked as though it needed a shampoo. Her fair complexion was red and blotchy with no sign of the usual carefully applied make-up, and she was using her gloved hands to attempt to stem the flow of tears tumbling from her swollen eyes. My alarm bells jangled – oh hell, real trouble, I thought wearily as my brain registered that it was a Saturday morning – she should have been getting ready to work. She was now secretary to Mr

Noble, a respiratory consultant, and I knew she'd arranged to work some overtime on a research project for him.

'Sara.' Janet said breathlessly through her tears as I shifted Jenny onto my other arm and then encouraged my sister into the hallway. She dropped the heavy suitcase onto the floor, came wearily into my arms and leaned her head gently against Jenny. I held her as close as I was able and patted her back, murmuring soothing noises. I felt sick with worry as loud sobs began to rack her slender body. I expected Jenny to start crying, but she didn't. I was relieved when, after a couple of minutes, Janet's cries gradually subsided into silent tears. I fatuously asked again if she was okay.

She let go of me and walked dejectedly towards the sitting room, then turned in the doorway and shrugged. 'I can't stand it anymore, I don't know what's going on, and we're growing further and further apart.' The words burst from her unpainted lips like projectile vomit. She heaved a soulful sigh and, as her anger changed focus, lifted her hand and smacked on her forehead with some force. 'I've made a bloody mess of everything, and I need to get away before I do something, I'll bloody well regret,' she gave me a pleading look, 'can I stay here, Sara, while I sort myself out?'

Peter came into the room with Paul in tow and took Jenny from my arms. He'd been listening. He gave Janet a sympathetic look, patted her arm and then took the children back upstairs, leaving us to talk.

'Of course, you can,' I said without thinking. 'What about the girls?'

'They'll be alright for now with Lyn looking after them. She's so good at it.' Janet looked thoroughly miserable and sounded somewhat sarcastic.

I knew that their relationship had been stormy at times, but I never dreamt that it was bad enough for her to consider leaving Simon. I suppose it was because they'd married too young and started life with all the pressures that an unplanned baby can bring. I felt afraid for them all, but my immediate concern was solely for Janet. She slumped onto our worn sofa. Her shoulder-length hair framed her thin face as she examined her wet hankie, folding its wetness this way and that, then sighing heavily, she mopped her eyes on her soft, sunshine yellow sleeve.

'I'll make a cuppa Jan,' I said softly and left the room, eager to do something constructive.

Janet gradually ceased to weep and ambled lethargically to the bay window where she drew back the blinds and peered out. She shivered while contemplating the misty moistness of the grey January morning. I came and stood beside her and watched the familiar sights of yellow and blue buses and numerous cars, conveying their occupants to work in the busy city. I'm not sure that anything was registering in Janet's consciousness as she didn't even react to the sound of a passenger jet, as it took off, from the nearby airport, with its engines screaming.

I went back into the kitchen as the kettle boiled, and my suspicions that had never really disappeared coalesced in my mind. I poured the water onto the tea bags feeling a sense of doom invade me. I was thinking how little it had taken for Lyn to provoke Michael into being used as her excuse for going to live at Janet and Simon's house. Had that been her scheme to live with Simon, I wondered, was it possible that she could be so cunning? No matter what Simon had said when I challenged him, I had seen evidence in the past of his promiscuous behaviour. I suddenly felt sure that I knew the reasons for the domestic upheaval that was causing Janet to cut herself into self-deprecating pieces.

I handed her a mug of hot tea with sugar and sat down next to her. 'Okay, tell me what's up?'

19

Tears flowed again as Janet said, 'It's Simon,' and gulped back a sob, 'we row all the time now. We've always had our arguments, but it's become worse and worse. I can't open my mouth without annoying him. Last night I thought he was going to hit me – he became so angry when I asked him to come to see a film that we'd both said we wanted to see. I don't understand.' She sat up straighter in her seat, took a sip of her tea, then scrubbed fiercely at her eyes and wiped her runny nose. She seemed to regain some of her confident manner as we drank in silence. After a few minutes, she went on. 'I don't think I can bear to be with him any longer. I love him so much, but now ...' She gave an involuntary hiccup.

I finished my tea and put my mug down. 'How's he behaving with Lyn and the children?' My suspicions clamoured for attention.

'Fine,' she said and touched her chest, 'it's just me that pisses him off.'

'Where are they now?' I asked as casually as I could.

'He said he wanted to go fishing with Tony, so he was planning on meeting him at Packington later this morning. Lyn was going to take Michelle and Karen to the park to meet up with her friend, who has two children who play with them. I packed my clothes last night,' she said. 'They were all still in bed when I left this morning.'

I was dismayed; I didn't need to hear any more details; my suspicions were confirmed – to my satisfaction at any rate. I'd seen Simon and Lyn and their sly glances, and even though I'd professed to believe Simon when he said that there was nothing between them, I realised that I'd believed what I wanted to believe. I had to come clean, and now I wished that I'd talked to Janet about it before.

'Y'know Jan,' I said, 'you need to go back home and kick Lyn out; that's where your problems stem from.'

There was silence for a couple of minutes while we stared numbly at each other. Our antique wag-at-the wall clock ticked us into another hour – its Westminster chimes seemed to spur Janet to speak.

'I don't think so,' she said and shook her head. 'Lyn's stuck up for me loads of times when Simon's turned nasty. She's helped around the house too. I told you. No, it's just me – I can't get my act together anymore.'

I shifted in my chair. 'No love, I'm not wrong or being unfair, Simon's always flirting with someone or other, you know that, and Lyn's spoilt rotten. We've all babied her.'

Janet shook her head vigorously. 'I know that he's been unfaithful at times, but I can't believe that Lyn would ...'

'You know she's looked after the girls since before you returned to work, she's loved playing happy families, and she's always had a crush on Simon. She was jealous of your family, and Simon's used her. He's a shit, I'll grant you a good looking one, but he knew that she had a crush on him, and he has absolutely no sense of right or wrong where women are concerned, has he?'

'No, but –'

'Lyn was jealous of your lot, and Simon's played on it so he could get his leg over.' My conviction that I was right was now firmly cemented in my head.

Janet stared in bewilderment at my intensely flushed face.

'You believe what you're saying, don't you?'

'I wouldn't say it if I didn't – it's the only rational explanation.' I thought for a moment then said, 'I don't think you should be the one to leave. Why don't you go home and have it out with them? I'll come with you if you'd like me to. Did you know that she has always had a crush on Simon – he once told me that you did?'

'No, I didn't – stupid, aren't I. Did he tell you that? When?'

'It's not worth going into now Jan, it was after I'd seen the way they looked at each other – I asked him about it.'

Janet's mouth dropped open. 'Why didn't you tell me?'

'The way he put it, there was nothing to tell, and if you already knew, it was none of my business. I'm now sorry I didn't, but I believed the lying bastard.' We sat looking at each other for a couple of minutes. 'What you going to do, hon?' I asked and tried to smile.

'I can't think.' She went to look out into the street again. I cleared the tea things away, leaving Janet alone with her thoughts. I heard her putting her coat on.

When I returned, Janet smiled wanly at me. 'I hope that you're wrong about them. But you're right. I need to leave my case here, go home and face the music. It's best that I go alone, but I'll ring if I need you to come and fetch me, okay?'

She dawdled down our short drive and turned once to wave. I knew that she'd already left me behind – mentally at home – anticipating the arguments which would surely come. She kicked dejectedly at a pile of dead leaves. I wished it was her husband that she was kicking.

The phone call came at around eight o'clock that evening.

'Can you come and bring my suitcase?' Janet asked in a dull but firm voice.

'Yes, of course, now?'

'If you could, I'd appreciate it,' she said and then rang off before I could reply.

Peter agreed that I had no option, yet again, but to go and leave him to mind our children. A short time later, when I rang their bell, Janet answered the door and said with a wry smile, 'It's okay – come on in, I'm on my own – Michelle and Karen are asleep.'

I followed her into her country style kitchen. It was all blue and white gingham with tasteful bits of pottery. She'd made a pot of coffee, and I sat at the pine table and gazed around while she poured it out. I noticed that she had a new Welsh dresser displaying her Denby Imperial Blue crockery. Yesterday we would have oohed and aahed over the new acquisition – today; it didn't warrant a mention.

'Where are they?' I asked in a shaky voice. I saw that Janet had changed her clothes and applied a little makeup at some time during this bloody awful day. There were tiny black blotches under her eyes where her mascara had smudged – they made me want to cry, but I swallowed hard – I needed to stay in control for her sake.

'Lyn ran out, and I'm worried about her,' Janet said.

'Simon's gone after her, and he seems to think that she'll be at the hotel on the other side of the park. They used to meet there sometimes. I've warned him not to come back.' She placed my coffee on a coaster and sat opposite.

I was surprised at how calm she seemed to be, but my mind was also touring around the roads trying to think where I could go to look for Lyn, who, no matter what had happened, would need some help.

Janet drew my attention back with her next words. 'I stopped at a cafe on the way home – you know the one by the bus garage – I needed to think. I was trying to convince myself that you were mistaken, but,' she paused, and her eyes took on a steely glint, 'I knew I was kidding myself when I found no one home. The note that I'd left for Simon was open on the kitchen table. His fishing tackle was still by the back door.

I felt as though someone was pouring cold water down my spine. 'Oh my God, Jan, I'm so sorry.'

It was as if I hadn't spoken as Janet continued in a level voice. 'I'd decided that after talking to them, I'd return to your place,' she said. She chewed on the inside of her bottom lip. 'I changed my clothes and sat in the living room. I sat there all day with my coat on – it became dark, and I got very cold.' She sighed heavily. 'I couldn't bring myself to get up and put the fire on, or make a drink or even go to the loo, I felt numb – I still do.'

There was a long spell of silence broken only by Janet drumming her long-polished fingernails on the table. I desperately wanted to know what had happened but understood that Janet needed to tell me as much as she wished. My anxiety escalated as I thought that Simon could return at any time.

Janet eventually continued with her story. 'It was when they all came through the front door together, laughing and joking, that I knew for certain.' She frowned and clenched her teeth – I knew she was remembering how she'd felt as the truth sank in. She gave me an unpleasant little smile. 'For a second,' she said, 'I wanted to kill them both.' I gasped, and my hands flew to my throat where a lump was threatening to close it. I couldn't have spoken – even had I'd known what to say.

After a minute, when she was back under control, Janet continued quietly with her explanation. I hardly dared to move a muscle for fear of interrupting her flow as she said, 'Lyn put the light on as she entered the room and screamed out when she saw me sitting there. Her startled face gave me the impetus I needed to move – I jumped up and shouted at her to get her things and fuck off out of my house. I thought that she'd be ashamed but,' Janet bit her trembling lip, 'the hard-faced cow shouted back that I should go, Simon loved her not me – I didn't deserve him – and she was pregnant with his child.'

I realised that my mouth was gaping as I stared at Janet in horror. I quickly shut it to and then asked unsteadily, 'What was Simon doing while all this was going on?'

'He'd taken the girls upstairs, and then he came into the room, but he just stood there looking sheepish. He wouldn't look at either of us – the spineless bastard. Lyn went over and put her hand on his arm and begged him to tell me that he didn't want me anymore, but he said that he couldn't. That's when Lyn ran out without even taking a coat, and I told Simon that he'd better go after her and not to come back.' Janet's head went down into her hands.

'What a pathetic pair of bastards! I'm so, so sorry, love.' I put my arm around her shoulders and hugged her to me. 'What now, how can I help?' I asked after the awful picture had sunk in.

'I dunno yet,' Janet said, 'but I know what I'm not going to do.' She sat up. There was a look of determination written on her tired face. 'I'm not giving up my home or my kids, and as for Lyn,' she shuddered, 'I'll never forget what she's done, but she is still our little sister. I'll try to forgive her, and I want you to forgive her too.'

I shook my head, thinking how much Lyn had hurt us all over the last few years. 'I'm not sure that I can.'

I didn't know how Janet could be capable of forgiving her no matter what she thought right now. She grasped my hand in hers and said, 'Please, Sara, will you try to find her and persuade her to come back? I think that she's going to need our support.' She took a deep breath and let go of my hand. 'I know one thing for certain I've finished with that lying bastard for good – it's a pity that I still love him.' A tear welled up, but she swiped it away with the back of her hand.

I hadn't known that Janet could be so strong, but I believed she meant what she'd said. 'Well, I hope that she'll finish with him too, but what if she won't?' I asked her.

'I'll face that when I have to. Right now, I'm concerned that our pregnant sister is possibly wandering the streets in this God-awful weather. Will you go and see if you can find her, Sara. I have to stay here with the girls, and you can search much quicker in the car anyway.'

'Of course, I just need the loo first.' I went upstairs and then got my coat. I didn't know where to start but thought that I'd drive around the local streets for a while then go to the hotel where Simon had indicated that she might go. I didn't fancy running into him, I'm not sure I could have kept my hands off him, but I'd have to try to find her. Janet was right anything could happen to her while she was in a state.

As I left the house, I could hear Janet in the kitchen as she washed our cups. She'll survive, I thought thankfully, and with a bit of luck, Lyn will too.

20

After two miserable hours searching the streets and asking at the hotel without locating either Lyn or Simon, I returned to Janet. 'I'm glad you've come back; she's here; Simon brought her back about ten minutes ago,' she said.

'Where is he? I want a word with him,' I said between gritted teeth.

Janet shrugged and shook her head. 'He's not here. He rang the bell and walked off down the path without looking back as soon as I opened the door. I don't know where he's gone, but Lyn's in here.' She pushed the sitting-room door open, and I followed her inside.

As soon as Lyn saw me, her lips curled in a sneer. 'What the fuck are you doing here?'

'Okay, Lyn, I don't know what I've done to make you have a go at me, but you can cut it out. I'm here because Janet asked me to help, and I'm not particularly bothered how you feel about it so you can stop swearing.'

'Oh, fuck off, you sanctimonious cow. I don't need your help. I wouldn't be here, only Simon insisted.'

'Is he going to look after you then?' I asked, with my lip curling.

'He will, he's promised.' Lyn looked very young. She couldn't believe that the man she loved had let her down. She started to cry.

Janet and I responded at the same time, as we had for all of her life, we both went and put our arms around her, and all three of us ended up rocking backwards and forwards while Lyn sobbed piteously.

I was the first to break away and said, 'It's late, and there's no point in me trying to help sort things out now. I think we should all get some sleep and talk in the morning. I'm off home.'

Janet nodded and said briskly, 'Come on, Lyn, why don't you go up and try to sleep. The girls will be up fairly early, and you don't want them to be upset, do you? However, you feel now, things will look better in the morning. I don't know how we'll go on, but both of us will try to help. Come on.' She took Lyn's hand and pulled her gently to her feet. I said goodnight and went out into the pouring rain after promising Janet that I'd be back early in the morning.

I just didn't know how Janet could still want Lyn in her house, but the family bonds were strong. She's probably the strongest of us, all I thought as I drove home and then listened gratefully to the gentle snores of my sleeping, tolcrant husband. I undressed wearily and climbed in beside him. I so wanted to feel the warmth and comfort of his strong arms around me that I was tempted to wake him, but I didn't. My feet were frozen, and I lay awake with unhappy thoughts chasing each other around in my tired mind until I gradually warmed up and fell asleep.

Sunday morning arrived too quickly after a restless night that I knew had been peopled by ghosts of the past, although I couldn't remember any details. As soon as Peter woke up, I told him my version of the previous evening's events. He listened with his mouth agape to the story and didn't interrupt once as it unfolded.

'Well, we all know what a shit he is, but for Lyn to be so devious and have the nerve to try to take Janet's place, quite frankly, I'm appalled and amazed. She's always been self-centred and wilful, but I would never have believed she could be such a rotten cow. What's Janet going to do now? She's not going to let her stay, is she?' Peter's lips curled, and he shook his head.

'I don't know, but you should have seen how calm she was, and in a way, so protective of Lyn. God knows how she could be like that – I know I couldn't. But I'll be guided by whatever she decides. I've promised to go back this morning and see how I can help. I can't say as I want to, but they are both my sisters, although Lyn doesn't seem to want my help. Oh, I don't know what to do – I've got to do whatever Janet wants me to. What do you think I should do?'

'I think you would be better off out of it, but I know you'll have to go. It's a good job that it's Sunday and I'll be here for the children. Try not to be away all day though I want to see something of you too.' He grinned and ruffled my hair, then took me into his arms.

'Hey, no hanky-panky, I can hear Jenny stirring. Any minute now, she'll be yelling for her bottle.' I rolled away as Peter pretended to be disappointed and went to shower before our hungry hoard needed us.

By the time breakfast was over, it was almost ten o'clock, so I quickly drove round to Janet's instead of walking. I thought I might need my car, and I was right. I did.

When I arrived, Janet and the girls were still eating breakfast in the kitchen, and Lyn was nowhere to be seen. After kissing Michelle and Karen, I asked where Lyn was.

Janet pointed to the ceiling. 'She's in her room and says that she doesn't want anything to eat. I've just left her to it at the moment, why don't you go up and see what she wants to do? If I'm honest, I feel too shattered to be sympathetic this morning.'

'What do you want her to do?' I asked after the girls finished their cereal and obeyed their mother by playing in the middle room. 'You don't want her to remain here, do you?'

'No, I bloody well don't, but I need to see that she's okay. I'm hoping that she'll go back home, but she said last night that she won't while Michael lives there. She is so spoilt Sara; she only thinks of herself and what she wants. She's not sorry for what she's done to me, you know.' Janet shook her head, she had applied makeup as usual, but it only served to emphasise the dark circles under her eyes. 'She is a nightmare, and I know I should hate her, but I don't. She can't stay here. I don't want her near my children anymore, even if it means I have to give up my job.' Janet sat down heavily on one of the pine kitchen chairs and put her head in her hands. I thought that she was crying, but when she looked up, she was dry-eyed.

'I'll help her with the baby if I have to, but she can't bring it here.'

'No, of course not, no one would expect you to have it here or her either. I'll go and talk to her, but I'm not sure she'll listen; she was quite antagonistic towards me last night.' I walked to the kitchen door. 'You're right she is spoilt, but we're all to blame. We've always babied her. I never thought she could do anything as awful as this, though, Jan. I'm so sorry, love – I'll try to get her to go home. Have you heard anything from Simon?'

'No, Lyn seems to think that he'll look after her, but seeing the way he behaved last night, I don't think the spineless bastard will.'

My heart was heavy as I climbed the steep flight of stairs, carpeted in a swirly blue pattern, and knocked on Lyn's door. Many times, I'd been asked to confront Lyn in her bedroom after she'd done something unacceptable, but she'd never done anything that I felt I couldn't cope with before. I was almost sorry when she opened the door and then walked back to the bed and sat down. I thought she looked dreadful; her face was blotchy and swollen from crying, and she'd torn quite a few tissues into small pieces which covered the bedspread like a scattering of snow.

She glared at me. 'I thought it would probably be you, but you've wasted your time, I don't want your help, and I certainly don't want a lecture. I know what I've done, but Simon will make it alright. Janet doesn't love him like I do, and he knows it.'

'Well, he's not here, is he, and you can't stay here, so what are you planning to do, eh?' I asked bluntly. When she didn't reply, I said, 'I'm not going to give you a lecture, Lyn, you don't need one; you're not a kid anymore. As you say, you know what you've done, and if what you've said to Janet is true, that you are going to have a baby, then there isn't only you to think of, is there?'

'It is true, and Simon said that he loved me and would take care of me and our baby. I don't know why he brought me back here last night, I wanted to stay at the hotel until I found a room to rent, but he said that this was best. Do you know where he is?' She sounded pitiful when she asked the question. She wasn't sure that Simon would look after her. She didn't seem to care that she'd torn Janet's life to shreds. I don't think she even considered that she'd done anything wrong. I resisted the urge to lay into her verbally and spoke impassively.

'Don't you think it would be best if you went home, Lyn?'

'No, I don't, I'm not going home while Michael is living there, I've already told Janet,' she exclaimed vehemently.

'Well, what are you going to do then?'

'I'm going to find a room if Simon doesn't come for me today.'

'How about if I ring Mrs Freeman, you know the dinner lady from the school, she sometimes lets out her two spare rooms, and perhaps she'll have a vacancy,' I said.

One Child Too Many

Lyn jumped at my idea and became polite. 'Would you please? I remember her; she was always nice to the other kids and me. Sometimes she gave us sweets that she kept in a paper bag in her pocket.' She looked wistful as if she'd like to return to the protection of being a schoolgirl. She'd said that she didn't want my help, but she looked so anxious when she spoke of Simon helping her that I could only see my little sister, who I'd always cared for and loved. I would have given much to turn the clock back and take more notice of the way things were heading between her and Simon. I should have been able to stop this from happening; I berated myself.

'Yes, I'll give her a ring, and if not, perhaps we can look in the Mail and see what other rooms are available. Are you sure you don't want to go home? It would probably be the best solution, Lyn – you'd have Mom to help you when the baby comes?'

Lyn shook her head. 'No, if Simon lets me down, but I know he won't – then I want to be by myself.' She began to sob, and I stayed quiet and waited until the sobs stuttered to a halt, and yet more paper tissues joined the detritus on her bed.

'Alright, you'd better start packing your things, and I'll go and see what I can do, alright?' I asked, resisting the urge to take her in my arms and comfort her.

'Okay,' she stood and picked up a dirty glass from the bedside cupboard, 'will you bring me a drink, please Sara, I'm thirsty, and I'm sure Janet doesn't want me to go down to the kitchen, does she?'

'I don't expect so, but I'll bring you some breakfast too. If you are having a baby, then you shouldn't starve yourself.'

'I've told you that I am, haven't I – you'd better believe it,' she said as I left the room.

Poor bloody baby, you'll have a lousy mother – then I remembered how good she'd always been with children. Everyone is entitled to make a mistake, so maybe it would be the making of her, and she'll have us to help her. It turned out that I was wrong on both counts.

21

Mrs Freeman didn't have a spare room; one had been taken recently by a student from Nigeria. I patiently listened while she wittered on about the course that he was taking at Birmingham University and his family circumstances. I asked if she knew of anyone else locally who had a spare room to let. She did and recommended that I go and see her neighbour, Mrs Willis.

I smiled inwardly and outwardly when I met Mrs Willis, who immediately insisted that I call her Florrie and offered to make me a cup of tea. She was quite a character. Her greying hair was done up in a bright blue scarf to cover the plastic rollers that adorned her head. She had on an old-fashioned, green, wraparound overall that had seen better days and a pair of cut off, black wellington boots on her feet as she shuffled along to show me the front room that she referred to as the best room. She talked non-stop about a host of topics making the cigarette that was wedged into the corner of her mouth wag up and down – depositing its ash at intervals onto the worn but reasonably clean carpet. I think that I fell in love with her, and offered to fetch my sister who I intimated could be very happy staying there. I said nothing of Lyn's circumstances.

I nipped home to bring Peter up to date and then returned to Janet's.

'I've found her a room,' I said as I entered the kitchen. I gave Janet the details, but she hardly seemed to hear me. 'Do you want to talk to her before I take her there?'

'I bloody well don't, and she's not to go in to see the kids either.' I could hear them playing in the living room. 'I need some time before I can see her, and I never want her to see Michelle and Karen,' Janet said. 'At the moment, I hate her – I hate them both.'

'Alright, I'll go up and help her as far as her room, but then I'm going home. God knows how Peter puts up with me.'

'Thanks, Sara; I'll be in the living room with the girls when she comes down. See you soon, eh?'

I helped Lyn bring her things downstairs and noticed that she'd put on some makeup, but her eyes were bleak.

As we reached the front door, Lyn said, 'Do you think I could say bye-bye to the girls?'

'Sorry, but no,' I said, and Lyn's lips set in a straight line.

'Okay, then let's go.' She turned the handle and hurried ahead of me down the path.

Lyn didn't seem to care what the room was like when I helped her take her possessions. As soon as I brought the last suitcase in and ensured that she had enough supplies for her immediate needs, I left and returned to Janet's.

I would have stayed with Lyn a little while, but she insisted that I go as she would let Simon know where she was as soon as I left. I certainly didn't want to meet up with him. At this juncture, I wanted to put my fist in his face, and I wasn't sure I would behave reasonably. It wouldn't have helped matters, I knew, so I was more than happy to leave her even though I was worried about how she would cope. Not physically, I knew that she had been very efficient when she looked after the Doctor's children and their needs, but mentally if Simon let her down yet again.

Janet seemed to be okay and very calm, almost too laid back to be believed. She thanked me for my help and said she was pleased to have Lyn out of her house but that she would go and see her the following day to talk. She still didn't think that Simon, who she called a weak-kneed bastard or worse every time she mentioned him, would look after Lyn.

Neither did I, but I shrugged and said, 'We'll see.' I was fed up now with all the turmoil and wanted to return to the sanity of my own home. I hugged Janet and left – promising to return the next day.

I didn't go back the next day, as one after the other, Paul and Jenny became poorly. They had runny noses and flushed faces and were very fretful, so I asked Laura, a friend who lived nearby, to take Dawn to school with her little girl, Julie, while I stayed home armed with the Calpol. She was happy to do it and said that she'd bring her home too. I had done as much for her in the past, so she appreciated the return of a favour.

When I phoned Janet towards lunchtime, she said that she would see Lyn later and let me know how she was. She sounded tearful, but when I asked her how she was feeling, she shrugged the question off and said, 'Simon's not been in touch – I wonder if he's with Lyn?' I thought that she'd probably had a dreadful night and felt awful that I couldn't go and comfort her.

'Would you like me to ask Peter to come after school? I don't think it's fair to ask him to mind Paul and Jenny, or I'd come myself, but I'm sure he wouldn't mind going with you to see Lyn just in case Simon's there.' I stopped talking as I wasn't at all sure that Peter would be happy to do this, but I thought that Janet needed some support.

'No, it's okay, I'll get Pauline next door to mind the girls for an hour, it'll only take me five minutes to walk there, and I've no intention of staying long whether he's there or not. I just need to make sure that she is okay. God knows why after what she's done.'

'It's because you're a good person, and she's still our little sister. I just hope that she feels some remorse.' Janet snorted, and I waited a couple of seconds, but she didn't speak, 'Will you let me know, love? What will you do if he is there?' I held my breath, imagining with dread the scene, which I thought might take place if he was.

'I don't know. I don't think that I could bear to be in the same room as the pair of them at the moment. If he's there, I'll know that she's alright so I won't go in. Don't worry, Sara. It'll all be okay – just look after the little ones, and I'll ring you later.'

After we'd said our goodbyes, I came off the phone feeling complete dismay at the way life can throw people about. We had all been chugging along in our little worlds, not perfect, but happy with our lot until Lyn and Simon pulled the curtain aside and showed us just how vulnerable our worlds are.

When Peter came home, I poured him a beer and drew him into the sitting room where Dawn was trying to amuse Paul by playing with his cars and making car noises. Jenny was asleep in her chair, her head lolling forward as she snuffled uncomfortably. I brought him up to date with everything, and as usual, his common-sense attitude had a calming effect.

'Try not to worry, love; you can't live everyone's lives for them. They are going to have to sort things out themselves. I know that they're your family, but this is where you belong, and there is no point in feeling guilty when you're needed here. What's your Mom said about it all?' He took a drink, and I thankfully snuggled up to him, inhaling his body odour that sometimes made my toes curl up. My toes remained relaxed; I was too stressed to feel sexy at the moment.

'She doesn't know anything about it unless Lyn's told her, but I don't think she has. I'm sure Mom would have been on the phone to me if she knew. I suppose I'll have to tell her at some point. She's going to be upset, but I don't know who she'll be upset most about, Lyn or Janet. Anyway, let's forget about it for now – I'd better go and start making dinner.

We both began to laugh as a minute later, we were joined by Dawn and Paul, who wriggled in between us on the sofa. I stopped mid-laugh as an unpleasant sensation crossed my diaphragm. Would our little family be next to be punished for being so happy, I thought? But I kept this to myself.

I knew that Janet had been to see Lyn three days running as she'd phoned to let me know how things were going, but Lyn hadn't been at all pleased to see her. She told Janet in an offhand way that she hadn't been out; she'd just been sitting reading magazines and waiting for Simon. She hadn't heard anything from him but was still firmly convinced that he wouldn't let her down. She'd tried to contact him by phoning his friend, Brian, and his brother Paul, but they'd both denied seeing him.

It was Saturday before I left the children with Peter and walked around to Janet's. It was cold and drizzly, but I appreciated the freshness and time to myself. After a quick hug, she put the kettle on and then, as usual, we sat either side of the kitchen table drinking tea when suddenly Janet burst out with, 'I don't know where he is Sara, and I couldn't care less, I never want to see him again, but I just hope he is going to look after Lyn. I certainly don't want to have to, and I won't ever let her see the girls again. She thought that she could replace me not just with Simon, but with my children too. The more I think about it, the more I hate her. She must have been laughing up her sleeve at me for being so gullible.' She ran a hand across her forehead and said, 'Stupid aren't I, stupid, stupid, stupid, not to have seen it?'

'No, you aren't; they were devious as hell. Even I wasn't thinking that they were involved until you said how bad things were. Then and only then it clicked. I don't think that she gave you or the rest of us any thought at all. She knew what she wanted and was determined that she was going to get it. She's selfish to the core.' I took a deep breath; I wanted to say what I thought about Simon too, but it seemed pointless to upset Janet further, so I didn't. 'I don't blame you for not wanting to see them. I'll go tomorrow and try again to make her see sense and go home. She won't be able to afford to stay in that room. I've paid a months' rent and given her money for food, but I'm not going to keep on doing that.'

'No, of course not. Why the hell should you. She has to go home. Mom needs to know what her precious baby has been up to.' Janet's voice was shrill, her face scarlet as angry tears gushed from her eyes that sparkled wildly. I had never heard her speak or look as she did. I was alarmed. Had she been pushed too far, was it possible that she would be able to? I didn't finish the thought. It was too frightening.

I quickly skirted the table and put my arms around her trembling body; she sobbed hysterically for a long time while I held her close and cried for all her hurt. She was the kindest, most gentle person in our family; she didn't deserve the disloyalty of her husband and sister, both of whom she loved. How I wished that I could wave a magic wand and make things better, but I didn't know what else I could do.

After a while, Janet calmed down, and I was pleased when Michelle and Karen came from their room. Janet could hear them as they walked downstairs, and she managed to grab some kitchen roll, run it under the cold tap and dab at her face. It didn't do much for her make-up, but it hid the worst of the ravages that crying had caused.

'Hi, girls, what have you been doing up there?' I asked them light-heartedly.

Michelle went to her mother and leaned against her. 'Have you been crying, Mommy?' She was nearly six years old now and bright with it. Janet shook her head, and Michelle stared hard at me. 'Why have you made my Mommy cry, Auntie Sara?'

I didn't know what to say, but Janet responded quickly. 'I'm sorry darling, it wasn't Auntie Sara's fault. I just learned something that I can't share with you at the moment. It's nothing to worry about, though. She gave a little wriggly dance to show she was okay and said, 'Come on sweetie pie, lean off my legs, and I'll make us some lunch. I'm getting hungry. Shall we have banana sandwiches?'

Michelle obeyed, but while we ate, I pretended not to notice that she occasionally gave me a quizzical look that made me feel unreasonably guilty. I was glad when lunch came to an end, and I could begin clearing the table. I think she'd forgotten her suspicions about my possible involvement in her mother's tears by the time she was allowed to go into the sitting room to watch a video. Thankfully I received my usual big kiss from both girls when I left after promising Janet that I'd go the next day to tell Mom what had been happening. Not something I relished, but somehow Mom needed to persuade Lyn to return home. I had no thought that Simon would look after her but felt certain that someone needed to.

22

'Sorry, love, I was just tidying up the old bean canes and sterilising some pots. There's nothing to keep me home now that your Dad's gone back to work – thank God. Why don't you pop round with the kiddies, and I'll make us some lunch,' Mom suggested, with an apology heavy in her voice.

'Okay, Mom, do you need me to bring anything in?' I'd already been at Mom's earlier to tell her about Lyn but had no luck as the house told me as soon as I inserted my key that no one was home. It's funny how houses always do that. It's a peculiar hollow feeling like dismissive vibrations in the air, fanciful, I know, but I've always felt it. I'd made myself a drink and waited a while in case she'd just gone to the local shops. But I left after ten minutes as I didn't want to waste my precious time. Now I'd have to go back as the awful facts still had to be told, and as usual, I'd got the shitty job.

'No thanks, love, I bought a fresh loaf on my way home. See you in a bit, eh?'

As soon as I put the phone down, it rang again. It was Janet, and my heart sank as I dreaded further bad news. But she sounded excited as she said without preamble, 'I've decided to do something positive; you know that Simons been teaching me to drive for ages, well I've booked a driving lesson, and I'm determined to pass my test and buy myself a car. I'll be buggered if I'm going to sit around and mope after that pair of bastards. What do you think?'

'Great idea, he can't stop you now, can he, and you've got your own money to spend. Good for you.' I chortled at the thought of her new-found sense of freedom.

'Okay, I'm going now, just wanted to tell you. Have you been to Mom's yet?'

'No, I'm just going. Catch you later, drive safely now,' I said. It was such a relief to end our conversation on a light note; everything had been doom and gloom for what seemed to be an age.

Later that day, I jumped into the gloom again as I gazed at Mom's impassive expression. 'You knew, didn't you?' I said quietly.

She put Paul down gently on the floor and followed him with her eyes as he promptly scrambled under the table and began to play with some cars that we left at Mom's house. They lived in an old, painted wooden toy box. that had belonged to us when we were small.

Mom looked up at my incredulous stare and shook her head. 'No, I didn't know, but I should have guessed.'

'Why, how could you have? Did Lyn tell you something? Why, oh, why didn't you stop her?'

'You're not listening to me, Sara, I didn't know, but I've seen the way they flirted with each other, and,' she put her head on one side, and her eyes flickered as though she was recalling some past event, 'he always stayed here just that bit too long when he collected the children. I'm a fool. I should have known. It's entirely my fault – all my fault.' She rubbed the back of her neck. 'All my fault.'

'Oh, Mom, it's not your fault don't upset yourself. What could you have done? It's what happens now that's important.' I held onto her hands and stroked them tenderly – I hated to see her like this. Jenny began to cry as I moved away from her on the settee. I picked her up, put her over my shoulder, and began to pat her warm backside soothingly, releasing an all too familiar smell, 'Phew, you're a stinky little girl, let's get you changed.' I stood and began to make my daughter comfortable. I was about to pluck up the courage to ask Mom about Lyn's father while I had my back to her, but I was relieved when the moment passed as she went into the kitchen.

I could hear the kettle as it came to the boil, and a few minutes later, Mom returned with the ever-ready teapot. She looked sad but composed as she filled our cups and then sat down. 'Is there anything else that you want to ask me, Sara?'

I met her troubled eyes. 'Erm, about Lyn, you mean? I asked, somewhat puzzled by her question.

'No, I know that your Dad told you he wasn't Lyn's father. He told me at Christmas. I've been waiting for you to ask me about it, why haven't you?'

Mom's whole body seemed to relax while she waited for my response, but I became tense with embarrassment. It was none of my business, really, but Mom needed to talk about it, so I had no choice. 'I wanted to ask you,' I said slowly, 'but the time never seemed to be right, and I didn't want to upset you either by raking up the past. Dad didn't tell me much, just that he wasn't Lyn's father.'

Mom took a deep breath. 'I always knew that he'd let the cat out of the bag one day. I'm surprised it took him so long. I thought that he'd tell Lyn when she was playing up, but,' she shook her head in disbelief, 'he was always patient with her. He never loved her, though, not like he loved you, and Janet and Michael.' She shut her eyes, and we were silent with our thoughts for a few minutes.

I felt so sorry for her. I stood and leaned over the coal scuttle to hide my glowing face and then carefully placed a few oval pieces of Coalite on the fire. It wasn't throwing out much heat, and the living room was chilly.

'Thanks, love,' Mom muttered.

'Look, Mom, you don't have to tell me any more about it, and I'm not going to tell anyone either; it's your business.' As an afterthought, I said without rancour, 'I don't suppose you set out to have Lyn, did you?'

Mom gnawed at her bottom lip and shook her head again. 'No, I bloody well didn't. I made a stupid mistake. I had one child too many, but I've tried to make it up to her – I've spoiled her – always given in to her and look where it's landed us. She's no good – no better than her father.'

'Oh, Mom, don't say that. She's made a mistake too.' I couldn't bear to think of the sister that I'd always treasured as being worthless.

'Face it, Sara, I was led into having a fling, I didn't plan it, but Lyn has schemed for years to get what she wanted, just like he did. He'd been trying to get me into his bed from when I was no more than a child.'

Paul broke the tension that crackled between my mother and me by demanding our attention for a few minutes. I listened to him with half an ear while I tried to cope with the dreadful feeling that Mom's revelations had stirred up in me. I didn't know what was happening to my close-knit family. Well, I'd always thought of us in that way, but I hadn't been very perceptive. I'd thought that I knew what was best for us all – now I didn't know what else to say or do.

Mom's next words confirmed my suspicions. 'You've met him, you know – Lyn's father.'

I inclined my head. 'Is it your cousin, Tony Gardener?'

Mom nodded. She looked composed, but her face was glowing as she said, 'I still fancied him, you know at my party, he wanted us to start having an affair, but I learned the hard way not to trust him.' She picked Paul up onto her lap and cuddled him to her until he squirmed about, wanting to be released.

'He seemed nice, Mom, and I could see the attraction. You know you don't have to tell me anymore; I get the picture. I just wonder if this is why Dad chose to be on the road so frequently, I suppose it is.'

Mom nodded again. 'We were never close again – not that I ever thought we were soul mates.'

I didn't want to hear too much of the nitty-gritty of my parents' relationship and quickly interrupted her flow. 'Look, Mom, whatever happened, happened, and there's no point in going over it now, is there? It's what we can do about the mess that Lyn's in now. She can't stay where she is, she needs to come home, but she still says she won't while Michael's here.'

'Well, it's his home, and I'll not ask him to go so that she can return.' Mom shook her head emphatically; she looked bewildered by the suggestion.

'I don't know what to say, I know that she still thinks Simon's going to come to her rescue, but I'm sure he won't. Jan's been to see his foreman, and he said that Simon has phoned in sick and taken a week's holiday that was due. No one seems to know where he is.' I glanced at my watch and realised that it was almost time to fetch Dawn from school. 'I'll have to go, Mom. Will you have a word with Michael? Perhaps he'll be able to persuade her to come home, but I don't think he should have to leave to accommodate her. I can't think of anything else, can you?'

'Don't worry, I'll talk to him tonight, and then I'll go and see Lyn tomorrow. No matter what she's done, she's still my daughter, and I want her here where I can keep an eye on her. I suppose I should tell her about her father now that you know, but I just can't face it at the moment – you're not going to, are you?'

'No, Mom, I'm saying nothing; I think you've both got enough to think about without that.' I shrugged my shoulders. 'We all have.'

One Child Too Many

It wasn't long before the topic of Lyn's father took a back seat in my mind. When I drove to pick Dawn up from school, I recognised Janet even though she was wrapped up from head to toe. It was bitterly cold, and she had on her blue duffle coat, black leather, knee length boots, and a bright green scarf wound around the lower part of her face. Her breath showed white through the loose stitches as she hurried to pick Michelle up from school. I pulled up alongside her, and she slid gracefully into the passenger seat.

'Phew, thank God you came. I'm feeling perished.' She lowered the scarf and blew on her gloved hands.

'Where's Karen?' I asked.

'I've left her with my friend Pauline. It's too cold to drag her out. How did you get on with telling Mom about Lyn?'

'Well, I told her, and she was shocked. She said that she'll have a talk with Michael and go to see Lyn tomorrow. She thinks that Lyn should come home, but she's not prepared to ask Michael to leave.'

'I should think not, bloody cheek. I think she deliberately picked that row with him so that she had an excuse to move into my place. I'm bloody sure of it.' Her hands clenched in her lap.

'You're probably right, but I don't think that we can do any more until Mom lets us know what's happening.' I braked carefully as near to the school as I could get.

'Stay in the car. I'll bring Dawn over.' She got out and walked rapidly towards the school gates, where a group of parents stood shivering. They looked like a gaggle of geese preparing to take flight as they flapped their arms about trying to get warm. I smiled to myself as I remained snug in my car.

A couple of minutes later, Janet's place was taken by Dawn as she threw herself into the bucket seat. She said something that I missed to Paul, who gave a delighted chuckle.

Janet and Michelle waved as they hurried past on their way to the shops. 'I'll be glad to get a car.' Janet mouthed and mimed steering, then blew us a kiss as I started the still-warm engine and drove home.

23

The following day after saying, 'Hello Sara,' Mom launched into an excuse. I could hear shuffling noises as she settled herself on the bottom stair by the phone. 'I still haven't had a chance to talk to Michael, so there's no point in me going to see Lyn is there? The more I've thought about it, the more I think I should let her stew for a while. It won't hurt her to worry about where her next meal's coming from – perhaps she'll be sorry for what she's done and be grateful to come home,' she said.

'Okay, okay, don't get your knickers in a knot, she's safe at the moment, so I don't suppose it'll hurt her to be a little insecure for a few days. Where's Michael then? Hasn't he been home?'

'No, he's been staying at Derek's all week, but he'll be back later, and I'll talk to him then. I know, I'm bloody sick of all this fuss our Sara, but I suppose it's payback time.'

'Don't be silly, Mom, it'll be fine; I'm going to talk to Janet now and find out if she knows any more. I'll ring you later, okay?'

It had only been two days since I'd told Mom what had happened, so I guess that she'd become more shocked as Lyn's treachery had sunk in. I didn't envy her; she was going to have to put up with Lyn and a baby just when she'd reached a time where she wanted less responsibility, not more. What a mess, I thought, glad that it wasn't my immediate problem.

I did have a problem, though, that I had to solve. It was nearing Peter's birthday, and I wanted to plan something special for him, but my head seemed to have been too busy with family troubles recently. I needed to concentrate on my husband, he was always kind and considerate, and I knew that he was sick of all the drama that Lyn brought into our lives. I decided that I'd stay away from her for a couple of days. I then rang Janet, who decided to do the same.

'Have you heard from Simon?' I asked.

'No, and I don't want to. I'll never forgive him for hurting, not just me, but the girls too.' I could hear the impatience in her voice as she quickly changed the subject. 'Anyway, I'm going back to work tomorrow, and I've now been taken on as Mr Hussain's secretary as well, so I'll be working full time. I'm not going to have time to worry about all this lot.' She sighed heavily, then went on. 'Barbara, next door, is going to mind the girls, and I'll be able to pay her the going rate, so Simon's welcome to Lyn – they deserve each other.' There was a short pause where I just couldn't think what to say, and then Janet filled the silence. 'Okay, you, I'm going; I've got too much to do. See you at the weekend?'

'Mm, yes, let's take the children somewhere nice, eh?'

'Okay, bye, Sara.'

I was left lost in thought with the receiver in my hand. Janet sounded composed, but I wondered if this was just her way of coping with a husband and a sister playing her for a fool. She'd never seemed to be the decisive, independent one, but she was doing a good job of giving that impression now.

Once more, I decided to get on with my life and stop worrying about my family, at least for a few days. I managed three, and then my conscience got the better of me. I went to visit Lyn on Wednesday evening after Peter had had his tea and the children were in bed. She was a mess, and I immediately felt sorry that I'd not been more supportive.

When Mrs Willis let me in, still dressed in the same garb that she'd worn when I initially met her, she took a cigarette from her lips and leaned towards me.

'She's not been out, you know, and she cries nearly all the time. I put tissue in me ears and turn the telly up to block it out. I've asked her what's the matter, but she won't tell me, and nobody's visited her, poor sod.'

She gave me a hard look and shuffled off in her cut off wellingtons, shutting her door sharply behind her. I knocked a warning on Lyn's door, then turned the handle and went in.

Lyn sat facing the dark window. She hadn't bothered to shut the curtains, and the street light threw an eerie, weird shadow on her magnolia coloured walls. She barely moved her head to see who had entered and quickly turned away as I said, 'Hello Lyn, why are you sitting in the dark?'

'Meter's run out, and I've no change.' She turned back to the window and tried to ignore me as I rummaged in my handbag and then fed the meter. As the light came on, I went to draw the curtains, but Lyn said abruptly, 'Leave them open and switch the light off – I like them open.'

I walked towards the light switch to do as she asked but caught my breath as I saw her face. I sat down heavily on a dining chair and stared open-mouthed at the swollen, bruised mess that was her forehead.

She pushed her hair away with a defiant gesture and exposed the damage. She had two black eyes, a cut across the bridge of her nose, and her forehead. Now that I could see it clearly, I was horrified.

'What's happened?' Has Simon done this?' I exclaimed.

'I haven't seen Simon – I haven't seen anybody except the crazy old bat who lives here.'

'What do you mean – have you done this, Lyn?' She nodded. 'Why? What's to be gained by hurting yourself?'

Lyn shrugged. 'The bottle was empty, and it was there, so I used it. None of your business is it?' She ran her hands through her hair and brought it forward, but it didn't conceal much of the damage that she'd inflicted on herself.

'Of course, it's my business, I'm your sister and I love you – you know I do.'

'Well, you've not been near, have you, so much for sisters, eh? You might as well go; I don't want to see you or Janet, and I don't need you spying on me either.'

'Don't be stupid. I'm not spying on you. I just wanted to see how you were and talk to you about going home. I've talked to Mom, and that's what she wants you to do. She wanted to talk to Michael before she saw you, but he's not been home for a few days.' Lyn didn't reply, and I could feel my patience dwindling as I asked, 'Has Simon been in touch?'

Lyn burst into tears and shook her head. 'No, and I hate him, how could he do this to me – he promised to look after me and the baby.' She looked and sounded like the ten-year-old Lyn that we had all loved and spoiled.

I took her stiff, unyielding body into my arms and held her close until she relaxed and slumped against me. She cried piteously while I rocked her backwards and forwards, and then suddenly, she pushed me away and screamed into my face. 'Just go away and leave me alone. I don't need your help.'

'Alright, Lyn.' I stood up, picked up my handbag, took a twenty-pound note from my purse, and flung it onto the small table that stood against the wall by the door. 'You need to get some help, Lyn, and you won't be doing your baby any good like this. I'm going, but I'll be back if you need me.' I walked out steadily and managed to wait until I was safely in my car before I, too, shed bitter tears. I needed to remember that she wasn't my sweet little ten -year- old sister; she was an adult who perhaps no longer needed me. She certainly didn't care about me or the rest of the family. For the umpteenth time, I drove home with her awful rejection whirling in my brain. It made me feel determined that I'd stop caring what became of her. I knew that it wouldn't be easy to detach myself completely, but I told Peter later that night that I would try.

'Well, at least for now,' he agreed, 'why don't you try sitting back and leaving the rest of them to sort things out? You might be surprised; give yourself a break, eh?'

I repeated that I'd try to stay away for a while, and I meant it, but I had to phone Mom the following day and tell her about Lyn's injuries.

'Oh, my Lord, I'd better go; God knows what she might do. I've talked with Michael, and he said that he doesn't care what she's done, she needs to come home, and he'd move out to live with Derek permanently. He's a good lad. I just hope she appreciates it,' she sighed, 'but I'm sure she won't. Will you help to move her things back home, Sara?'

I wanted to refuse, but old habits forced me to say that I would. 'She hasn't agreed to come home yet, Mom, but give me a ring if you need me. I don't want to be in her company at the moment. I'm beginning to think that she's got the devil in her she was such a bitch last night.'

'Alright, love, I'll let you know what's happening. Thank you, Sara, you're a good girl; I don't know what I would have done without your practical head all these years. You've always been sensible. I'll phone you later – kiss the kiddies for me.

24

A couple of days later, the frustration of not knowing what was happening became too much, and I called Mom. The phone rang and rang, and I was just about to end the call when she picked up and said a breathy, 'Hello.'

'Hello Mom, it's me, Sara; I thought you were going to ring and let me know what was going on. Has Lyn come home?'

'No, she hasn't. I'm sorry, I should have rung you, but it's been awkward. I've been round at Lyn's since I last spoke to you. You nearly missed me; I've only come home for a change of clothes. I'm going back round there now.'

'Why, why won't she come home?' I asked, feeling annoyance grabbing at me.

'It's no use you feeling angry, Sara. She's in a bad way, and Dr Modern has been in to see her. He's going to try and find her a place in that new special unit in Hall Green. It's an assessment unit – he thinks that she's having a breakdown. Well, he said something like a psychotic break, I think, but he talks so quickly that I'm not sure what he said. Anyway, Lyn has agreed to go as soon as there's a place for her. She'd been hitting herself again before I got there and,' Mom gulped noisily, 'she's such a mess, Sara.'

All my good intentions to stay away went flying out of the window as I said, 'Do you want me to come with you, Mom?'

But as soon as the words were out of my mouth, I regretted them. I couldn't leave Paul and Jenny and go anywhere.

'No love, she doesn't want to see you or Janet, God knows what she thinks you've done to her, but she became hysterical when I suggested asking for your help. She seems to think that Janet wouldn't have gone back home without your encouragement. She blames you for everything. She's just not thinking straight at the moment – she still believes that Simon loves her and he will come to her when the baby's born. I bloody well hope he doesn't. He's done enough damage.' I didn't know what to say. I felt hurt and angry to be getting the blame for any of this, but before I could speak, Mom said, 'I'd better go, love; I'm a bit afraid to leave her on her own.'

'Alright, Mom, have you heard from Janet?'

'No love, perhaps you could give her a ring and bring her up to date, but ask her to stay away from Lyn's until after I contact you.' There was a long pause, then she said, 'Don't worry too much, love, everything will be okay. I'm missing all the kiddies, but there's nothing to be helped, is there? Gotta go – bye, love – take care.'

'Bye, Mom,' I said quietly, but I knew that I spoke into the ether. I walked blindly into the kitchen and poured myself a tall glass of white wine. It was far too early, but I thought, what the hell. After listening to Mom telling me that the fault was mine. I needed something to pick me up

I think the wine did the trick as I spent the remainder of my day enjoying my two little ones, and we happily went off to collect Dawn, who I now called my big one, much to her amusement. I knew that Peter would be late home, so I prepared salad and cold chicken and ham for tea. Dawn loved cucumber, so she was happy as she said that it was her favourite food in the whole world. Even the two little ones enjoyed their mashed-up tea and were tucked up in bed before their Dad arrived home. Dawn took advantage of her big girl status by staying up later and eating a second helping of cucumber while Peter and I ate our meal.

At this point, I felt pretty relaxed and happy within my little world, but for the second night running, as soon as Peter and I settled down to watch one of our favourite programmes, I began to sob. I really wouldn't have blamed him had he lost patience with me, but he didn't. He held me at arm's length and peered closely at my streaming eyes. 'Okay, what's happened now?'

I dashed my tears away impatiently with my sleeve and gave him the gist of my telephone conversation with my mother.

He held me to him and brushed my hair out of my eyes where it had stuck – wet with tears. 'So why are you crying, do you know?'

I shook my head but then tried to tell him how hurt I felt that I was getting the blame for having any part in my sister's troubles.

'Well, who's blaming you, only Lyn, and as your Mom pointed out, she's not thinking clearly at the moment, is she? You daft 'apporth no one with any sense is going to blame you for anything. Stop beating yourself up, or I'll have to get my riding crop and beat you for real.' He laughed, and I began to smile. Of course, he was right, and I was overdramatising the importance of Lyn's words.

'I'm sorry, love, I know you're right, and I didn't mean to turn on the waterworks again.' I could feel my neck muscles relax. We sat in silence for a few minutes.

'I tell you what though, my love – I am sick and tired of you being upset by your family – perhaps it's time for us to move further away, what do you think?'

My stomach gave a nasty jolt as though I'd drunk some iced water too quickly. I still liked where we were living and didn't want to move away just yet.

'Not yet, please, Peter, I know that both our Moms would miss the children, and I'd miss my family too. We're just going through a bad patch – all families do.'

I could feel my eyes start to sting again and was relieved when Peter said, 'Okay, but no more crying, eh? Otherwise, I will have to beat you.' He gently pushed me away and went from the room, returning a couple of minutes later with glasses of wine. 'Come on, let's have an early night, and we'll take these up with us.'

I did phone Janet the next day as Mom had asked me to, but we didn't chat for long, and I got the impression that she couldn't be bothered to talk – hopefully, it wasn't just to me. I decided that I wasn't going to ring anyone again – I'd wait for them to ring me. I stuck with it and found it difficult to believe that two days passed before I heard from a family member. I couldn't remember being out of touch for so long in my whole life and was amazed that they had flown by without me being upset.

Mom told me when she eventually rang that Lyn was in the assessment unit and seemed to be coping well. She could only stay there for six weeks, and then she would either be transferred to a long-stay psychiatric placement or be discharged home. Probably the best that could happen, I thought, but when she told me that Michael and Derek had already moved Lyn's belongings from her room to Mom's house, I felt useless. I'd been no help to any of them, and rightly or wrongly, I was upset not to be needed. I tried to shrug the feeling off and took the children round to Mom's for an hour after I'd fetched Dawn and Julie from school. Laura and I had arranged to do the school run every other day. It suited us both as the weather was so cold.

I'd missed seeing Mom, and so had the children, and so we spent the time laughing and playing with them. I deliberately steered the conversation away from my siblings as I was still unable to come to terms with my negative feelings, and Mom didn't seem to have much to say either. She did tell me that Dad was coming home the next day, and I promised to make an effort to see him, but I felt ambivalent about how hard I'd try. Two days running, getting the little ones ready to go out when Dawn would be brought home by Laura didn't seem to be worth the effort somehow.

It turned out that he was home for a few days, so Peter and the children came with me the following Sunday, and we had a family day just as though the trouble with Simon and Lyn hadn't happened. I had hoped that Janet and the girls would put in an appearance, but Mom said that she'd spoken to her briefly the day before, and she seemed to want to keep close to home when she wasn't at work. I couldn't understand why she hadn't phoned me lately, but I wasn't about to go chasing after her. I wondered if, deep down, she too blamed me for not seeing what was going on with Simon and Lyn and giving her the chance to stop things going too far. I dismissed the notion; I wasn't to blame, and I was letting my thoughts become paranoid.

A few days later, I did ring her to invite them to come for tea – a belated celebration of Peter's birthday. I was stunned when she refused.

'What on earth's the matter Janet, have I done something to upset you?' I asked. My stomach was full of glass marbles that were trying to hit each other.

'No, don't be silly. What could you have done, we've hardly seen each other lately, and I know it's my fault.'

'Well, why are you behaving like this. Why can't you come to Peter's tea? You've always got on so well; is it something he's done?' I knew I was clutching at straws, but I just didn't understand why Janet would refuse the invitation without a good reason, and she didn't seem to have one.

Janet took a deep breath and said slowly, 'I'm sorry, Sara, I should have told you before that Simon's home.'

'Oh my God, you mean he's back living with you?'

'Yes, and before you say anything, he's my husband, and I love him no matter what he's done,' Janet said, 'that's why we can't come. I'm sure that no one in the family wants anything to do with him, but he's Michelle and Karen's father, and that's what counts. He's promised never to see Lyn again, and I think that we'll be selling the house and moving away as soon as the weather gets warmer and people start looking to buy.'

I felt my legs slide from under me, and I sat gracelessly on the hall floor. My mind wouldn't take it in. It'd been the last thing that I thought Janet would do.

'I've got to go and see why Jenny is upset, Jan; she's starting to cry. I'll ring you tomorrow,' I said and replaced the receiver with too much force.

25

I didn't ring Janet the following day, nor did I go to see Dad again, as I'd promised before he went back on his travels. I think that I was too stunned and upset by a feeling that my whole family had somehow betrayed me. I just wanted to be with Peter and our children and lick my wounds, real or imagined; it made no difference. Rather than have a party, I persuaded Peter to drive to North Wales the following weekend to revel in the mountain scenery as his birthday treat. It's something that we both liked to do, and it helped me stop feeling sorry for myself and gain a better perspective regarding both Janet and Lyn's behaviour.

Driving through Llanberis pass was always magical for me. The giant boulders and rocks scattered haphazardly on the grey-green slopes just made me think of the power of nature, and I loved it when we parked the car and climbed over the low wall to collect stones from the Afon Nant Peris, the small stream that trickles at the bottom of Snowdon. Perhaps I shouldn't have, but I always brought a few small rocks home and put them in our garden. Peter moaned about the extra weight in the boot, but I just laughed and reminded him that we didn't weigh too much, so it should be okay, and of course, it was. We had booked for one night into a family room at the Pont y Pair Inn in Betsw-y-coed. It was also a pub and a bit noisy, but it was clean and suited our budget. After having a good night's sleep, we drove home in high spirits, and by the time the welcome sight of our house appeared, I was feeling happy again and determined to re-establish good relations with my family. I knew that I shouldn't allow Simon to prevent me from seeing Janet, and taking on board Peter's good advice, I determined that I would try to treat him as though nothing had happened. I wouldn't be seeing very much of him, so I felt sure that it would be for the best. I also decided to go and see Lyn and try to make my peace with her.

I waited until the following Saturday when I hoped that Simon might be at the club where he had always spent his time, and then I phoned Janet. She began to weep when she heard my voice, and I felt sorry that I'd thought she didn't want to see me anymore. I could have kicked myself for not being more understanding. She hadn't wanted to tell me about Simons return because she knew full well how I would feel about him being back in her life. She hadn't known what to do.

'Don't cry, Jan – please don't cry – I'm sorry for being so stupid, it's taken me a while, but I understand now.' I could hear quiet sniffles and could picture her mopping her eyes as I spoke. I waited a few seconds and said, 'am I forgiven?'

'There's nothing to forgive; I just thought that I'd probably lost you forever. I'm stupid too, but I do love him, you know. I know he's sorry for what he did, and he's trying hard to make it up to me and the children. He hardly ever goes out these days except to work. He was fortunate that they gave him his old job back.' She spoke quickly, and I realised how much I'd missed her company. We'd been close since we were tiny, and I wanted to see her, and put my arms around her, and not let go.

'Can we get together soon?' I asked, crossing my fingers as I waited for her reply.

'How about if I come to yours and bring Michelle and Karen? They'll be excited, they've been asking where you all are, and Simon has gone to the club.'

'That would be great, come now, this very minute, I can't wait.' A thought suddenly struck me. 'Hold on, do you need me to come and fetch you?'

'No, I have a car now, I passed my test two weeks ago after only three lessons, and I love the independence of being able to go anywhere when I want to.'

'Whoop, whoop, clever you – okay, I'll get the kettle on – see you in a min.' I danced into the kitchen, and Dawn danced behind me, laughing to see me so excited.

'Auntie Janet and the girls are coming to visit,' I told her. She grinned widely and came to hold my hands then we jigged around together. I hadn't realised before how my estrangement from my family would affect the children, too – I'd been too wrapped up in how it affected me. I realised just how selfish I'd been when Janet and the girls arrived. Dawn and Michelle flung themselves into each other's arms, followed closely by Karen and Paul. They ignored Jenny and chattered joyously together while I hugged Janet, and we laughed as we told each other how much we'd missed our time together.

'I can't stay too long, Simon will be home at two for lunch, and I would rather let him know that I've seen you in my own time.'

I flinched inside at the sound of his name but recognised that I needed to accept Janet's decision to keep her marriage going. Later, when we were drinking our inevitable cups of tea, I asked Janet if she'd seen anything of Lyn. Her face became impassive as she told me that she hadn't seen either Lyn or our mom since the news that Lyn didn't want to see either of us.

'I'd better ring Mom and find out what's going on. We can't let this break our family apart; it would be too awful,' I said, and Janet nodded.

'Go on then, phone her now while I'm here, and will you tell her about Simon? I can't face it?'

'Okay, do you want to see what the kids are up to?' I said as I went into the hall and dialled Mom's number.

'Hello, Mom, its Sara. How are you?' I found that I was trembling slightly inside as I made the call. I'd no idea how annoyed with us she would be. I soon found out as the phone went down with a bang at her end.

I rang back, and this time she spoke first. 'Is that you our Sara? Just remembered that we exist, have you?' She spoke quietly, but I could hear the tension in her voice.

'I'm sorry, Mom, I've kept meaning to ring, but there's been a lot going on, and Peter and I have been on a little holiday,' I wasn't about to say that it was only overnight.

'Oh, have you now?' You still could have rung, couldn't you?' Mom said tersely.

'Well, I know it's no excuse, but I must admit that I've been a bit peeved with the way we were told to keep away from Lyn.' I could hear the exasperation as Mom exhaled. 'How are you and Lyn anyway?' I asked hurriedly, wishing that the phone call was over.

'I haven't heard from Janet either, have you?'

'Well, yes, but only today. She's here, and she wants me to tell you that Simon is now living back at home with her and the girls. She didn't know how to tell you herself, so that's probably why she hasn't phoned.' I ended lamely, not knowing what else to say. I thought that Mom could have phoned us, but I also knew that she would have expected us to make the call after any trouble. She always had expected us to be the first to make amends whenever anything upsetting occurred.

'Well, you both should have let me know that you were alright. I've been worried, and I'd enough to cope with visiting Lyn every day and trying to make sure that she was okay.'

'Well, is she?' I asked.

'Mm, well, she's much better, and the doctor has said that she can come home next week if she continues to remain calm and attends group therapy. She knows that Simon is back with Janet. He wrote to her and told her that he couldn't see her any more, but he'll help to support the baby when it's born.'

'How bloody kind of him,' I said. 'I wonder if Janet knows that he's written.'

'Well, Janet told him to write according to Lyn, so she must do. Lyn's been asking to see both you and Janet.'

'Well, that's good, I'll tell Janet, and we'll make arrangements to visit her and try to make things better before she comes home. Well, I hope Janet will agree anyway.' I wasn't at all sure that she would, and I wasn't sure that I wanted to go either. 'Look, Mom, I'm going to go now and tell Janet what we've talked about, and we'll come and see you soon. All the children have been missing you, and so have I.' She gave a deep sigh. 'How are Dad and Michael?'

'They're okay. Your Dad's home for a few days now, and I've been missing the children too. Give them kisses from me and bring them to see me soon, won't you love.'

'Of course, love you, Mom.' I said, and ended the call. All her anger had dissipated, and I felt grateful that she had always been an understanding and forgiving mother.

When I brought Janet up to date with the phone call, I was relieved that she agreed to see both Mom and Lyn.

'Thanks for doing the dirty work, Sara. I'll phone her myself later on now I know she's not going to make a fuss about Simon. It'll be nice to see Lyn too – I don't hate her, you know.'

'I know you don't; she's still our sister.' I mentally crossed my fingers that Lyn had got her head straight and wanted to see us and make her peace. I wasn't banking on it, though; I thought it was more likely that she had an ulterior motive behind her request. I'm becoming more and more cynical, I thought, and gave myself yet another mental slap.

26

It was barely six o'clock on Sunday morning when the phone demanded attention. I put Jenny over my shoulder and patted her back gently as I lifted the receiver and heard the sob in Mom's voice as she said, 'Hello, is that you our Sara?'

'Oh dear, what's up, Mom, is it Lyn?' I asked, feeling sure that it was.

Mom took a deep breath, and her sobs turned to sniffles as she said, 'No, it's your Dad; he's had another stroke.' She began to sob again in earnest, and I could see my fingers turning white where they squeezed the phone as I tried to take in what she'd just told me.

'Mom, hey Mom,' I called firmly, 'come on, love, get a grip, tell me what happened ...'

'He's on his way to Selly Oak hospital. The ambulance took him a few minutes ago; he was unconscious, and they said it would be better if they didn't wait until I could get dressed to go with him, and I'm scared he's going to die.'

'Alright, Mom, try to calm down; he'll be alright. I'll just go and wake Peter and get dressed, and then I'll come and take you to the hospital, okay? Go and make yourself a cuppa and get dressed – you need to get some things together to take with us.'

I almost burst out laughing when Mom said, 'Food you mean?'

'No, you daft 'apporth, pyjamas and his washing gear.'

'Yes, of course, I'm all confused; it's been such a shock waking up and seeing him with his face all twisted up. I don't know what woke me because he wasn't making a sound,' her voice was barely more than a whisper as she continued, 'I think it was the smell.' She began to cry quietly again.

I waited for a minute and then called her back to the present.

'Come on, Mom, I need to see to the children if I'm to take you to see him, don't I?'

'Yes, sorry, love, I'll make some tea. You're a good girl.' The phone went down, and I hurried upstairs to rouse Peter.

I wrinkled my nose as I entered our bedroom, which was redolent with a night's worth of cabbage smelling farts; infinitely better than the smell that had greeted my mother, I thought in my silly fashion. Peter opened one eye, held out his arms, and I passed our tiny daughter to him. She immediately fell asleep.

'Who was on the phone at this time in the bloody morning?' He grumbled with his eyes shut sleepily. They flew open when I told him it was Mom. 'Oh no, what's the matter now?' He sat up carefully, trying not to wake Jenny.

'It sounds bad this time, Peter.' I sat down on the side of the bed and felt tears well up behind my lids. I quickly brushed them away – no time for weeping. I repeated what Mom had told me.

'Are you going to the hospital with her?'

I nodded. 'Yes, is that okay?'

'Try not to worry, love, he'll be alright,' he said. 'It's a good job it isn't Monday, I have an important meeting that I have to attend, but I can have the kiddiewinks all day today if necessary, just go and get ready. Have you phoned Janet?'

'No, I'd better do that now.' I leaned over the bed and kissed him hard on the lips. I loved him so much; at times like this, I felt overwhelmed by it. I turned away and went into the bathroom as Peter shut his eyes.

Once she'd got over the initial shock, Janet made arrangements to meet us at the hospital. I was relieved as I didn't fancy coping with Mom on my own, and I wasn't ready to face up to how my Dad might look. Mom's description had made him sound grotesque.

I hadn't realised how low the outside temperature had become and was unprepared for the task of scraping thick ice from my windshield. By the time I'd finished, and the glass was sufficiently clear for me to drive safely, my thick, woollen gloves were sodden, and my hands were frozen. I pulled the gloves off and replaced them with a pair of musty smelling, green leather ones that I found in the glove compartment. I tucked my fingers under my oxters until they were warm enough to grasp the steering wheel and then carefully negotiated our driveway. Thankfully the road had been gritted overnight.

I tooted the horn as I pulled up outside Mom's house. She soon appeared, bundled up as if going on an Arctic expedition. Sensible my Mom – I gave her a reassuring pat on her arm as she sat in the passenger seat. I'm sure she barely felt it through her layers. She smiled though and thanked me for coming to fetch her. We didn't talk much on the journey; we were both absorbed with our thoughts and fears, well I was full of apprehension, and I'm sure that she was too. When we reached the hospital, Janet was waiting for us in the reception area, and we were quickly joined by Michael and Derek, both of whom were decked in their leathers, each carrying a motorbike helmet by its chin strap. I wasn't happy to think that they'd biked here, but I said nothing. They were adults, and it seemed pointless to interfere even though I wanted to tell my little brother off. Michael now towered a good ten inches above me

– he's now my big brother, I thought. As usual, my mind was performing its frequent dance of irrelevance.

We knew that we couldn't pile into the ward en masse, so Mom and I went to the main reception to ascertain where Dad was. The receptionist quickly flicked through some papers and then turned to a chart on the wall behind her. 'They've admitted him to the stroke trauma ward,' she said and pointed.

We hurried along several dimly lit corridors that were alive with cleaning trolleys and blank-faced people until we found the correct ward. We pushed the double doors open and gazed in on a scene resembling a disturbed ant's nest. The daily routine of breakfast and bed changing was in full swing. We approached the nurse's station to enquire if we could see my father, and a nurse in a dark blue uniform, who I later found out, was the sister-in-charge, came from behind the long reception counter and took my mother's hand in hers.

'Mrs Davis?' she enquired with a charming smile, as though she knew by some supernatural means the identity of every person that entered her ward.

Mom nodded. 'I've come to see my husband.' She shook her head and frowned. She seemed confused.

'Will you come with me, and I'll just ask the doctor to come and have a word with you,' she said, and then turned to me, 'and you are?' She raised eyebrows that I thought were far too bushy for a young woman. I tried to focus my mind.

'I'm Sara, his daughter – has something else happened?' I could taste iron filings in my mouth, and I instinctively knew that something worse had occurred.

She didn't answer my question. 'I'll just get the doctor.'

We followed her to a side room where she indicated that we should be seated, and then we waited. Mom sat with her hands, writhing in her lap, as they always did when she was stressed. I couldn't think of anything to say that would be reassuring, so I remained quiet with my mind doing summersaults.

I glanced at my watch; five minutes had passed. My unease grew. After ten minutes, I knew that something was very, very wrong, and I got to my feet, determined to go back out into the corridor and insist that I see my father. I was almost at the door when it flew open and a tall, black man in a white coat entered. He introduced himself as Dr Aburewell and lowered his imposing height into the armchair next to Mom.

His voice had shades of Paul Robeson, as he said, 'I am so sorry to tell you, Mrs Davis, that your husband had another stroke about an hour ago and,' he paused for a second and took Mom's trembling hand in his, 'and I'm afraid that he didn't recover.' He slowly shook his head from side to side. 'There was nothing that we could do.' Mom began to cry and utter peculiar little mewling sounds. 'I'm so sorry,' he said again and turned to me. 'Are you his daughter?' I nodded, and he said, 'Your father didn't regain consciousness – sadly, there was nothing to be done.'

'Thank you,' I said. I went to comfort my mother, who had ceased crying but now sat in stunned silence, her face a pasty white – unlike her normal all-weather tan.

'Is there anything that you'd like to ask me?' Dr Aburewell said, after a couple of minutes of silence – that seemed to me to be more like a couple of hours.

I began to panic as I tried to think about what I should want to know. My mind screamed repeatedly; he's dead, he's dead, we were too late. I could feel a lump in my throat that I knew presaged tears. They sprung unbidden, and I tried desperately to get control as I dashed them away, and I thought, oh my God, how am I going to tell Janet and Michael.

My mind threatened to shut down, but instead, I heard myself say – in a cold, clipped way – 'What happens now?' I thought again of Janet and Michael downstairs, waiting for their turn to come and see their father.

'Well, I'm going to arrange for one of the nurses to bring you some tea, and they will answer that for you.' He turned to go.

'My sister and brother are downstairs. Can I ask them to join us here – they'll need to know too.'

'Yes, that's fine – please take whatever time you need.' He smiled and said quietly, 'And now I really must go.'

I dropped a kiss onto Mom's greying hair and sat down beside her. 'I'm sorry, Mom.' I felt guilty that I hadn't been able to get her here before he died.

Mom sniffed and wiped her eyes with a tissue from her handbag. 'I don't know why you are sorry for me,' she said, 'I lost him years ago, but I'm sorry that you've lost your Dad; he always loved you.' Tears welled up in her red-rimmed eyes again, and she mopped them away.

'I know he did, and I loved him – so did Janet and Michael. Will you be okay if I go and fetch them?'

Janet knew by my face that something awful had happened. Her hand clutched at her throat, and she mouthed, 'No,' as I walked towards them.

I felt my energy drain away and slumped onto one of the grey, plastic chairs before I spoke.

'We were too late,' I said. I began to say that our father had passed away, but the words dried up in my throat, and I sobbed as if my heart would break. It had suddenly hit me as though a door had banged shut in my face – he was dead, and I would never be able to talk with him again.

27

After listening carefully in the hospital to the procedure that the sympathetic male nurse explained to us, Michael surprised everyone by saying that he would make all the arrangements for Dad's funeral. I was grateful, and I'm sure that the others were too, as no one disputed his right to take over. It finally made me realise that he was no longer just my little brother – he was a man – and a very responsible one too. Sometimes a crisis can bring out the best in people, I thought.

It didn't bring out anything except disquiet in me when Janet and I went with Mom the following day to see Lyn and tell her about Dad. I was expecting her to have one of her hysterical fits, but she didn't. She accepted the news of his death calmly and asked when the funeral would be.

'We don't know yet, love, but if you are feeling well enough, you should be able to come home before it takes place. Do you want to come home yet, Lyn?' Mom asked.

'Of course, but I don't know if the doctors will let me. Will you ask them for me?' She looked directly at Janet and said, 'I'm sorry for everything, and I want to go home to have my baby. Please ask them if I can. I won't do anything stupid again,' she said.

Janet's face crumpled as she nodded. She went to where Lyn sat by the long dining table in the communal room and hugged her. Then she stroked Lyn's baby bump and said, 'It's okay, you're my sister, and I can't wait to become an auntie again, but you stay away from my husband and the girls until they are older, they – are – not – yours – do you understand?' Lyn nodded her affirmation and lowered her head as Janet sat beside her on another dining chair.

I walked over to them and gave Lyn a quick hug and then said to Janet, 'I'll go with Mom, and see if we can make arrangements for Lyn to leave here if that's what you all want? I couldn't quite bring myself to be as completely forgiving as Janet had been. I don't think that a leopard can change its spots, and I had just watched Lyn exercise her old manipulative skills on Janet.

I kept my reservations to myself as Lyn nodded her head vigorously, indicating her wishes. Mom and I then went to find the person in charge, leaving Janet talking to Lyn as though nothing untoward had ever happened.

It was agreed that Lyn could be discharged the following Thursday after her group therapy session. Unfortunately, none of us was able to supply transport during the daytime, and so after much discussion, it was arranged that Peter should pick her up after school finished.

Janet and I both popped into Mom's during the next week to see if Lyn was settled or if she needed anything. It felt as though she'd never been away except for her very apparent baby bump. She seemed happy, and Mom told us that she was being helpful around the house and getting on very well with Michael when he visited.

When we got together a couple of times that week, both Janet and I talked about our surreal feelings. We found it hard to believe that our father's cremation was in a few days. There had always been long gaps when he wasn't at home, and that's what it felt like now. I couldn't shake off the feeling that he might walk in the door or be sat by the fire reading his paper when I visited Mom's house.

I expect that's how most people feel in the time between someone dying and their funeral. It was a feeling of being in Limbo for us – but not for Michael – he had taken the brunt of reality. I was so glad and touched that he was in the here and now when I realised that he'd remembered, without being reminded, that Karen's birthday was on the fifth and Michelle had hers on the seventh, and so he'd booked the funeral for the eighth of March.

Michelle cried when we told her that her Granddad had died and said that she didn't want any birthday presents, but Karen didn't understand the concept, and we persuaded Michelle that we should celebrate their special days for Karen's sake. She was okay with that, but no one felt like celebrating, and it was all very low key.

Dad's funeral was how I think most funerals are – mainly boring, sad affairs. We did try to make it a celebration of his life, but I found that my anger at his early demise was paramount throughout. I was glad when it was all over, and we were back at home where each of us could remember our own relationship with him.

For some reason, Peter had a yen to holiday in Europe that year, so we found ourselves spending Dawn's eighth birthday in a private apartment in Benidorm. It was in a gated tower block mainly inhabited by Spanish people. We had a great time. The weather was hot and sunny, and we had the kidney-shaped swimming pool to ourselves most afternoons as the locals were invariably working or enjoying a siesta in the cool of their apartments. When we returned home after ten days, it was to be met at Birmingham airport by torrential rain pouring from a miserable, overcast sky. Dawn and Paul were tired from the flight and fed up at leaving the sunshine behind, so it wasn't long before they were squabbling and set Jenny off crying. I don't think that I'd ever noticed before that England has a distinctly cold smell and feel about it. I couldn't wait to get home, get the children off to bed and settle into a nice warm bath. Peter was his usual humorous self, and in no time, had located our car, loaded the luggage and driven us home. I don't know how he does it, but he hardly ever seems to become impatient with situations that cause me to tear my hair out.

Later that week, we all met up at Mom's house, where Michael had arranged a tea party to celebrate his twenty-third birthday and give us the news that he and Derek were going to live in Canada for two years. They had friends there who had arranged jobs in the logging industry for them. Everybody was delighted, but I felt a little sad as I'd only just begun to appreciate having such a loving, supportive couple in our lives. I said as much to Michael later that evening, but he said that two years would fly by, and perhaps Lyn might have settled down and stopped making everyone miserable by then. I hoped he was right.

Days rolled past until we reached August fourteenth, and it was with excitement that we received the call to go to Good Hope Hospital, where Lyn was in labour. It was ten past eleven when Mom came to find Janet and myself, where we waited impatiently in reception.

'Lyn's had a beautiful baby boy. He weighed seven pounds exactly,' she said. She was beaming, and I felt so happy for her and Lyn that it had gone well.

I stood up and took her hands, and we did a little jig. 'Blimey, that was quick; she's only been in labour four hours.' I wanted to see and hold my new little nephew. I glanced across at Janet, who I realised wasn't saying anything. It dawned on me that Lyn had achieved something that she hadn't – she'd given Simon a son. The news was doubly unwelcome for her.

I didn't know what to say and was relieved when Janet went to Mom and took her by the hands as I had done and said with a smile, 'Well, congratulations, Grandma.'

'Don't think that I don't know how you must feel, Janet love,' Mom said. I'm sorry that it's all happened, but we have to make the best of it. It's not the baby's fault, is it? He deserves to be loved no matter who his parents are, doesn't he?'

Janet shrugged. 'I know you're right, Mom, but it's very hard to take. Don't worry, though; I'll play the good Auntie. I told Lyn that I would, but I wish she'd had a fucking girl instead.' She sat back down and turned her head away from our eyes.

'It's bad blood, that's what it is, but it's not the baby's fault,' Mom whispered. I could just about catch the words, but I was pretty sure that Janet hadn't heard them.

'Come on, let's go home, I don't think we'll be allowed in now, and I'm sure Lyn needs to sleep. We can return tomorrow, can't we?' I said persuasively.

'She doesn't know that you are both here, so I'll just nip up and say goodbye to her, then I'll meet you at the car,' Mom said, in a tone that brooked no argument.

'Okay, see you in a few minutes,' I said. Janet looked at me and smiled through clenched teeth. I grabbed her arm and tugged at her. 'C'mon, let's go; it'll feel better after some sleep.'

'Will it?' Janet said and rolled her eyes up to the ceiling.

'Oh, c'mon, there's no point in sitting here.' I got up, and she followed me out to the car. After sitting in silence for a few minutes, I turned the radio on and listened to some people talking about climate change so that I wouldn't have to speak to her. She seemed lost in thought, and I didn't think anything that I could say right now to comfort her. I was glad when Mom joined us a little later. Her breathing was laboured, as though she'd hurried back from seeing Lyn.

I started the car and began to drive before she got her breath back and began to talk animatedly. 'I told her that we'd all come and see her tomorrow, and she was pleased with that. She wanted me to tell you that she is going to call the baby Freddy even though she knows that Fred wasn't her real father –'

'When did you tell her?' I asked. My eyes were steady as they gazed at Mom.

'Well –'

'What, what do you mean, more bloody secrets, eh? I've just about had enough of this fucking family,' Janet interrupted.

I swerved to avoid hitting the kerb, causing both of them to gasp in fright. I was aware that my concentration had flown out of the window when Mom dropped the bombshell that had made Janet swear, and it scared me.

'Oh, shit, sorry,' I said. 'But will you please stop talking about secrets and stuff until we're home – I need to concentrate on driving.'

They lapsed into silence, but I could feel the tension in the car and had to force myself to ignore the pair of them. Fortunately, we arrived at my house, where Janet had left her car a few minutes later.

As we pulled onto my drive, Janet opened her door and spoke in a tight voice. 'I can't cope with anymore tonight. I'm too tired. I'll phone you after work tomorrow. I can't have another day off.'

I switched the engine off and waved as she got quickly into her car and drove away. 'Oh my God, I forgot that she didn't know – how could I be so stupid?' Mom said.

I started the car up again. 'I'll take you home as well Mom, it's late, and I need some sleep before the kiddiewinks wake up. Is that okay?'

'Please, dear, I've had enough tonight too.'

As she got out of my car, she spoke in a somewhat shaky voice. 'Thanks for the lift love, I'll see you tomorrow.' We blew each other a kiss, and I watched her go safely into the house. I sat for a couple of minutes gazing in wonder at the streaky, blue-black sky. It was after midnight, but it was still so light that I thought, fancifully, that Mother Nature didn't want to go to bed. I laughed out loud at my imagination, and it quieted me down somewhat. Why shouldn't my thoughts be a little bit crazy; after all, it had been a crazy, stressful evening? I laughed again and then thankfully drove home, thinking only of my sleeping family that waited for me.

28

Mom rang the following day to say that she would visit Lyn in the afternoon, and perhaps Janet and I could go in the evening. Of course, we did as we were asked, and Lyn was so pleased to see us and show Freddy off that I couldn't be anything but pleased for her.

He was a beautiful baby with a mop of fair hair and a tiny button nose. I held him for a little while, and then Lyn told me not to be greedy and give Janet her turn. Lyn was chattering away, giving us a rundown on the birth and how difficult it had been, and never noticed the look of sheer dislike that passed briefly across Janet's open face as she gazed at her wriggling nephew.

I thought that Janet had done an excellent job of hiding her true feelings. By the time we left Lyn to rest with her baby cuddled up in her arms, Janet was able to kiss Lyn warmly and tell her how beautiful her son was, but I had seen the look that exposed her soul, and I felt so very sad for her. I thought that try as she might, she would always be deeply hurt each time she saw the result of the betrayal by her husband and her sister. Conversely, it seemed to me that if she couldn't have Simon, Lyn was quite content to have Simon's baby. She behaved as though the baby was her achievement alone, and for the sake of peace, we allowed her to do just that.

Looking back on it, the end of nineteen seventy-three and almost the whole of seventy-four seemed to disappear as if it only consisted of Christmas, daffodils, school holidays, birthdays and then Christmas again. The children were all healthy and growing out of their clothes at the usual rate that children do. Janet and I visited Mom's about once a week, but we never stayed long. Lyn seemed pleased to see us at first, but when Freddy was about fourteen months old, her attitude changed. Sometimes when Janet and I visited together, she would make us a cup of tea and then take Freddy into the front room, leaving us to talk to Mom. She made it clear without saying so that we weren't welcome to follow her. Mom told us in confidence one day that she thought Lyn was becoming more guarded, as she'd found herself a boyfriend. She'd sworn Mom to secrecy; she didn't want Janet or me to know that she was seeing a man called Mark, someone she'd known since her school days. We promised not to let on, and I was pleased for her. It explained her behaviour anyway.

As we left, Janet looked back at the house. 'Bloody secrets, stupid bitch,' she said. Just that, and without saying goodbye to me, she got into her car, waved her hand and drove away.

I knew how she felt. I, too, was sick of Lyn's silly secrets. I wondered why she'd never grown up. But I decided that what we saw was the way it was always going to be and tried not to dwell on her behaviour.

I regularly took my children to see their Grandma and Aunt, and on these occasions, Lyn remained with us, but Janet never took Michelle or Karen. I thought that perhaps that omission had something to do with Lyn's behaviour. If Mom wanted to see Janet's girls, she had to visit them at Janet's when Simon wasn't there or occasionally, they would meet up at my house. I didn't mind, it seemed to be working okay, and Janet was determined that Lyn would have nothing to do with Michelle or Karen even if she felt that she was entitled to do so. It hadn't been easy, but, except for keeping the children away, Janet seemed to have come to terms with Lyn's betrayal, and everything was okay between them, at least on the surface.

We did occasionally see Simon, but we managed to avoid this whenever possible. I spoke to him when I had to, but he wasn't fooled; he knew I'd as soon spit in his face. I could never forgive the spineless bastard for not being able to keep his cock in his pants, but I had to be civil; otherwise, I knew that we would lose Janet, and I didn't intend to let that happen.

I remember how worried I'd been just after Lyn had given birth to Freddy. Janet had brought Mom to have a cuppa at my house where, thanks to Peter taking Dawn and Paul to see his mother, I was on my own except for Jenny, who was having a nap. I was surprised but pleased to see them. We chatted easily for a while until Mom began to explain to Janet about Lyn's conception. Janet had listened intently, her face stiff. I remember looking out of the window and watching the rainbow behind the house opposite lose its brilliance as the colours faded.

I can still hear Mom's faltering voice and the exact words she spoke as she ended by saying to Janet, 'I know I should have told you before, and you can't blame Sara she's given me every chance to tell you myself – I'm sorry, but there it is.' Her face and chest were red as a beetroot by the time she'd finished talking.

'I might have guessed that there was something different about her; she's not like us, is she?' Janet had retorted.

'Hold on, she's still –' I'd exclaimed, bringing my eyes and mind back to the family drama that was playing out in my sitting room.

'Well, is she?' Janet had interrupted as she'd leaned forward in her chair and glared into my eyes. 'Is she?' I remember thinking apprehensively that she looked and sounded somewhat deranged.

I'd taken a deep breath and told her to calm down and then said, 'You're right, she is a bit different from the rest of us, but we can't all be the same, can we. It doesn't mean that she's any less Mom's daughter and the little sister that we've all indulged. We know what she's done, Jan, but you're the one that said we should all be supportive and, yes, forgiving, if only for Freddy's sake. He's our nephew and our children's cousin, for goodness sake.' I'd ended lamely.

'Oh, he's more than that, much bloody more.' Janet had sounded anything but calm.

Mom had put her cup down unsteadily onto the side table and said, 'Now give over our Janet, I know what she's done, and I know how hurt you are and,' she cried out, 'and it's all my fault. I shouldn't have been so stupid, but I was, and it's not Lyn's fault that she's different, she can't help being the way she is, and she's still my daughter no matter what she's done.' She'd then groped in her polka dot handbag and retrieved a tissue. 'And,' she'd continued with a sniffle, 'I love her just the same as I love you and Sara and Michael.'

They both had tears running down their flushed cheeks. Mom was wearing Youth Dew, her favourite perfume, and as she had become heated, the smell of it had permeated the room. I hated it. I still do. It reminds me of that day as soon as I get a waft of it. It had been awful, and I remember asking them if they wanted more tea. I hadn't heard their reply, I couldn't wait to get into the sanity of my kitchen where the air smelled fresh, and the only things that had been broken recently were eggs.

When I returned, they were sat side by side on my tired, brown leather sofa. I had seen it through new eyes, and remember thinking that it was time that we bought a new one. My mind, as usual, had been trying to think of mundane things to put off tackling further recriminations from Janet.

One Child Too Many

As I'd put the tea tray down, Mom had said softly, 'What did you mean, Jan, when you said that Freddy's more than the children's cousin?'

My heart had hit rock bottom as I had thought that Janet might still be feeling angry, but I needn't have worried; they'd been talking while I was out of the room.

'Well, he is,' Mom's eyebrows had drawn together, but I'd guessed what she meant before she'd explained in a controlled way, 'he's also Michelle and Karen's half-brother, isn't he.'

Mom's mouth had become a perfect O as the penny dropped, and she'd said thoughtfully, 'Yes, I suppose he is – oh dear, I'm so sorry – such a mess.'

I remember being glad that Janet had calmed down when I looked from one to the other and asked, 'Do you think that we could have a break from Lyn for now and talk about what we're all going to do for Christmas?'

They'd both smiled gratefully, and I'd felt my shoulders relax. I didn't lose her then, and I knew that I would do everything in my power not to allow anything to come between us in the future.

At Christmas, which once again was held at my house, Mom told me in confidence that she thought Lyn might be pregnant.

'Oh my God, are you sure? How do you know? I asked.

'Well, she hasn't said anything, but I've heard her in the bathroom this week – and she's been crying a lot. I haven't asked her about it because she'd only tell me to mind my own business. I know she would,' Mom said.

'It's a bit soon, isn't it – she's only been going out with Mark a few months, hasn't she?

'Well, it's not very long, but it doesn't take long, does it. I think this might mean she makes a go of it with Mark, I've only met him once, but he seems nice. Anyway, she is happy enough, so perhaps we can stop worrying so much about her.

Freddy is such a sweet little boy and no trouble. I won't mind having another grandchild to cuddle – they grow out of my arms so quickly,' Mom said.

'I know what you mean, and I don't suppose for a minute that either Janet or I will have any more.

29

At the end of the month, Janet came to babysit with Michelle and Karen as Peter and I had arranged to go for a meal with some of his school colleagues. It was a tradition in the making, and we were looking forward to the evening. Peter was upstairs getting ready, and I was in the kitchen, having a glass of wine with Janet. After generally chatting about the children, Janet suddenly came to the point. I'd felt that something was bugging her.

'I went to see Mom last night, and Lyn was in the kitchen making a drink. She only had on a thin nightie – and I couldn't help noticing her belly. She's putting on weight again, isn't she?' Janet said.

'Erm ... I think she could be pregnant again.' I hoped the conversation would end there.

'She looks about four months,' Janet began counting on her fingers, 'bloody hell, Freddy's only eighteen months old, stupid bitch.'

'Well, Mom said Mark seems to be very nice, and he's making Lyn happy so –'

'We'll be late; love, come on.' Peter called from the hallway.

I blew Janet a kiss, stuck my head around the sitting-room door, warned the children to be good, and then joined Peter, who'd already gone out to the car.

We had a great evening, and when we arrived home, all the children were asleep, and Janet was snuggled under a quilt on the settee watching late-night television. Peter and I said goodnight to her and then went straight up to our room and fell into bed. As usual, I'd had more than enough alcohol to make me tipsy. Peter moaned the following day that he'd had to put up with my snores until he gave me a dig in my ribs, and I turned over. I just laughed.

Janet and the girls went home after Peter cooked them all a fry up as a thank you to Janet for babysitting. Something she said she didn't need any reward for, but he insisted. I teased him as he likes to show off his culinary skills, but I was happy that he enjoyed cooking. I didn't.

At the beginning of March, Auntie Freda had again produced the cash and invited Mom to accompany her to Australia for three months. Freda's twin brother William had emigrated there in nineteen-forty-eight with his wife, Helen, and their daughter, Trudy. They had kept in touch by phone and letter, but Mom rarely mentioned them. I had seen photos and thought they looked like two comfortably off, happy families. Trudy had married an Australian, and they had two children, a young boy named Dennis and a leggy girl called Kirsty. They lived in sprawling bungalows next door to each other – on the coast just north of Perth.

Auntie Freda and Uncle William wanted to see each other before they died, Freda told us in her usual forthright manner, but she didn't want to go on her own. Mom took some persuading as she was scared of flying and had never been away from her family. But thankfully, when she phoned me after they landed, she was no longer afraid, she was exhilarated.

We had all gone to the airport to wave them off, and just as we were dropping her home, Lyn asked us if we'd phone and make sure she was going to be in before visiting. She explained that she would be spending time at Mark's house because she often looked after his dog while he was at work. Neither Janet nor I were bothered – Lyn had become quite a stranger lately. I just smiled and told her to ring if she needed me. Janet ignored her. Not one of us mentioned her very obvious pregnancy.

While Mom was away, the time passed very quickly. I didn't see much of Janet, and other than making one phone call to Lyn to make sure she was okay, we didn't communicate. Except for the odd phone call from Mom and an occasional one from Michael, I was content with being a wife and mother. Michael was enjoying working in Toronto. So much so that he and Derek were contemplating staying over there. He made their lives sound fun, and I felt a little pang of jealousy which lasted for all of a minute. I appreciated the simplicity that our little family was enjoying, too much to want to uproot ourselves. I might have known that it couldn't last.

At the beginning of May, Janet rang me. 'Hi Sara, you okay?'

'Mm, we're all fine, you okay?'

'No, I'm not. I've just found a Barbie doll in Karen's room, one I've never seen before, and I don't know where it's come from.'

'Well, we bought both Michelle and Karen Barbie dolls that they'd said they would like. I know they're a bit of rubbish, but it's become a favourite –'

'Yes, I know, but this is another one, and when I asked Karen where she'd had it from, she began to cry and refused to answer me. She looked scared of me Sara, I've never seen her look at me like that before,' Janet sounded upset.

'What did you do?'

'I was so taken aback by her behaviour that I just grabbed her and hugged her until she stopped crying. I told her it didn't matter, that it wasn't important, and then sent her off to watch telly with Michelle.'

'You don't think she's taken it from school or anywhere, do you?' I know I sounded startled at the thought.

'No, I think that it's much worse than that – I think it's off Lyn,' Janet said.

A feeling of dread took hold as I said, 'No, surely not, they haven't seen her, have they?'

'I bloody well hope not,' she paused, 'I suppose Mom could have given presents to the girls from Lyn before she went and told them not to say. I bet that's what it is, but she shouldn't have; it's made Karen scared of having to keep it secret. I can't stay on the phone; something is boiling over. I'll ring you later.' The phone went down.

Here we go again, more trouble, I thought. I went into the kitchen and distractedly picked up a fairy cake from the batch that I'd just made with the children and stuffed it wholesale into my mouth. I suddenly realised what I'd done, ceased chewing, and went and spat the cake, which I'd promised myself I wouldn't eat anymore of, into the rubbish bin.

'Oh, gross Mother,' Dawn said and wrinkled her nose as she passed the kitchen door.

'Well, I need to lose this again, don't I?' I patted my stomach.

'Well, don't put things in your mouth then.' She laughed uproariously and ran over to hug me. 'I like you cuddly anyway.' She kissed my belly and skipped away, giggling.

She'd taken my mind off Janet's phone call, and I thought no more about Barbie dolls as I collected the never-ending, dirty laundry from the bathroom and tried to overload the washing machine. Defeated, I left half the load on the floor and went to spend some time with Peter and the children. They were lying on the sitting room floor building with Lego and trying to stop Jenny from wrecking their efforts.

One Child Too Many

'Mommy tell her to go away,' Paul demanded and pushed Jenny, none too gently, with his foot. She began to wail.

'Don't be spiteful to your sister; she only wants to play,' Peter said firmly and wagged a finger under his nose.

I scooped Jenny up and sat on the sofa feeling tired yet happy with my family, but at the back of my mind, I knew that all wasn't well with Janet and Lyn – I felt heartily sick of it.

Later that night, when Paul and Jenny were in bed, I went up to Dawn's room with an armful of clean linen that lived in a chest in her room. She was sitting doing homework at her desk by the open window. A gentle breeze lifted the curtains and ruffled Dawn's long hair. I could smell the medicated shampoo that she used; it smelled clean. I glanced around her room and admired the way that she kept it. Everything had a place, and with no help from me, everything was in its place. A thought suddenly struck me as Dawn jumped up and offered to put the ironing away.

'Yes, please, love.' I went and sat at her desk. 'Dawn, I wondered if you knew anything about a Barbie doll that Auntie Janet has found in Karen's room? She doesn't know where it came from, do you know?' I asked and watched her face.

'Yes, it was from Auntie Lyn; she sent one for Michelle too, but Michelle said she didn't want it, and Uncle Simon took it away. Why do you want to know? It was for their birthday,' Dawn said.

'Did Grandma give them to Michelle and Karen before she went to Australia?' I asked, hopefully.

'No, Auntie Lyn gave them to Karen when she went to Grandmas, but it was a secret and Michelle doesn't like secrets, so she wouldn't have it. I don't like secrets either, and I don't like Auntie Lyn or Uncle Simon anymore. They tell lies.' Dawn finished putting the linen away and sat on her bed. 'Can I have my chair back now, please Mom, I've got to finish my homework?' Dawn and I changed places.

While Dawn continued to write something in her notebook, I stared at the wall trying to make sense of what my straightforward daughter had just told me. She hadn't seemed to be bothered about answering my question, so I decided to ask her another important one. One that I knew could have far-reaching consequences.

'Dawn, sorry to interrupt you again and please don't answer if you don't want to; I won't mind – does Uncle Simon take Karen and Michelle to see Auntie Lyn?' I held my breath as I waited for her answer.

Dawn swivelled in her chair. 'Yes, he does take Karen, but Michelle won't go. Karen has to keep it a secret, though, and it sometimes makes her very sad, and she cries. That makes Michelle upset, and I don't think she should have to go without Auntie Janet knowing. Do you, Mom?'

'No, love, I don't. Do you know how long it has been going on?' I asked.

'No, I don't, but it seems like a long while – should I have kept it a secret, Mom? Will Auntie Janet be cross with me?' Dawns face crumpled as she realised that there could be consequences to being honest.

'No, my love,' I said and hugged my ten-year-old daughter, who was becoming aware of things that I would like to protect her from. 'No, she won't, but I will have to tell her what you've just told me, and it will cause some upset, but it'll stop Karen and Michelle having to keep secrets that they shouldn't have to keep – so it's for the best. I tried to control my feelings, but I was fuming – the crafty pair of bastards.

30

I put off telling Janet what I'd learned for a couple of days, hoping that she'd have discovered the truth herself. But as she didn't phone me, I knew that, once again, I was going to be the bearer of devastating news. I left a message asking her to pop in whenever she could. She did the next evening after work.

'I can't stay long; the kids will want their tea. What's up?' Janet asked after shouting a greeting to Peter and the children.

I shut the kitchen door. 'Have you found out where the Barbie doll came from yet?'

'No, I'm going to wait until Mom returns – why have you?'

My face must have betrayed my feelings. 'I'm sorry, Jan.'

'Oh no, not again, please God, not again.' She banged her fist down on the work surface. 'I should have known better than to trust the conniving pair of snakes. She is pregnant, isn't she, and it's Simon's, not some imaginary Mark's. I could kill the pair of them. He promised, and I believed the lying bastard. And he's been taking the girls there.'

'Apparently, Michelle refuses to go, so it's only Karen. You can't blame her; she's been so close to Lyn all her life.'

'I don't blame her, she's just a little girl, but he must have thought I was fucking stupid. Well, no more, he's out. She wanted him; she can have him. I've shed enough tears – fucking pair of bastards.' Janet sank back against the cooker,

199

and I quickly fetched a glass of water. Her face showed pale under her light makeup.

'For God sake, sit down,' I shoved a barstool towards her. I could hear the clock ticking louder than ever before as Janet gulped the water and swiped at the drops that dribbled down her chin.

'How did you find out?' she asked.

I told her what Dawn had told me. 'I'm so sorry, Jan.'

'Stop saying you're sorry, none of this is your fault; it's my own – I should never have been such a bloody idiot.' She stood up and smoothed her skirt down.

'What are you going to do?'

'Tell him to fuck off to that piece of shit that he's never stopped screwing. Had his cake and eaten it, hasn't he? Well, he's going to get a shock – can I bring the girls down here to stay the night, Sara?'

'Of course, bring them now. I'll give them their tea.'

'Okay, see you in a bit,' Janet said and left.

It wasn't until after she'd gone that I realised she hadn't shed a tear. Good for you, I thought – stay angry.

I was angry too and went into the sitting room to where Peter was, as usual, playing games with the kids.

'What was all that about? Jan shut the door sharpish, didn't she?' Peter looked up, and I beckoned to him to follow me. As we entered the hall, Dawn was hanging over the bannisters, and even her hair looked pale.

I smiled at her. 'It's okay, love, please don't worry about it. Auntie Jan asked me to thank you for telling the truth, and she's bringing the girls round to stay the night. Can they both sleep in your room on the blow-up?' I asked. Janet hadn't said thank you, but a grin replaced the pinched look on Dawn's face. An excusable lie I felt.

'Yes, of course, I'll see to it,' Dawn said and ran down to get the blow-up from the hall closet. She blew me a kiss as she disappeared upstairs.

'What on earth's going on?' Peter asked, and I drew him into the kitchen.

Peter's jaw dropped as I quickly filled him in. He shook his head repeatedly. 'Do you think I should go and see if Jan needs any help? I can't believe how bloody devious people can be.'

'No, she'll be back soon with Michelle and Karen, so they'll be out of the way. Mind you, maybe you should ask her – it wouldn't be the first time he's hit her – that I do know.'

'When did he –'

'It's not important now – it was when Janet wanted to return to work.'

'What a wanker – do you think she'll be strong enough not to have him back this time?' Peter asked.

I shrugged. 'I've no idea. I just hope so.'

A little later, I made coffee, and Peter went to open the front door to two very excited girls with their rucksacks. They tumbled into the hall to be greeted by our equally excited children. The noise was deafening.

'I'm not staying a minute,' Janet said. She located her two, kissed them goodbye, and went off into the warm June night with a wave of her hand. Peter had no chance to ask her anything.

'Okay, you lot,' Peter said, 'line up against the wall.'

'Oh Daaad,' Dawn moaned, 'I'm too old –'

'C'mon, all of you line up in height order.' Peter grinned. There was such a scramble, but they all did as he ordered.

'Well done, now follow me,' he said. He led the way into the garden where he produced a ball, and they spent the next half hour kicking it about. Even Jenny, who wasn't yet three, ran about getting in the way until Peter scooped her up into his arms and continued the game.

By the time they trooped in like a line of sweaty monkeys, their tea was ready. After they were all fed and the little ones washed and into their pyjamas, Peter went to take a shower while I cleared up in the kitchen. Thank God for the goggle box, I thought as the little ones settled to watch *The Magic Roundabout,* and Dawn and Michelle went into the conservatory. I couldn't keep my mind from alternating between what was possibly happening at Janet's and being thankful for my lovely family.

I didn't have to wonder for long. When Janet picked the girls up the next morning, she said that she was having a day off work and would be back later when the children were in school.

I don't know if I expected tears or anger when I let her in, but she showed neither. She followed me into the kitchen, where I was busy trying to get some chores done, and perched on a barstool.

'Make us a cup of coffee will you sis,' her hand went to her neck, 'my throat's a bit sore, all the bloody shouting last night, I expect.'

I threw the dishcloth that I'd been wiping surfaces with into the sink and put the kettle on. 'Are you okay?'

She yawned. 'Yes, surprisingly enough, I am.'

'Well, you seem calm anyway – want to tell me about it? I presume he's gone?'

'Oh yes, he's gone alright and this time, for good. I don't know where, and I no longer care. He's a cheating, lying bastard, and I was a fool to think I could trust him again. Our fucking sister has got more of a hold than I realised. Spineless, that's what he is.' Janet's face twisted into a bitter smile. 'Well, she did give him a son, didn't she? Do you know he even had the gall to tell me that I couldn't expect him not to see his own son? But when I accused him of still fucking her, he denied it.'

I passed her a mug of coffee. 'He must think we're all stupid.'

'Well, he certainly thought I was. I tell you what, Sara, he even denied taking Karen there and said that Michelle was telling lies. How could he be such a bastard to use his kids like that? I don't understand him. But I want to kill her. After the way I forgave her and tried to help her. She's been spoilt, yes, but she's rotten inside to do what she's done to me. I hate her guts.' Janet sipped her coffee, and her shoulders slumped.

I didn't know what to say. I couldn't blame her for how she felt. I'm not sure I would have been able to keep my hands off either of them. 'Did he leave last night or this morning?' I had to say something to break the tension.

'By the time he'd agreed to leave and packed a case, it was ten o'clock. I stayed in the kitchen while he made a phone call, and then he came and stood in the doorway and said goodbye just as if he was going on holiday. I threw a mug at him – it just missed and smashed on the tiles. I'm sorry I broke one of my set now.' She smiled with her tongue tucked in the side of her mouth. 'He looked sad, walked to the front door, turned and closed it quietly behind him.'

'I'm sorry Jan.' I felt like crying for her. I refilled our cups and offered the biscuit barrel. 'Do you want one?' I asked.

'No, thanks.' She shook her head.

'Well, what now?' I said.

'I don't really know Sara, but I know that I won't have him back again. Somewhere along the line, the love that I had for him has disappeared, but I don't hate him; he's weak, and I knew that. He's the stupid one – he's thrown away a loving family for a neurotic, selfish bitch.'

I scratched my head. 'Well, I don't know how you are managing to be so sensible, but I'm glad to hear it.'

Janet stood up and placed our cups into the dishwasher. Oh, I know I'm not going to get over this so easily. I never slept at all last night, but I'm relieved it's over. So, we'll see what happens. I'm glad I've got you, Sara – you've never let me down, have you.'

'No, and I never will; you can depend on it.' We hugged, and then she picked up her jacket from a peg by the door.

'I'll probably ring you tonight, but don't worry if I don't, I've some catching up to do. I'll let you know if anything else happens.' Janet kissed me and left.

31

After Janet went home, I began to wonder where Simon had gone. I just hoped that he hadn't moved in with Lyn while Mom was away. I decided to visit her; it would be nice to see Freddy again; he'd be coming up to twenty months old, a lovely age – and I could find out what she was up to. I rang her on Monday morning after Dawn had gone to school.

I let it ring for a few minutes, but there was no answer. I left it for an hour and tried again.

'Hi Lyn, long time no see how are you and Freddy?' I said brightly.

'Oh, hello Sara, we are okay, but I can't talk now; I'm just going out.'

'Oh dear, I was hoping to come and visit and bring Paul to get to know Freddy. Are you going to be out all day?'

There was a long silence. 'You can't come here, Sara; don't pretend you don't know that Simon lives here now.'

Well, now I knew for certain. 'Have you asked Mom if he could, Lyn?'

'Not that it's any of your bloody business, but no, I haven't. But I'm having our second child in August, and I need him here to help me. You and Janet haven't been much help lately, have you?' she said.

I wasn't in any mood to argue at this point, so I tried to keep the vitriol out of my voice. 'You made it pretty clear that you didn't need us, Lyn – but you knew I was here for you if you needed me.'

'I don't fucking need you or that other snooty cow, so mind your own business and stay away. I have all I need.'

'I hear you, Lyn, and I'm sorry for you – but I will come and visit Mom any time I want to, and you won't stop me.'

'Fuck off.' Lyn banged the phone down.

I was shaking as I hung up. She's becoming worse and worse. Why did I ever care about her? Over and over, my thoughts churned. I made myself a cup of coffee and took it into the conservatory where Paul was playing with his cars, and Jenny was smiling as she napped. I couldn't believe that she'd let Simon move in while Mom was away. I didn't suppose that Mom would agree to him staying there, and I knew that I wouldn't visit while he was there – no matter what I'd said to Lyn. Mom was right; she did have one child too many, I thought and tried to shut her out of my mind. I was almost relieved when Jenny woke and began to cry. I took her with me into the kitchen and made up a picnic to take to the park. As I was buttering bread, I wondered if Laura would like to come too. I phoned her, and she jumped at the offer of company. It was a lovely sunny day, and being in the fresh air, and the beautiful surroundings and chatting to someone who knew nothing about my sisters and their problems was just what I needed.

Dawn was a bit jealous when she knew that we'd had a picnic without her, so I told her that I'd take her with me to see Janet after Peter came home and we'd eaten tea.

'I want to talk to your Aunt privately, though, so you'll have to stay in the sitting room with Michelle,' I said.

'Hmm, I expect it's about Uncle Simon and Lyn, isn't it,' she raised her eyebrows and looked sideways at me, 'it always is when it's private,' she said.

I raised my eyebrows back and grinned. 'Well, yes, it is – I don't know what you know or don't know my detective daughter – but I'm sure that you will know the details soon enough. Now is it going to be sausage, egg and beans or spaghetti?'

'Spaghetti, please – I'll go and do my homework first, though – I haven't got a lot tonight; I think that Mrs Simmonds was too busy flirting with Mr Pritchard at the end of biology. She completely forgot to give us any.'

I laughed at my clever daughter as she ran upstairs with her ponytail swinging. She's growing up too fast, I thought for the hundredth time.

Later on, after tea, that included spaghetti and cucumber to please Dawn. I kissed Paul and Jenny goodbye and said to Peter, 'We won't be long, love, and I'll tell you all about it when we're in bed.'

Peter grimaced. 'Must you,' he grinned.

'Oh, you – see you later.'

It was nice to be taking Dawn somewhere on her own, and I made myself a promise that I would try to arrange some more outings with her. She was entertaining and good company. But I wasn't looking forward to telling Jan how my day had gone.

I had phoned to make sure she was in, so she'd already poured me a glass of white wine and handed Dawn a soft drink as she joined her cousins who were watching a cartoon.

'Come on, then what's happened. I can tell something has.' As usual, she settled herself opposite me at the kitchen table and watched me intently as I sipped my wine.

I told her what Lyn had said, and she shrugged. 'Well, I guessed it. She's welcome to him, Sara. They're as bad as each other. Sly.' She refilled her glass and held the bottle out to me.

I put my hand over my glass. 'No, I'm driving – I'll have a coffee in a minute, though.' I got up and put the kettle on.

'At least I know for definite that there is no Mark, well not a boyfriend anyway. He exists because Mom's met him. Talking of Mom, have you heard from her this week?'

'No, and I just wonder what she's going to say when she finds out that Simon's living in her house. She won't stand for it; they'll have to get out and find somewhere else to live.'

'Oh, that's what you think – I bet you that she lets him stay. Lyn will be able to get her way as usual. Mom won't throw Freddy out, and the other fucking kid is due in August, isn't it? No, she'll stand for anything so long as Lyn isn't upset again. Mom was terrified when she lost it last time and started hurting herself. She still blames herself; she won't risk it.'

'Oh, hell, I hope you're wrong. Lyn was so aggressive, and I'm just about sick of her affecting my life. It'll mean we won't be able to go there anymore. It makes me mad – she's our mother too.'

'You know what, Sara, I won't let that happen. I shall go to see Mom whenever I want, and so will you – she's got my husband – I'll be blowed if she's having my mother too. No, she can fuck herself, and he'd better stay out of my way too.'

I looked at Janet's set expression. I couldn't help but admire her. 'You're right, and she can't have mine either.'

'Hang on,' Janet laughed, 'have we got different mothers now?'

I joined in the laughter, and it dispelled any tension in the room. I made coffee for us both and asked Janet about her job. She was very enthusiastic, and I began to feel a desire to return to work myself. I didn't share that feeling, though. I didn't want sympathy; I didn't deserve any. My life was going well. After another half hour chatting about generalities and trying to keep away from the topic that was probably uppermost in both our minds, we said our goodbyes and I returned home with Dawn.

'Mom, can you tell me what's going on? Is Uncle Simon living with Auntie Lyn now?' Dawn asked.

'Afraid so, but don't let it worry you, love, grownups can behave very badly at times. How about we sing and chase nasty thoughts away?'

We launched into a rendition of "Yellow Submarine", Dawn's sweet soprano voice counterpointing my slightly off-key contralto. It worked, and by the time we got home, my mood was lighter.

As soon as we arrived, Dawn headed for her bed, and after checking on the little ones, Peter and I did too.

'Okay, what's happened, as ever I'm the last to know?' Peter said with a grin while he arranged his clothes over the valet stand that I'd bought him for his birthday.

I reluctantly brought him up to date – I was sick of talking about Lyn's rotten behaviour and kept this rendition as brief as possible.

Peter climbed into bed and pulled me onto his arm. 'Oh, is that all? I thought it was something serious.'

My head shot up, but he was grinning. 'Well, I'm glad you're not serious,' I said.

'In a way, I am serious, love. You can't affect the lives of other people. They just have to get on with it. You've done your best to keep everyone happy, but it's not possible, is it? It's time to sit back and let them work things out for themselves,' he paused and looked thoughtful, 'and I wonder what your Mom will say when she returns to find someone who she dislikes waiting for her?'

'I know you're right, love, but no matter how hard I try, I seem to get sucked into it. I feel so sorry for Janet, but Lyn can go to hell as far as I'm concerned. She's turned out to be a right bitch, and I just don't understand her. As for Mom…'

I eased up off Peter's arm, drew my nightdress over my head and slung it towards the bedroom chair. It fell short, and

I considered getting out and picking it up in case a spider crawled into the fold. I told myself not to be so stupid – spiders get on chairs too – and left it where it was. I lay back down. 'It's too warm in here, and I can't sleep like that.' I blew my breath out. 'I'm tired, and I don't want to think about anything more tonight' I turned to Peter and kissed his cheek. 'G'night, love.'

Peter chuckled. 'Oh no, you can't become nude and expect me not to take advantage.'

He began to kiss me, and I kissed him back, then I became wide awake.

32

It was very early on Saturday morning when I met Mom at the airport at the beginning of June. She and Auntie Freda looked tanned and bursting with health, but they also looked tired. The time had gone quickly for me, but I felt as though I hadn't seen Mom for a year. I hugged them both and helped them deal with their luggage. Once it was safely stowed, I suggested that perhaps they'd like to come to my place where I'd make breakfast for them.

'Oh, no, thank you. I want you to take me straight home. I've missed my house. I'll get my own food,' Freda said.

'Thanks love, but I'd like to go straight home too,' Mom said.

I glanced in the mirror. 'I'll take you first, then Auntie.' I started the car and tried to think about what to say to warn Mom about Simon and Lyn. I decided I could wait until I'd settled Auntie Freda. 'Do you need to get shopping first, Auntie?'

'No lovely, it's all arranged. Mrs Drindle, down the road, is seeing to everything. You don't need to worry your head about me. As soon as you've dropped me, you can get your Mom home; she's exhausted after our long flight. Mind you, we did manage to get some sleep on the plane, didn't we, Nora?'

'That's good. Did you have a great time out there then?'

'Oh yes, we did, love,' Mom said, but it's nice to be home. I can't wait to see all the children. I bet they've grown.'

They filled my ears with the sights and sound of Australia until I pulled up outside Auntie Freda's house and helped her in with her luggage.

'Thanks, Freda,' Mom said, as she kissed her, 'let's get together again soon.'

'No, thank you, Nora, for keeping me company – I wouldn't have gone without you. I'll phone you next week. Get some sleep.'

We waved. 'Mom, I need to talk to you before you go home, and I'm taking you to my house first. I can't talk while I'm driving.'

'Oh my God, what's wrong? Is it Lyn?'

It's not serious, but I need to explain something, just hang on for a few minutes. The children are dying to see you again after all this time. Paul asked me if you died.' I laughed to stop her from making guesses. A few minutes later, we were at my house.

I left her cases in the car, and Peter came from the conservatory with Jenny in his arms, closely followed by Paul, who threw himself at Mom's knees. Jenny began to cry, and I took her from Peter as I kissed him on his cheek. 'Thanks, love. Will you have them just a little longer while I have a word with Mom?'

'Of course, welcome home Nora, would you like a cuppa and something to eat,' He asked.

Mom nodded. 'Please love but,' she looked at me, 'tell me what's the matter, will you? I'm worried to bloody death now.'

'Where's Dawn?' I asked Peter.

'She's at Laura's with Julie. Why don't you both go into the sitting room, and I'll keep Paul and Jenny in the kitchen?' Peter said.

'C'mon, Mom,' I led the way and sat by her side on the settee.

Mom's hands were doing their usual dance in her lap. 'If you don't tell me this minute, Sara, I'm going to be very angry. What the hell's wrong at home? Is it the baby? Has Lyn lost it?'

I told her about Janet finding the doll and throwing Simon out when she realised that it was his baby that Lyn was expecting. Mom's hands cupped her cheeks that became redder as the tale unfolded, but when I told her that Simon had moved in with Lyn, she jumped to her feet and shouted, 'No, I'll not stand for it. He's not living in my house with her – the fucking crafty pair of buggers.' She walked over to the fireplace and thumped her hand on the mantel shelf making the three framed pictures of my babies' jiggle.

I was glued to my seat. I'd never seen Mom so angry or heard her swear like that. Peter pushed open the sitting-room door and came in, followed closely by Paul. 'What's the matter – is everything okay in here.' He looked at Mom, who was still standing by the fireplace. 'Are you alright, Nora? Mom didn't answer, but she was now pale under her tan.

Peter went from the room and came back with some golden liquid in a small glass. 'Here, drink this and for goodness sake, come and sit down.' He led her to an armchair. 'Are you okay, love?' he asked me. I was shaking as Paul held onto my knees. His eyes were like a Lemurs as he gazed from one to the other of us.

I nodded and took a breath. 'Yes, I'm okay.'

'Do you need a brandy too; shall I get you one?' Peter said. I shook my head as Mom took a sip and gasped as the liquid brought tears to her eyes. She searched for her hankie, which she always kept tucked under her bra strap, sneezed repeatedly, mopped her eyes and then placed her glass on the side table.

'I'm sorry for swearing, but it was a shocking thing to hear. I still can't believe they would do such a thing.' She picked up her glass and held it out to Peter. 'Thank you for this, but would you be a love and make me a cup of coffee instead.' She leaned back in her chair and closed her eyes.

Peter smiled and went into the kitchen, returning a little later to where I was trying to distract Paul by stealing his nose and replacing it with my thumb.

'Come on into the kitchen. I've made toast and coffee,' Pete said.

Mom's face had become an attractive tan colour again. I took her hand and pulled her up, then continued to hold it while we went to join Peter. Paul needed no telling; he only heard the word toast, and he was off to get his second breakfast. I smiled inwardly. Was I raising a Hobbit?

I kissed Mom's head as she sat down at the breakfast bar. Then I unceremoniously grabbed a piece of brown seeded toast and began to eat it dry. I was too hungry to butter it. I pushed the butter dish and a jar of Silver Shred towards Mom, and she began to eat slowly.

'Are you okay, Mom?' I said.

She blew on her coffee and took a drink. 'Yes, love, I'm okay, and I'm sorry I lost it and swore in front of Paul.'

'Never mind Paul,' I laughed, 'you shocked me. I've never heard you use such bad language before.'

Her eyes twinkled. 'Well, I have on special occasions.' She'd regained her sense of humour, and I was relieved to hear it.

'What are you going to do, do you know?' I asked.

She took another bite of toast and said, 'I'd like you to run me home in a little while if you will, Sara. I don't know what's going to happen when I get there, but,' her voice became firmer, 'he's not staying.'

'Try not to upset yourself, Mom; it's not worth it; it's your house. Just say your piece, and if you need any help ...'

Mom smiled. 'It's alright, Sara, I'm calm now, but I'm glad you told me. If I'd walked in and found out ... well, who knows?'

'There's one more thing that I haven't told you, and I probably need to.' I told her about my row with Lyn. 'She made it clear that she expects me and Janet to stay away, but I more or less told her to get lost. I'm peed off with her, and to be quite honest; I don't know what to do for the best.'

Mom's chin jutted forward. 'I know what you'll both do Sara, as you rightly said, it's my house, and I get to choose who enters it. Not Lyn and certainly not Simon. You've to visit whenever you like, of course, you can.'

'I'm glad to hear it, but I wouldn't let anyone stop me from seeing you anyway.' I picked Jenny up and gave her a cup of juice to drink. She promptly threw it towards Paul. 'That's naughty, Jenny,' I said, as Paul picked her cup up and handed it back to her. My mind just wasn't on my children at the moment.

Mom turned to Peter, who was stacking the dishwasher. 'I wonder if it would be better if you took me home, love. I just don't know what's going on, and I might have trouble telling Simon to go. Do you think it would be like waving a red rag at a bull to get Sara involved?'

'Might be wise – what do you think, love?' Peter blew his cheeks out.

'I don't mind, either way, I'm not scared of Simon or Lyn's moods come to that. But if you don't mind and if that's what Mom wants ...'

'Yes, please, love,' Mom said.

Just then, the phone rang. I strode into the hall. 'Hello, yes, okay. It's Jan Mom. She wants to say hello,' I called then returned to the kitchen.

215

At first, I could hear Mom's quiet voice, and then it became perfectly audible as she said, 'No, Jan, he can't stay, and I don't bloody care where he goes to either.' There was silence, and then – 'I know the baby's due soon, but they can find somewhere else. Look, Jan, I'm too tired to talk any longer, love. I'm going home, and I'll see you tomorrow at some point, I hope.' It went quiet again for a moment – 'okay, love, bye.'

She looked as though she could tear her hair out as she joined us in the kitchen. Peter picked up his keys. I'll just transfer your luggage to my car, and then if you're ready, I'll take you home. I'll give you a shout.'

Mom smiled as he went out. 'You are lucky, Sara – you chose a good one there.'

'Don't I know it, he's kind.'

Mom picked up her handbag as Peter called to her. She went to the car, and Paul, Jenny and I waved her off. 'Is Grandma coming back?' Paul asked.'

'Yes, love.' I was too distracted to answer him correctly. I was glad that Peter had taken her, but I hoped he'd hurry back. I settled Paul and Jenny in front of their favourite cartoon and spent my time between looking out of the window and doing bits and bobs of chores until he returned about an hour later. Had she carried out what she said, would Simon have gone? It took me all my time not to bombard him with questions as soon as he set foot in the house.

33

After kisses all around – Dawn had come home shortly before Peter did – I made tea and sat looking expectantly at him as he drank. 'I know you're dying with curiosity,' he said, 'so I'll tell you what happened, but you're not going to like it.'

'Not going to like what?' Dawn said.

I considered sending Dawn out of the room but thought she couldn't be shielded from family problems forever. 'Shh, you'll know in a minute, go on, Peter, what's happened?' I gazed wide-eyed at him and absent-mindedly held the knife that I'd been using to peel potatoes out in front of me.

Peter ran his hands through his hair and snuggled Dawn into his side as he said, 'Well, he's still there, or at least he will be when he returns from the club. He's sitting on the committee now and was at a meeting.'

'Yes, but what did Lyn have to say? Stop being obtuse, Peter.'

'Sorry, love, I don't mean to be, but it sticks in my craw to repeat the scene I just witnessed.'

'Jenny will be up in a minute, so tell me please, Peter.'

He took a deep breath, and his brows drew together. 'Okay, when I took the cases in and dropped them in the hall, I followed your Mom into the sitting room. Lyn got up and hugged her and said that she was pleased she was back and she'd missed her. She's quite big now, you know.'

'Well, she's about seven months – she must be – did you see Freddy?'

'Yes, he's really cute, and he hid behind the sofa, so I didn't see much of him – then it started. Your Mom asked where Simon was; Lyn told her and then said that he lived there now. She then sat back down.

'Your Mom went ballistic and told her that no way was she having him living there. She told her that she was a lying bitch for having pretended that it was Mark's baby. You should have seen Lyn. She was white around her lips and eyes, and she had two bright red patches on her cheeks. She said she was sorry, but she couldn't help it – she loved Simon.'

I shut my mouth with an audible snap. 'What happened then?'

Dawn stood up. 'I've heard enough, Mom. I'll be up in my room,' she said.

'Okay, love,' I said as she left the room.

'What happened though, Peter?'

'Well, Lyn began to cry piteously, and Freddy crawled from his hiding place and held onto her skirt. He was howling, and his little face was all scrunched up. Your Mom went to pick him up, but Lyn told her to leave him alone, and if she didn't want her to be happy with Simon, she'd find somewhere else to live, and she'd make sure that she never saw Freddy or the new baby again.' Peter took a deep breath.

'I bet you felt awful having to listen to it.'

'Well, it wasn't exactly my idea of Saturday morning entertainment, but I didn't feel I could just walk out. Anyway, all the fight seemed to go out of your Mom, and she told Lyn that she could stay because of the children, but they would have to use the front room when Simon was there.'

'I knew she'd give in. Lyn has always made her feel guilty.' I realised that my lips were clamped in a straight line and relaxed them.

Peter smiled. 'You know what, Sara – your Mom's not as soft as you might think. The last thing she said to Lyn before I left was that you and Janet would come and visit whenever you wished, and if she caused trouble or created a bad atmosphere when you were there, then she would make her and Simon leave and take the children with them. She said that she wasn't having Lyn dictate who could come and go in her house and that you and Janet deserved to be there more than she did. Lyn cried even harder, but I don't know any more because I carried your Mom's suitcases upstairs. When she saw me off at the door, she asked me to tell you that she'll ring you tomorrow and not to worry.'

'Well, I can't see Jan wanting to visit if he's there, or me either. But I don't see why I should let Lyn dictate when I can or can't see my mother – so I bloody well will go.'

'Okay, love, but I'm tired of the drama now, so do you think we can go and shop. Then I'd like to relax with a beer or two and watch the football.'

'Come on then, will you give Dawn a shout, and I'll get the kiddiewinks ready. I'm sick of it too.'

Mom rang the following day, just after breakfast. We were getting ready to go out for the day to Bourton-on-the-Water, and I was checking my list to make sure I didn't forget anything important, so I almost didn't answer. I was glad I did, though, as Mom sounded like her old self again, happy and relaxed.

'Hello, love you all okay?'

'Mm, yes, you?'

'I just wanted to tell you that I've had a long talk with Simon and Lyn, and I feel happier now about them staying here.'

'That's good; what changed your mind?'

'You know Sara; they really wouldn't be able to manage if I threw them out. Simon insists that he wants to support all his

219

children, but his job doesn't pay very well, and between you and me, he's not brainy enough to earn more than he does. I don't believe that he would get a better job, so I have no choice but to let them stay here. God knows what would happen to Lyn and the children if I didn't.' She sighed deeply.

'I know what you mean, and you are probably right, but will you be able to put up with it all?'

'I'll have to, won't I, but they are clear that they live in the front room. I don't want to see him more than I have to.'

'Did they agree to that?'

'Yes, and Simon said to tell you that he will always make himself scarce when you visit, so don't stay away on his account.'

'Hmph, that's kind of him – anyway, Mom, I must go, we're just on our way out.'

I told her where we were going and then said goodbye.

'Okay, love, see you soon and thank you, Sara.'

When I told Peter what was said, he grimaced, his lips compressing downwards. 'It'll never work out, but I don't see what else she could do.' He picked up our cool bag and headed for the door. 'Come on, and let's get on our way and forget about your family for now. I told my Mom that I'd pick her up in half an hour.'

I glanced around and felt a little sorry that we were going without Jenny, who had a heavy cold. Laura had volunteered to mind her for the day, and I had taken her there a little while ago. I knew that she would have been miserable, and I didn't want to stop everyone else from having fun. I gathered the rest of our necessities together and joined the children who were already in the car. I was looking forward to being in the fresh air, and I'd arranged to meet Janet there as a surprise for Dawn.

The day was warm and sunny when we found a parking space and walked to where we'd arranged to meet by the first bridge over the River Windrush. The girls and Paul threw themselves at each other. Peter and I hugged Janet, and we headed for a bench. A cup of tea was always first on Janet and my menu, so we crossed over the road to the cafe and Peter and his Mom took the children off to have ice creams while we indulged ourselves. It was such a relief to be away from all the recent worries that I hoped Janet wouldn't bring up anything about Mom's situation. But she did.

She took a sip of her tea. 'I didn't think that Mom would let Simon stay, did you?'

'I did, actually. She's never been able to be tough with Lyn. Well, any of us, now that I think about it.'

She turned to face me. 'He came to see me last night.'

'Who – Simon?'

'Yes, Simon.'

'Oh.'

'He told me that it was me he loved, said that he was sorry and asked if I would let him come home.'

My jaw dropped open. 'What did you say – you haven't let him have you?' I wasn't thinking straight.

'I told him that this wasn't his home, and he would never again be welcome to step foot across the doorstep – let alone live there. He made a move to push past me, but Michelle came downstairs, and he stopped when he saw her. He said that I must hate him, but I told him that I felt nothing for him.'

I bit my lip. 'And ...?'

'He began to cry, but you know what, Sara – I didn't care. I told him to go back to the sly cow that he deserved. He turned around and went.'

'What about him seeing the girls?'

'Oh yes, I told him that he could ring up when he wanted to see them, and I'd make arrangements – but not when he was with Lyn. I've felt so tempted to ring Lyn and tell her what he said, but that would make me as spiteful as she is, so I've resisted. I wasn't sure if it would bring on another breakdown either.'

I could see Peter and his mom, who was holding Paul by his hand, returning with the girls flying ahead of them. 'Well, I'm glad you didn't have him back this time – but our lot are nearly here, so don't let's talk about it anymore for now.' Jan nodded.

We moved outside and found a picnic bench where we ate lunch. Then after taking a tour of the model village and letting the children dangle their feet in the shallow river, we headed home. I couldn't help but wonder what the next crisis would be and when it would arrive.

34

There was no crisis, so I could stop worrying and get on with my own life. I went to Mom's on a couple of occasions, and Lyn just stayed out of my way. Then at the beginning of August, just after Jenny's third birthday, we took a little break as a family while the children were off school. As a treat for Dawn, we drove to the Lake District. She'd pressed for this destination as she wanted to see where Beatrix Potter had lived and visit the museum that she'd read about. Neither Peter nor I had been there, so we were looking forward to it too.

After we parked the car, Peter picked Jenny up and put her into her pushchair, and I shepherded Paul and Dawn up the small gangplank onto the boat that would take us on a trip along Lake Windermere to Bowness. It was a pleasant day, warm with a gentle breeze, and the water seemed alive with multicoloured jewels that bounced off the wake of the boat. We found seats easily enough, but Paul was becoming a real handful, and I had to watch him every second – I had visions of him diving overboard.

I thought that the scenery was spectacular and enjoyed the motion of the boat. I could have stayed doing nothing else all day. For the first time in a long while, I wasn't thinking about my sisters and their problems.

When we arrived in Bowness, we trekked the short distance to our overnight stay. The town was quaint but geared up for tourists, and it was crowded. We constantly had to step off narrow pavements to allow visitors in wheelchairs to pass by. But we spent a comfortable night and did all that Dawn wished the next day. Then back on the boat again for our return journey to Lakeside and on to Blackpool, where we spent another night and half the next day so the children could enjoy the Pleasure Beach. All in all, we had a great time with nothing to worry about, but it started again the minute we got home.

As soon as I opened the front door, the phone began to ring. I just knew it would be Mom. I rubbed the back of my neck as I picked up. 'Hello, Mom.' I rolled my eyes at Peter, who'd followed me in with Jenny asleep in her car seat.

'How did you know it was me?' She didn't wait for me to answer, 'I'm glad you're back; Lyn's in hospital.'

'Oh my God, why?' Here we go, I thought.

'She's in labour, and Simon took her in last night. I phoned the hospital this morning, and they said she was comfortable.'

'What do you want me to do, Mom?' I heaved a sigh.

'I wondered if you could mind Freddy for me so I can go to the hospital – I promised her I'd be there – but Simon's not come back.'

'I've just walked in the door Mom, I don't see how I can, and I thought she wasn't due until the end of the month.'

'She wasn't; it's coming early.' She went quiet. 'Please, Sara, I'd ask Jan, but you know how she is.'

'Well, can you blame her? Hold on a minute, I'll speak to Peter. Look, I'll call you back in a minute.' I put the phone down.

I stood for a minute, trying to decide what I felt and what I wanted to do. I'd been so content having a break with just my own family that I almost felt assaulted by this intrusion, and I wanted no part of it. I went and found Peter where he was pouring juice for everyone.

'What was that all about?' He glanced up at my face as I told him. 'Well, how about we sell the house and go and get back in the car and live in the Lake District, eh?' He laughed at his joke, and that made me laugh too. 'Seriously, love, don't let's turn this into a drama again, just go and fetch Freddy, and we'll look after him until Lyn's home. He's a nice little kid, and we should get to know him.'

'I don't know how you can be so sensible and kind, my love,' I said and went back to the phone.

Half an hour later, Mom put Freddy into my car and handed me a bag with his clothes. 'Do you need anything else, Sara?'

'Does he have anything special to eat?'

'No, he'll eat anything usually.'

'Well, I don't then.' I started the car, and Freddy began to bawl. He cried on and off all the way to my house. I wondered what I'd let myself in for – he didn't really know us.

'Poor little chap,' Peter said, as Freddy sat on the floor by Jenny and Paul, who seemed fascinated with this new addition. 'It's nearly his second birthday, isn't it?'

'In two days, and I don't suppose Lyn will be home by then. I've told Mom we'll keep him until she is.'

'Well, he's not crying at the moment – it'll be alright, and it'll do Jenny good not to be the baby for a while.'

I glanced across to see Jenny pass Freddy, one of her treasured teddy bears. 'Once again, you're probably right, but Paul looks as though he might take it fro ... there he goes,' I said, as Paul snatched the bear from Freddy and gave it back to Jenny.

'That's not kind, Paul,' Peter said, watching as Jenny handed it back. 'Don't you dare do it again. Jenny is being kind.' Paul surveyed his father from under his beetled brows but then passed Freddy one of his toys. 'That's a good boy.'

Paul looked pleased with himself and smiled at his father.

'Daddy will you look after my yastic band,' he asked and handed Peter a rubber band that he often played with but never succeeded in making it fly across the room.

Peter automatically said, 'It's elastic, my son.' Then proceeded to make it fly for him with all the children trying to catch it as it passed.

I flopped down in an easy chair and watched them for a while, then felt my eyelids drooping. The next thing I knew, Peter was gently shaking my arm. I startled awake, only ten minutes had passed, but things had changed. I now had a mug of coffee on the table by my side, and I could hear Dawn moving about in the kitchen. A few minutes later, I heard the washing machine begin a wash cycle, and Dawn came into the sitting room with a big grin on her pretty face.

'What's making you so happy?' I asked and smiled.

'Well, I've been good, I've sorted the things that we took with us and put a load of whites in the machine, and I've made up Jenny's cot for Freddy to sleep in,' she said and tilted her head to the side.

'Well, you're a little duck; that's what you are, my love. Thank you for letting me doze. I needed it.'

'Thanks for taking me to the Lakes Mom – I enjoyed going to see the museum and everything else. Is it okay if I go round to Julie's now?'

'Yes, love, but come back for your dinner, won't you?'

'Okay.' She skipped out and left me remembering what a wonderful age ten was. Practically no worries and excitement around every corner, but I shook my head as I thought briefly that not every child had the advantages that Dawn did. I looked over at Freddy, who seemed happy enough playing with Jenny and Paul.

Peter came back into the room. 'Do you think she's had it yet?'

My mind jumped back into gear. 'No, I shouldn't think so; Mom would have rung. She's been in labour a while though now, hasn't she?'

'Hm, yes, but it's no use worrying about it, let's have some dinner, shall we, I don't know about you, but I'm hungry.'

'Stews nearly heated up – do you think Freddy will eat it?'

'Course he will, Jenny used to when she was his age.'

He was right, and once I'd got the hang of getting the food to stay in his mouth again, he enjoyed eating with us. I was more than a little worried about how he would be when I put him to bed, but he sucked his thumb and was soon asleep. I breathed a sigh of relief when first Jenny, then Paul, joined him.

Dawn had popped home for dinner and told me that Laura wanted to know when she could come and catch up.

'Mom, can I have a sleepover at Julie's? Her Mom said it's okay?'

As she left, I called, 'Tell Laura I'll phone her tomorrow.'

Peter and I relaxed at last with a glass in our hands as we watched Coronation Street's latest episode. Then we switched the television off and enjoyed chatting about how much we'd both like to tour America when the children were old enough to be left. After a while, I said, 'I think I ought to phone Janet and tell her that Freddy is here and Lyn's in the hospital.'

'Maybe you should. You don't want her to think you're keeping anything from her.'

'Will you get me a refill then?' I walked into the hall as the phone rang. 'Thank God for that she must have had the baby.' I hurried to answer it. 'Hello, Mom.'

It wasn't Mom. It was Janet. 'I was just about to ring you.'

'You're back then – was it good?' Janet said.

I brought her up to date with all the news, and she laughed when I told her that Freddy was here.

'I hope he's not staying too long. I wanted to come and see you all tomorrow after work. Hasn't she had the brat then?'

The bitterness in her voice shocked me. 'It's not the baby's fault, Jan – and no, she hasn't – but she's been in labour a long time now.'

'I hope she's in a lot of pain.'

I gasped. Was this my caring sister?

'I tell you what, Sara, I really hate her, and I just can't think about her with any kindness right now. I'll call you tomorrow.' I could hear that she was crying as she ended the call.

I replaced the receiver, and the phone immediately rang. 'I've been trying to call you Sara, Lyn's had a little girl, and she's only small, but she's beautiful. Is Freddy alright?'

'He's fine, and I'm glad it's over. Is Lyn okay?'

'She is, but she had to have a caesarean in the end. Anyway, it's over now, and I have another granddaughter. She's going to be called Simone. I'd better go as other people are waiting for the phone. Will you keep Freddy until she's home, love? I'll be able to look after them then. I need to do some gardening and see to the allotment too. Simon's useless, but at least he's here and making Lyn happy.'

'Do what you have to do Mom, we're alright, but I don't relish the thought of telling Janet that she's calling the baby Simone.'

'Nothing to be done. She's decided that's what she wants. Simon suggested other names, but she'd have none of them. Anyway, I'd better go. I'll phone soon, hug the children for me. Bye, love.'

I said goodbye with a heavy heart. Children should always be welcome news, I thought, but to call Simon's child, Simone was spiteful to Janet. Lyn was proud of her ability to take Janet's husband and didn't mind who knew. I had a fairly deep-seated faith in divine justice and believed that Lyn would, in some way, be punished for her selfishness.

35

I think that it was Lyn's ruthless determination to call her baby Simone that finally made me realise I had no love left for my youngest sister. I didn't hate her as Janet did, but I wanted nothing to do with her. I couldn't bring myself to send a congratulatory card, and I did not want to see the baby either.

A week later, Mom asked me to bring Freddy home, and I asked Peter if he would take him for me. I'd become used to having him with us, but I wasn't sorry to see him leave as I knew that Janet wouldn't be visiting me while he was there. Nor could I visit her with him in tow, and I didn't think it was fair to ask Peter to mind him. He probably would have, but I just couldn't ask him to. Silly, really, because I had no hesitation in asking him to pop him back to Mom's. When he returned, I asked if he'd seen the baby, but he told me that he'd handed Freddy over to Mom at the door. For no reason that I could understand, I was pleased that he hadn't gone in.

As the weeks went by, Janet and I established contact again, and our lives continued as before. We rarely mentioned Simon, Lyn or their two children, although Dawn spoke about Freddy to Michelle and Karen. She told me that they couldn't understand why they had a half-brother they weren't allowed to see. She said it made them sad. Dawn said that she understood, but she'd like to see Freddy again.

229

One day towards the end of November, Mom called in on her way to the allotment to get some vegetables. She was excited because Michael and Derek were coming home to spend Christmas.

'That's lovely news, but where are they going to sleep? Lyn's turned his room into a nursery, hasn't she?'

'It's okay they're staying at Derek's Moms. But I am worried about Christmas dinner though Sara. Where is it to be?'

'I'm sorry, Mom, but I'm not a magician, and I won't be able to decide what everyone is doing. It's too complicated this year. I'm happy to have you, Michael and Derek and Jan and the girls here, but that leaves Lyn. I'm sure you wouldn't want to leave her on her own with just Simon, and even if I wanted her here – which I don't – then Jan wouldn't come.'

'I know, do you think that we'd better stay at home this year, love?'

'It would be best, but I hope that Michael will come here at some point. I think that I'll leave it until Jan tells me what she wants to do. I can't believe how Lyn and that bastard have affected our family.'

'I know, but we just have to get on with it. I spoke to Jan yesterday, and she sounds okay. She says she still won't come to visit anymore so I'll have to go there to see them. I don't want the girls to forget me.'

'Don't be daft, Mom; they're too old to forget; they love you, just as much as this pair do.' I indicated Jenny and Paul, who were both crawling around her feet playing at being dogs.

'Well, let's see what happens, shall we. You should come and see Simone – she's really a pretty little thing.'

I could feel my lips tighten. 'She might be, but you should have heard Janet when I told her what the baby's name was. She was furious – I think she still loves him, you know Mom.'

'Well, I hope not; he's no bloody good.' She gave a loud sigh. 'Why don't you come and bring Dawn after school for an hour tomorrow. I'll make some tea, and perhaps Peter could join us.'

I frowned. 'I don't – '

'Lyn stays in the front room most of the time, and I miss seeing you at home. Please come, Sara; the longer this goes on, the more I think things will never be right again. I wish your father was alive. He'd have known what to do.'

Mom was beginning to look her age, I thought. All the bloody worry, no doubt, and I didn't want to add to it. 'Alright, we'll come at about four, but I don't know about Peter. I'll let you know.'

'Okay, love,' she smiled. 'I'll see you tomorrow then. Come on, you two get up and give me a kiss bye, bye.'

After she'd gone, I berated myself for being so soft where she was concerned. No wonder Peter had been prepared to make us move house rather than have me fly into every upset that Mom had. I thought those days were over but apparently not. I still didn't want to see Lyn, and I was also afraid that Janet would think I was being disloyal to her, but Mom's pleas were my downfall.

As promised, I took the children to Mom's when Dawn arrived home, and Peter joined us later for tea. Initially, we saw neither Lyn nor the children, but Lyn carried the baby in after we'd been there for ten minutes, and Freddy trailed behind her. As soon as he saw me, he beamed and then went to Jenny and kissed her.

Lyn stood in front of the television and quietly said, 'Hello, stranger.'

I could feel my throat become dry as I tried to greet her. My words sounded squashed as I said, 'Hello yourself. Are you okay?' Did I care – I don't know, but old habits and all that.

'Thank you for looking after Freddy for me while I was in the hospital. Would you like to see my daughter?' She held Simone out towards me, and I took her. She was indeed a pretty child; small and lively, she kicked her legs and waved her arms about while I held her. 'She's beautiful, and Freddy is a lovely, sweet-tempered child; I enjoyed looking after him.'

I handed Simone back to her, and she smiled. 'He's not like me then.' She smiled again, took Freddy by the hand and left the room without a backward glance. Freddy began to cry as he wasn't being allowed to play with his cousins.

I found the whole episode surreal. There was silence in the room after the door closed until the little ones began their noisy play again, and Dawn gave me a raised eyebrow look.

'I'm sad I didn't get to hold her,' Dawn said. I don't know what I've done to her – she's still my Aunt, isn't she?'

'She's not very happy at the moment, Dawn – it's not you – take no notice,' Mom said.

Peter arrived shortly afterwards, and we had tea and then headed for home. I thought it wasn't the best visit I'd ever had, but at least it broke the ice.

When I saw Janet a few days later, I told her about my visit.

'You've always given in far too easily to Mom and Lyn, but I promise you that I won't be following in your footsteps. I can't see me ever going to Mom's again while they are there. Mind you, he came to pick the girls up and take them to the cinema on Sunday, and he asked me again if I'd changed my mind.'

'What did you say?' I thought I'm sure we've been here before.

'I told him to fuck off. But I think that she'd better watch her step. I know what he's like, and he isn't happy with her. He loves his kids, but he's not interested in babies until they can hold a conversation. I think he's probably already looking around.'

'Well, he'd be a fool, wouldn't he? He's already paying support for Michelle and Karen, and he'd have to pay rent if he moved out of Mom's plus pay maintenance for Freddy and the other one.' I couldn't bring myself to say Simone's name. 'He's trapped himself financially.'

'Well, it serves him right. Let's talk about something else, eh?'

I thought I could see a tear in her eye, so I quickly changed the subject. 'Okay, love, what are you thinking about doing at Christmas? Are you and the girls coming to me?'

'I'm not sure what to do; it's awkward, isn't it? Do you want to go to Moms? Michael and Derek will be there, won't they?'

'No way, we will be staying at home, and I hope that they'll visit after dinner. I've already told Mom that Lyn isn't welcome and she's staying home – but Mom says that she'll come to mine later.'

When Christmas day dawned, that's precisely what happened. Michael had hired a car, and they drove Mom over to join us after dinner. He hadn't changed, and Derek was quite handsome now his acne had disappeared. They both spent the majority of the day on the floor playing with the children who, until Paul or Jenny had one of their moments, were becoming quite a civilised band of cousins and siblings.

Except for the sad fact that Michael and Derek had flown back to Canada promising to return later in the year for their main holiday, New Year's Eve was similar to Christmas day up until Big Ben boomed out its countdown. We sang Auld Lang Syne, and everyone who was there was in high spirits. Peter did the usual first footing as he hurried out the back door and came in the front carrying a piece of coal, a slice of bread and some salt that he sprinkled in the hallway. I, for one, had high hopes for 1976. Hopefully, the drama of the last few years would now recede into the background. What did I know? I would have wished for anything other than what the future held for us.

36

I felt somewhat guilty three days later when it was Lyn's birthday, and I hadn't sent her a card. I was so torn. One minute I wanted to try and heal our relationship, and the next, I just wanted to keep well away from her. I eventually behaved like an ostrich and concentrated on making arrangements for an overnight stay at a London hotel for Peter's birthday. We had stayed there before, and as his birthday fell on a Sunday, I booked train tickets for the first of February so we'd be in London until late on the second. I took a chance and didn't tell him we were going until Janet and the girls arrived very early on Saturday morning to babysit.

I'd already packed a case for him and hidden it, so it was a big surprise. He swung me up in the air, just as though we were still teenagers. It was a fabulous weekend and just what we both needed – freedom from responsibilities.

Our holiday buoyed us up for a while, and I was happy with my lot. Even Janet seemed to be getting on with her life with no bother.

My bubble burst one Monday morning in April that year when Mom visited unexpectedly. She was soaking wet, and her umbrella showered our hall with water as she placed it in a corner to dry. I could tell by her face that it wasn't just a casual pop in for a cuppa visit.

'What's up, Mom,' I asked as I led her into the kitchen. She just smiled and went to make the tea. I was folding washing, so I was happy that she didn't expect me to leave my chores.

Paul came running in and yelled, 'Grandma,' and then shook Jenny, who was staring at raindrops that were trickling down the glass in the back door. She shouted too and headed for Mom's open arms. She chatted away to the children and smiled a lot, but I knew the signs. We all went into the conservatory and sat watching the clouds as they scurried across the dismal sky and poured icy cold rain onto our miserable looking garden.

I tried again after a couple of minutes. 'You look worried, Mom. Is something the matter?'

'I think so, but I'm not sure, Sara.' She glanced at Paul to make sure he was occupied and then whispered, 'I think Simon is hitting Lyn, but she denies it, and I don't know what to do.'

I shook my head slowly. 'No, for goodness sake – what makes you think so?'

'They row a lot, especially after I've gone up to bed. I don't think they realise that I can hear almost every word.'

'That doesn't mean he hurts her, Mom. Why would he?'

'I can tell you why. She thinks she's pregnant again, and she hasn't lost the weight she's gained from having Simone. He keeps telling her she's a fat pig and how could anyone fancy her. I can hear him, and I can hear Lyn crying and telling him he's a bastard.' She spelled the last word out.

'But why do you think he's hit her?'

'I'm sure I've heard him slap her, and then sometimes there's a scuffle, and I think they're fighting. It's driving me loopy, Sara. It's not as if they stick to the front room now. I suppose I knew that wouldn't work for long. They only go in there most of the time if I make a fuss.'

'Do you think she's pregnant again then?'

'I hope to God she isn't, but she thinks she is. Oh, I don't bloody well know. I need to get my life back together. I'm not getting any younger, and I wish they weren't living under my roof. I've even agreed to mind Freddy and Simone so that Lyn could get a job – but now.'

I stared at Mom's hands. They were tearing her paper hanky into shreds. That's where Lyn gets the habit from. I remembered the way her room had sometimes looked like a snowstorm when she was upset.

Jenny grabbed onto my knees, bringing me sharply into focus. I picked her up, grateful for the breather. 'I don't know what to say, Mom. I suppose I could ask her if he is – but she's not going to tell me anything, is she? To be quite honest, I'm tired of Lyn and her troubles, but he hadn't better be hitting her. Although I'm fairly sure he hit Janet at least once.'

Jenny put her hand across my mouth. 'Alright, love, what do you want?'

'Drink.'

'Do you mean drink please, Mommy?' I said automatically. Jenny grinned, and I got up.

Mom stood too. 'You're right, Sara, I know she won't tell you. I just needed to talk to you about them. I'm sorry, love, they're not your problem.'

'They shouldn't be yours either. Try not to worry. Shall I ask Peter to have a word?'

'No, it'll be alright, but if it goes on much longer, he will have to find somewhere else. He can live under a railway bridge as far as I'm concerned. Anyway, you go and see to Jenny, and I'll ring you soon. You're a big help, you know, Sara.'

I smiled, and with kisses all round, she left. Leaving me thinking that it was a pity Mom hadn't drowned Lyn at birth.

Reluctantly, I phoned and told Janet what Mom's last visit had been about, and she said that she hoped he did hit her. I knew that after a while, she'd soften, and in the next sentence, she did. I was glad I couldn't see her face, though.

'I hope she gives as good as she gets, and with her temper, I bet she does,' Janet said.

'Yes, but I don't think anyone should be striking anyone else. If I knew for sure, I'd want to do something about it.'

'I just find it so hard to forgive her. There are times when I'd like to lay into her, you know. She destroyed my family. Oh, I know he was partly to blame, but it was more because he was cock happy than vindictive. She schemed from when she hit puberty – I know she did. Anyway, I'd best go before I say something that will see me burn in hell. See you soon – take care.'

By the end of May, I had begun to think that Mom was mistaken about what she could hear at night. I'd seen her a few times, and she'd said no more about it.

It was a Saturday evening a few weeks later. I'd just put the little ones to bed when Mom called, sounding so distraught that I called for Peter to come to the phone.

Peter listened for a second, then spoke firmly. 'Okay, Nora, calm down. I can't understand what you are saying,' there was a long pause, then he said, 'is she bleeding? Well, calm down. I'm coming – make a cup of tea; I'll be there in a minute.'

I let go of his arm and realised that I'd been holding on so tightly my hand had pins and needles. 'What's the matter, what's happened?'

'He's hit Lyn, and she called the police.'

'Is she alright? Has he been arrested? Is Mom okay?' I could feel bile threatening to flood my mouth. I swallowed repeatedly.

'Lyn refused to press charges, so there was nothing they could do. Your Mom sounded so upset that I'm going to go and have a word with him. I don't see why she should have to put up with his behaviour.' He picked his car keys off the hook and went out. I don't think I've ever seen his face set in such grim lines.

I kept trying to imagine what was happening and constantly walked to the window to see if he was back.

'For goodness sake, Mom, will you please sit down? You're making my head spin,' Dawn said. She put down the book that she'd been reading. 'Why don't we go and bake some cakes ready for tomorrow's tea, eh?'

I could have kissed her toes; she was so grown up now, and I was grateful for the distraction. 'I'm sorry, love, I'm just so worried.'

'I know, and I can't believe how Uncle Simon can be so wicked. He shouldn't hit Auntie Lyn, should he? Do you think Dad will hit him?'

Would that be possible, I wondered? 'No, I'm sure that won't happen, so don't worry – let's go make those cakes.'

The chocolate cakes were on a wire rack cooling by the time Peter returned.

'Did you hit him, Dad?' Dawn asked. I thought that she sounded hopeful.

Peter smiled. 'No, I did not, and this is not something that ever should have involved you.' He dropped a kiss on her forehead. 'C'mon, let's have you tucked up in bed – scoot.'

'Aww, Dad, I want to know what happened. Do I have to go?'

'Yes, love.'

Dawn scowled, but she picked her book up, took a can of Pepsi from the fridge, kissed us goodnight and did as Peter said.

I felt proud of her restraint; I was sure that I'd have argued with my father. I poured us some wine, and we sat in the conservatory.

'What went on, love? Is it all okay? I've been so anxious?'

'Do you think I don't know that; I presume from the wonderful smell that you've been baking?'

'Dawn's suggestion, I know she's too young to be involved, Peter, but she's not daft; she knows what's going on.' I took a drink.

'Hm, well, I don't have to fill her young mind even more with how shitty adults can be. She'll find out soon enough.' He scratched his head. 'There isn't an awful lot to tell you. By the time I arrived, your Mom had calmed down, and Simon had gone into the front room. Lyn was ironing some of the children's clothes that she wanted to take them out in tomorrow. She has a black eye and a cut lip, but she seemed unbothered by them. I asked her if she was alright and why didn't she tell the police that she wanted them to charge him with assault. She said that she didn't want him taken away; she just wanted him to stop hitting her.'

'What did Mom say to that?'

Peter shook his head. 'She just held her hands out and shrugged. She seemed at a loss. I could feel myself getting quite uptight and went into the front room. It was obvious that Simon wasn't used to anyone knocking then walking in there – he jumped a mile as the door opened.'

'Oh my God, what did he do?'

'He stood up and asked me what I wanted. I walked towards him and told him that if he hit Lyn again, I would make sure that he found himself out on the street. He stuck his chin out and asked me how I thought I was going to do that. I just told him that he would see, and Nora shouldn't have to put up with his carrying on. Then I walked out, said goodbye to your Mom and Lyn and came home.'

'I'm glad you didn't hit him anyway.'

'So am I,' he lifted his hands to his eyes, 'I don't want to hurt my pretty hands,' he smiled.

I laughed. 'What will you do, though, if he does hit her again?'

Peter's smile disappeared. 'Not sure, but I won't allow it to carry on. I think we should visit more frequently. Dawn's responsible enough to leave with the kiddiewinks for an hour. We should get into the habit of dropping in there each evening and at the weekends as well. What do you reckon, eh?'

'Well, it'll certainly send him the message that he can't do as he likes while he's at Mom's, and I think you are right about Dawn. She amazes me sometimes how responsible she is.'

Peter swigged his drink. 'I think we should vary the times we are there. Now shall we forget about it and try and relax before I drag you off to bed?'

37

Peter and I took the children on holiday to a small hotel in Llanberis at the beginning of August. Jenny and Paul always loved the miniature train rides that are part of the scenery there. As always, whenever we go away on holiday, and I think that we've left everything nicely settled at home, something changes. Before we went, we had carried out our plan to visit Mom's frequently, and it seemed to be working. There had been no more bruises that we could see, and Mom and Simon spoke civilly to each other.

This time the upset was Janet. She had put her house on the market in June without telling us. There hadn't been a for sale board, so I had no chance to know. I sat in her kitchen and listened open-mouthed while she told me that she'd accepted an offer for it and was moving to Inverness before Christmas. I could hardly take her words seriously. I thought she'd been happier recently – she'd even gone out on a couple of dates with men that she'd met at work.

My stomach churned, and I said, 'Oh why – please don't go that far away, Jan.'

'I'm sorry, Sara, but it's for the best, believe me – I can't take any more.'

'What do you mean?' I scratched my head. My scalp felt so dry – I must buy some different shampoo. My mind was off on its protective wandering.

'You mean, you don't know?'

'Know what? Don't tell me you're having him back?' I uncrossed my legs that had been moving with a life of their own.

'You must be fucking joking. Have him back – I'd as soon choke the life out of him.' She looked furious.

'What, for Christ sake – tell me and calm down before you burst a blood vessel?'

'A while back, I let him come here while I was at work so that he could have the girls for the day. Do you know what he did?' I shook my head as her lips puckered, and she clenched her teeth. 'He brought Lyn and the children round, and they spent the day here. Here, in my bloody house with my bloody girls.'

'Oh my God, no.'

'He swore them to secrecy and,' she laughed derisively, 'he was stupid enough to believe that one of the girls wouldn't tell me. I hadn't been in the house more than half an hour after he'd left full of smiles – when Michelle told me what a good day they'd had. The girls no longer like Lyn, but they enjoyed seeing Freddy and Simone.' She leaned back in her chair, and her face relaxed a little. 'I couldn't believe his gall. It made me so angry. I'm making damn sure it won't happen again.'

I watched the changing expressions on her face and wanted to cry. I stopped myself because I knew tears wouldn't help.

'Well, bang goes our close family, and I can't begin to tell you how sad it makes me feel. Did you have to go so far away though Jan – and what about your job?'

'Our family was fractured as soon as Lyn began to grow up. As for Inverness, I've been offered a job as secretary to another respiratory consultant who's a friend of Mr Nobles. That's why I've chosen to go there.'

'But I shall miss you so much, Jan, we've certainly been and stayed close, haven't we?' My lips were trembling, and Janet came and put her arm around my shoulders.

'I know, I'll miss you and Peter and the kids too, and of course Mom, but I can't stay. I hate both of them so much. I don't want my girls mixing with them. Now Simon and I are divorced, if he objects to where we live, I will apply for sole custody, and I'm sure I'll get it too.'

I tried to be positive. 'I understand, and it's not as though we can't visit, is it? Does Mom know what you intend to do?'

'Yes, love, she does, I told her as soon as the sale went through, but I didn't want to spoil your holiday. She's sad too, but she understands.'

'It's funny that you are the one to go. Peter and I enjoyed being in Kent so much that we talked about going to live there. But there was always something to stop us. Fate, I suppose. Well, get a place big enough for us all to stay, will you?' I grinned.

After another half an hour of small talk, we parted with hugs as always. My heart was heavy as I drove home. As usual, I told Peter and allowed my tears to flow. Towards Christmas, we waved goodbye to Janet and the girls and promised to visit early the following year. I felt heartbroken, and Dawn sobbed her tender heart out too.

Lyn had her third child, another boy they called David, on the second of January the following year. He was a beautiful baby, and Lyn proudly showed him to me and even allowed me to hold him. I can't say that I felt any closeness, though, which made me sad. I still loved little Freddy, and I had become quite fond of Simone too. I suppose it was inevitable as Peter and I had maintained our frequent visits. Mom told me that things had improved between them all, so much so that they rarely kept to the front room now. I was pleased for them and began to feel welcome when we visited. Not that either of us wished to speak to Simon any more than we did before.

There were tears again when Michael let Mom know that he and Derek had decided to make Canada their permanent home. Peter said that we should follow suit, just up sticks and relocate to Kent as we'd promised ourselves that we would. But I wouldn't hear of it. I didn't think that we should leave Mom while Lyn and Simon lived there. Mom had told me that she could listen to them rowing again at night, and I still felt more than a little concerned.

December 14, 1977, is forever etched in my brain as the day my world spun out of control. Dawn kissed us goodbye after the little ones were in bed, and Peter and I strolled round to Mom's house. It was a crisp, clear evening, and the heavens had put on a spectacular show to amaze us. We hadn't been there for more than ten minutes when Mom asked Peter if he would fill the coal bucket for her while we were making a cup of tea. Lyn was busy ironing, and Simon was sitting in the fireside chair facing the fire and warming his toes while he read the *Evening Mail.*

Peter went out into the yard, and I could hear him shovelling the coal into the bucket. Then I heard Simon's raised voice followed by Lyn's piercing scream. Peter must have dropped the shovel because I heard it clatter on the ground, but I never noticed Mom drop the tray full of cups. I shoved the living room door open and burst in just as Lyn brought the heavy electric iron down on Simon's head. I stood, transfixed as he slumped forward and watched open-mouthed as Lyn smashed it again and again down onto his exposed scalp, each successive blow landing with a dull *thwack*. Then she pushed the still steaming iron into his ruined face and held it there. A nauseatingly sweet smell filled my nostrils and made me gag. Lyn's screams were unholy.

Managing to move my paralysed limbs, at last, I crossed the room and tried to take the iron from her, but she shoved me away, and I staggered back against the table. She continued to reign blows on Simons unmoving head until Peter elbowed past me and wrenched the iron from her. She continued to scream as she slumped to the floor. My screams nearly matched my mothers. Both have faded. But I can still hear Lyn's demented ones at times.

Peter tried to find Simon's pulse but couldn't, so he left him where he was and phoned the police. Mom tried to help me with Lyn, but we couldn't get her to budge or stop screaming. We eventually collapsed onto the sofa, but neither of us spoke.

As Lyn was arrested and placed in handcuffs, she stopped screaming.

'Why Lyn, why? I asked.

She looked into my face and said without emotion, 'He didn't love me, and now he won't call me a fat pig ever again.'

Epilogue.

We stood with a noisy clattering of feet then became silent as His Honour, Judge Claremont, made his way along the bench. He gathered his black and purple robe together, pushed his spectacles up the bridge of his beaky nose and sat down. We all sat. Peter took my trembling hand in his steady one and began gently stroking it with his thumb.

A female security guard indicated to Lyn that she should sit. Lyn looked annoyed and shrugged away from her hand, but she sat down. Her lank hair hung forward as she bowed her head until I could no longer see her face.

I waited with dread as the jury bailiff led the jurors in, and they filed back into their seats.

The judge removed his spectacles, wiped them on his tippet and then replaced them.

He watched solemnly as the court clerk asked the foreperson, a middle-aged woman dressed in a red jumper, 'Have you reached a verdict?'

A bubble of nervous laughter threatened to burst from my lips as she, too, pushed her spectacles up the bridge of her nose before answering, 'Yes.'

'Do you find the defendant, Lyn Margaret Davis, guilty or not guilty of the charge of manslaughter?'

All eyes were on this nameless woman as she said, 'Guilty.'

'Is that the verdict of you all?'

'Yes,' she said firmly and sat down.

Lyn gasped, and her head fell to her chest. I wondered if she had fainted. My breath became shallow as I fought to control the urge to vomit.

After ordering that Lyn should be remanded into custody, the judge thanked and dismissed the jury. He adjourned the trial for a pre-sentence report and left the bench.

Lyn was led from the dock, but as she started down the stairs, she stood still and gazed sadly into my eyes as she mouthed the word 'please.'

I couldn't respond. I just watched as she disappeared from my sight. I was numb.

The End

Acknowledgements

This was a difficult book for me to write, but thankfully with encouragement and help from Susie, I brought it to fruition.

Thank you to Theresa Howley, my lady in the sink, a true story. She was a great character and taught me how to laugh at the extraordinary things that happen.

A big thank you to my super family, who have continued to offer support and love.

Thanks again to Mary Mooney, aka Lisa, for being my reader and soundboard.

Last but not least, thank you for purchasing this book. I know you could have picked any number of books to read, but you chose one of mine, and for that, I am incredibly grateful.

Your feedback and support will help me significantly, so I hope you could take some time to post a review on Amazon and maybe share it with your family and friends on social media. For more information about me, please visit my website at www.lesleyelliot.co.uk

By the Same Author:

The Copper Connection
www.amazon.co.uk/dp/B085WDCBX5

In May 1995, life changes forever for twenty-one-year-old Heather Barnes when an abhorrent crime fractures her life. Not willing to rely on the justice system, she vows to exact revenge. Is she strong enough to carry out her plans? Is she smart enough to avoid detection? We follow the highs and lows of her family life and relationships as she grows from a helpless victim into an independent, resilient woman. Will she ever be capable of putting the trauma behind her and finding the happiness she deserves, or will her need for vengeance destroy her?

Sally-Secrets and Lies
www.amazon.co.uk/dp/B088Q1XD96

Happiness can be hard to find and even harder to hold on to. In February 1916, when Sally Brooks is twenty-five months old, a family argument changes her life forever. Lied to since childhood and unaware of secrets that will cause her heartbreak, will she ever be able to make sense of past events and gain the happiness she deserves? Follow Sally's family life and relationships as she grows from naïve child to protective mother, learning about betrayal and loss, friendship and love on the way.

Love and Beyond
www.amazon.co.uk/dp/B08L9GCRDQ

Stella is special, but she doesn't find that out until she dies and arrives at the Waystation. There she is given the opportunity to return to her life with the woman that she loves if she agrees to carry out a mission. Find and intervene in the lives of four people to safeguard one who is significant to the future of the world. But there is a problem. If anybody discovers her secret, the deal is off. Stakes are so high that failure is not an option, but even being an angel does not convince Stella that she has the power to succeed.

Printed in Great Britain
by Amazon

Printed in Great Britain
by Amazon